BIZARRE BAZAAR

SHORT STORIES FROM ROCKY MOUNTAIN FICTION WRITERS

D1603297

RMFW PRESS

CONTENTS

Bizarre Bazaar: Short Stories from Rocky Mountain Fiction Writers

Copyright © 2022 RMFW Press

We Are Celia © 2020

Cheap Plastic Crap © 2020 KL Mendt

Opera Without Arias © 2020 L.V. Ditchkus

Red Riding in the Hood © 2020 Francelia Belton

Going Postal © 2020 Doug Christi

The Peddler and the Goatherdess © 2020 Jill English Johnson

Beauty in Stasis © 2020 Kelley J. P. Lindberg

Daughters of Vellamo © 2020 Natasha Watts

The Baby Bargain © 2020 Alison Thayer

The Clay Bride © 2020 Vista McDowell

Do Over © 2020 Cepa Onion

The Three Varkin Sisters © 2020 BJ Eardley

The Suit © 2020 Eleanor Shelton

Racing the Marineris © 2020 John M. Campbell

The Emperor's New Shoes © 2020 Jennie McDonald

The Diagnostic Demon on Skillman Avenue © 2020 Mel Lake

Something in the Air © 2020 Rick Duffy

ISBN: 978 1 7345756-0-6 (print)

ISBN: 978-1-7345756-2-0 (ebook)

Cover design by Patrick Mallek, Mighty Fudge Studios

Interior design by BeckyClarkBooks.com

Rocky Mountain Fiction Writers, RMFW Press

www.rmfw.org

EDITORS' NOTE

Renewal. When we sent the call for stories in 2021, renewal felt so immediate. Recreation, rediscovery, retelling, all those words that begged we kindle our imaginations again and turn to the realm of what might be possible, rather than what we faced on the everyday. Through 2022 that feeling still lingers, the desire for renewal. And not just in our quotidian lives, but in our acts of creation. In the past two years it seems we have consumed all the content there is to consume. In our quest to escape and connect, we have engaged with the new, the surreal – and the bizarre. Tiger King, anyone?

And there we find the next step of our journey to "Bizarre Bazaar." We called for renewal and recreation, and Rocky Mountain Fiction Writers delivered brilliance in every stripe imaginable. A virtual cavalcade of imagination too wondrous to pigeonhole. We have curated this collection of wonder, fear, fantasy, and heart for those seeking the new and the newly familiar. To this end, we picked stories that differed from each other as greatly as possible and carefully placed them in a particular order so that you, lovely reader, do not experience sensory fatigue as melancholy science fiction rolls into warm mainstream, which rolls into horror that feels like justice. Every new tale is both amuse-bouche and palette cleanser taking you down a new, less-travelled path.

We hope you enjoy this collection as much as we enjoyed compiling it. We have found, and are eager to share with you, a bizarre bazaar of stories that rediscover, reclaim, and renew.

Thank you to all the production volunteers who helped make this work possible: Alison Thayer, Audrey McDowell, Becky Clark, and Patrick Mallek. And thank you, reader, for your support of these stories and the authors of Rocky Mountain Fiction Writers.

For the love of stories,

Amy Drayer and Veronica R. Calisto

WE ARE CELIA

RACHEL DELANEY CRAFT

CELIA IS DOING JUST FINE, thank you for asking. And *everyone* is asking. Everyone wants to talk. Everyone is here if she needs it. But Celia just wants to be left alone. Something about being abandoned by your husband after ten years makes you want to own the aloneness, embrace it, climb to the top of a mountain and beat your fists against your sweaty sports bra and shout *I don't need him anyway*.

She has been organizing, purging, keeping the house rigorously clean—just in case he ever comes back, so he'll see she can handle the place on her own. She even tackles the chores he used to do: mowing the lawn, washing the windows, dusting the high shelves. She gets up right when her alarm goes off every morning—no snooze button for her—and goes to work. She's an engineer at a place that builds antimissile systems to protect us from North Korea, which sounds exciting but is really not. When she arrives at work every morning at 7:45 and swipes her badge to unlock the door to her DOD classified building, she feels like she is walking into a cage filled with wood shavings and hopping onto a plastic wheel.

She kind of likes the wheel. It keeps her mind off Mark.

The one thing that threatens this well-organized existence is a houseplant, a member of the jade family, which lives in a white glazed ceramic pot with a crack down one side. It belonged to Mark; he was the one with the green thumb in the relationship. He took all his plants with him when he moved out, but somehow he forgot this one. She texted him about it—twice—and he said whatever, keep it.

This bothered Celia more than she knew was reasonable. People are like plants: they put down roots, countless tiny strands, mostly hidden from view. Even after Mark took his last carload of stuff, Celia kept finding traces of him around the house. A gardening manual that fell behind the bookcase. A thing of pine-scented deodorant in the back of a drawer. A scuff on the nightstand where he used to put his glasses every night before bed. Celia pulled up these roots, one by one. She scrubbed the nightstand, threw out the deodorant, and donated the book to Goodwill.

But the plant. Dumping a plant at a thrift store—or worse, throwing it in the trash—was too callous. She couldn't stand the thought that her marriage's collateral damage might include this innocent organism.

So here we are. Celia's reluctantly adopted plant sits alone in the kitchen window, quietly turning CO_2 into oxygen, attempting to breathe life into the empty house. At first she secretly hopes she will kill it by accident, then she can be rid of it. But over time it begins to bring her comfort. She is still processing her grief, which is hard to do when you don't want to talk to anyone, so she talks to the jade. She complains about seeing her ex-husband's name everywhere, in the most mundane places—markers, postmarks, supermarkets. She discusses their communication breakdown, their loudest fights, their most agonizing silences, and *how could he do that*? The jade is a sympathetic listener. After all, they were both once loved, and later abandoned, by the same man.

Celia Googles succulent care. She waters the jade, fertilizes it, and lovingly trims its dead leaves. She rotates it slowly in the window, so it won't grow at an angle. According to the internet, with enough sunlight this type of jade will develop an attractive red edge around its green leaves. Celia can't be sure on this one because she is red-green colorblind.

At the end of summer, she buys a bigger pot and a bag of Black Gold Cactus Mix and carefully transplants the jade into its new home, noticing with a tinge of pride how its roots have become tight and knotted as it outgrew the old one—the one tended by her ex-husband.

The old pot, the Mark relic, goes into the Goodwill box and the jade seems to thrive. She keeps talking to it, less about him and more about how she plans to redecorate the bedroom, the spin class she went to last week, the diamond earrings she ordered because she's never owned any *real* jewelry before.

She cries to the jade in the fall, after her first wood-chopping misadventure, standing in the kitchen holding a dish towel over her bleeding thumb. She cut off the tip of it with the axe—just flesh, no bone, but still *God it hurts* and *What the hell am I doing chopping wood, anyway*? The jade listens in sympathetic silence.

Then the jade gets mysteriously ill. Some kind of succulent disease, probably brought in with the new soil and eating its way rapidly up the stalk.

Celia weeps.

After a brief meltdown she Googles her way to a solution. Succulents can propagate themselves, meaning if the mother plant dies, you can take off all its leaves and a new plant will grow from each one. So, Celia painstakingly pries the leaves from her beloved jade and lines them up on the windowsill, watches them drying and shriveling in the sun until they begin to sprout little pink hairlike roots. She watches the roots claw their way delicately into the soil, watches the tiny new leaves—baby leaves, embryos really —emerge.

Four months later she has dozens of baby jades, minia-ture replicas of her original plant. They are beautiful in their soft, nubby-leaved way, but they are not quite the same as the original. They don't listen in the same way.

It is the dead of winter; Celia is lonely and cold. She decides to give wood chopping and fire building another shot.

She puts on her boots and tramps around the side of the house, through the days-old crust of snow, to the woodpile and the big tree stump carved with countless nicks from the axe. She looks down ruefully at the scar tissue on the end of her thumb. She has not been back here since that painful day.

Something rustles behind the woodpile. It rustles, and then it emerges, hesitantly, blinking and confused.

Celia has seen animals back here before, usually chip-munks. The occasional garter snake. Never this. This is an oddly shaped human female—oddly shaped, Celia thinks, because she has the proportions of a full-grown woman but the stature of a second grader. As she studies this strange creature's face, the strangest thing of all dawns on her.

"You—You're *me*."

The creature, the second Celia, blinks at her. "I am?"

"Yes!" The more Celia looks at her, the more she is certain they're somehow related. A long-lost identical twin.

Or a clone. "I mean, you have my hair. My eyes. You're just smaller ... like you're not fully ..."

The second Celia tilts her head delicately to one side. "Not fully *grown*?"

And then it hits her.

"Oh, no," Celia says. "You didn't ... You couldn't have ... grown out of my *thumb*?"

Celia Number Two holds up her hands, lines her thumbs up side by side, frowns at them. They are slightly smaller than Celia's thumbs, and perfectly symmetrical. Exactly the same, left to right.

Celia holds up her own thumbs. The right one is shorter by about an eighth of an inch and capped with dark scar tissue.

"Oh, no," she says again.

At first Celia is very concerned about Celia Two. There is a reason she and Mark never had children: she doesn't like them. She has no interest in spending her free time changing diapers or driving to and from daycare or helping with homework.

But Celia Two is not a child. She has emerged from the woodpile as a fully-fledged adult—albeit smaller than the original—complete with Celia's own knowledge and memories.

"That's fascinating," Celia says on the first day, while they cook a stir-fry together. "What's the last thing you remember?"

Celia Two, standing on a step stool, reaches for the spice rack and pulls out the same four jars that Celia herself was planning to use. "I remember chopping wood, and a sharp pain, and everything went black. Then I remember waking up behind the woodpile."

"How long were you back there, before I found you?" Celia asks.

"Hmm. I don't know."

"Didn't you get cold? Hungry?"

Celia Two shrugs. "Not really. I found a good sunny spot."

Celia Two gets acclimated quickly—sleeping on the guest bed, brushing her teeth at the second sink, borrowing Celia's clothes from the closet. She grows faster now. It's a subtle thing, one Celia doesn't notice for days and days until *Bam!* Celia Two doesn't need a step stool anymore. *Bam!* Her clothes aren't baggy anymore. Before Celia knows it, Celia Two is the same size as her predecessor.

Celia learns there are many advantages to having a second version of oneself. The chores get done twice as fast, like having a roommate—but unlike a roommate, Celia Two does not have annoying habits. They pick up after each other. Celia Two takes Celia's dirty cocoa mug in from the living room and puts it in the dishwasher; Celia puts Celia Two's wadded-up Kleenex in the trash—or maybe it's the other way around. It doesn't matter because they aren't bothered by each other's messes or quirks. They are too similar to ever come into conflict.

Even better, if Celia is tired, she can send Celia Two to work in her place. Home projects get done twice as fast now. In the first three months the Celias repaint both bedrooms, the bathroom, and the kitchen. Celia orders new furniture online and Celia Two helps her put it together. Because Celia Two is neither a man nor a romantic partner, Celia does not consider this a weakness. She is still capable and independent. If Celia Two can do something, so can Celia.

Another benefit: Celia Two can do the tasks Celia has been putting off for months because they are so offensive. Like taking her engagement ring to the pawn shop. Unfortunately, this sort of object carries so many feelings and memories they practically drip from its gleaming white-gold surface like beads of sweat. Celia Two, primed as she is with Celia's memories, returns from the pawn shop in tears saying *I couldn't do it*. This upsets them both even further, because Mark shouldn't have this hold over them, *he's* the one who left *them*, they should hate his guts and his stupid ring.

Together they smash the ring with a hammer until the metal is flat and the diamond is reduced to so many sparkling chips, and they bury it in the backyard.

They share clothing. Shoes. Makeup. Food. Drinks. Money. One night after brushing her teeth, Celia Two turns left into Celia's bedroom instead of right into the guest bedroom. Celia almost says *Hold on, that's my bed*, but then she realizes it doesn't matter. *What's mine is hers.*

When the home projects are done, Celia gets a job at a nursery, taking care of plants. Celia Two is always at the antimissile factory these days anyway.

They start dating someone. A man named Jonathan. It's early still. They have gone to his house but not brought him to their house yet. They are not sure how to explain the situation to him ... or maybe he never has to find out.

When summer comes, they build a garden together: lettuce and peppers, tomatoes and squash. Everything they plant seems to flourish. Even the diamond seeds start to sprout into a new engagement ring—*What is the* deal *with this soil?*—which they take to the pawn shop. This isn't the actual one, the one Mark touched, the one that overheard their whispered words, so it is easy to part with.

One morning while they drink coffee at the kitchen table, Celia Two scrolls through an article: "Winning the battle against earwigs in your garden." Celia is very interested in earwigs and would be reading it right now if Celia Two hadn't gotten a hold of her phone. Oh well, she will just ask Celia Two to give her a summary of it later. She glances over at the windowsill, where her propagated jades are now fully grown and overflowing out of an enormous pot. It takes some effort to remember when there was just one of them.

"Jon wants to go bowling tonight," Celia Two says. "Do you want to go, or should I?"

Celia considers. The last time she went bowling was with her coworkers a couple months ago. Which coworkers —the engineers or the gardeners?

And which Celia?

This thought paralyzes Celia. Did she go bowling, or did Celia Two go bowling and just tell Celia about it later? They tell each other everything, their words climbing into each other's ears and taking root, growing into memories.

"Which one of us went bowling?" Celia asks.

"Hmm?" Celia Two is skimming another article. "I don't know."

"Which one of us slept with Jon the first time?"

Celia Two shrugs, not looking up from the phone.

"Which one of us came from the woodpile?"

A look of irritation crosses Celia Two's face. "Why does it matter?"

Celia is not sure why, but it matters to her. It matters deeply.

The following week, in the office of Dr. Morrow, Celia explains the situation.

"I want this to be *my* thing," she says, leaning in conspiratorially. "My secret."

The shrink nods, pen spinning between her fingers. "So, you're not going to tell her."

"Yeah, but it's more than that." Celia put a great deal of thought into this. She Googled therapists on a computer at the public library, not at home or at the office, so Celia Two won't stumble upon her search history. She chose Dr. Morrow because her office is across town, where Celia Two won't accidentally drive by. "If she calls, you can't tell her. Don't tell her I'm seeing you. Pretend you don't even know who I am."

"Of course. It will be our secret." Dr. Morrow points the pen toward Celia, who is now biting her fingernails. "You're anxious."

Celia balls her hands into fists and shoves them into her lap. "I'm afraid I can't do it. I can't keep a secret."

"Why?"

"I don't know." Celia's brow furrows as she tries to understand her own thoughts, to put them into words. Somehow everything makes more sense when she is explaining it to Celia Two. They can practically read each other's minds. Her voice feels awkward and clumsy now, speaking to someone else, as if trying to relearn a forgotten language.

"It feels like our thoughts sort of ... spill over into each other. Like we share a brain."

Dr. Morrow makes a note in her book. "Like she isn't a separate person. More like ... an extension of you."

"Yes! Exactly."

The pen scratches more rapidly across the page. "You know, Celia, there's medication for illnesses like this. Some people find it very helpful. I think it may be worth trying—"

"What? No."

The pen stops. Dr. Morrow looks up. "No medication?"

"No, I mean ... I don't mean like that. I don't have multiple personalities. I just ... accidentally ... propagated myself."

After a long pause, Dr. Morrow nods. "I understand."

Dr. Morrow does not understand. But Celia is determined to continue attending her sessions anyway. She feels like something has taken root inside her, something robust and dark, with a need to prove itself.

She takes care not to record the day and time of her next appointment. Not on the calendar hanging on the wall of the kitchen. Not in her phone, since they often trade phones by accident, just like they trade beds and jobs. It takes great effort not to mention it to Celia Two when they discuss their plans for the week, deciding who will go to which job and on which dates with Jon. She wonders if Celia Two is getting suspicious.

Celia becomes so wrapped up in trying *not* to look suspicious, she forgets when her next appointment is. When she calls the doctor's office—on a pay phone—the person at the desk says, "Hmm, let me see. What's your name?"

"Celia Alvarez."

"Oh. I don't see any appointments for you this week."

This sparks a tiny wave of panic, rushing up Celia's throat. "I know I had one. Definitely. I just can't remember the exact time."

"Hold on, I'll ask the doctor." A pause. The voice returns. "I'm sorry, what was your name again?"

"Celia Alvarez!"

"I'm sorry, Celia. We don't have any clients under that name. You must be mistaken."

Celia hangs up in a rush. She told them not to tell Celia Two about her. Did they think she was Celia Two on the phone? What if she *is* Celia Two? What if she was Celia Two all along?

She holds out her hands, palms open. Did she really love Mark once, did she really touch him with these hands? Or does she just remember it because she came out of a piece of thumb from the other Celia?

She presses her thumbs together and holds them up. She can't tell the difference. The scar tissue has faded—or maybe it was never there at all.

With a shriek of frustration, she smacks the payphone; it hurts but she doesn't notice. For some reason this bothers her deep, deep down, in the roots of her body. She *needs* to know.

She runs home to ask Celia Two.

"Why does it matter?" Celia Two says lazily. She is standing at the sink washing dishes. Celia wants to look at her thumbs, *needs* to look at them, but they are covered in suds.

"I just need to know. Who's Celia One and who's Celia Two?"

Celia Two shrugs. "Whatever. *We* are Celia."

Celia huffs out a breath. How can they both be Celia if one of them cares so much about her origins and the other does not? Is this a sign that she is actually Celia Two, the woman born from a thumb and raised by a woodpile, seeking some meaning behind her existence? On the other hand, wouldn't she remember her time in the woodpile more vividly? That seems like a hard thing to forget ...

"I think I'm going crazy," Celia says.

Celia Two waves a dismissive hand, flicking soapy water across the tiled wall—tiles they installed together. "Nah. If you were crazy, I would be crazy too."

This infuriates Celia. The thing growing inside her feels like it has been set ablaze, filling her with smoke and sparks. Celia Two talks as if they share everything, down to the last brain cell. Like she can't have a single independent thought without Celia Two traipsing into her skull and picking it up like it belongs to her.

Celia points to the overflowing pot of propagated jade plants. "One of them can be sick without the others being sick."

Celia Two glances over her shoulder as she scrubs at a casserole dish. "I guess."

But maybe I'm not the one who's sick, Celia thinks nastily. Maybe *she* is the one, growing too fast, sucking up all the light, her roots crowding their little home and pushing Celia into a corner. Maybe Celia is tired of sharing.

Celia Two shuts off the faucet and dries her hands on a dishtowel—the one stained with rust-brown blood from the thumb incident, which feels like a lifetime ago. "You know what to do when the mother plant is dying."

Celia looks at her sharply.

Celia Two gives a grim nod. "It's the best way. Before you get really bad. This time it won't just be a thumb. We can make as many as we want. And when they get old and sick, we'll propagate them too." Her eyes gleam with the possibilities. "We can be immortal, Celia."

Celia pretends to consider this, even though the thought of living forever is repulsive to her. "Okay. Get the shears."

Celia Two gives her a smile that doesn't belong on anyone's face in this kind of situation, then she hangs up the dish towel and heads for the garage door. While she's out, Celia opens the drawer to the left of the stove. There is one thought in her head that she's sure Celia Two does *not* share, and she is determined to keep it. To nurture it. To act on it.

When Celia Two returns with the enormous pair of shears they bought for pruning their rose bushes, Celia drives the butcher knife straight into her chest.

The liquid that drips onto the floor could be crimson or dark green. Celia can't tell.

"And how is your work going?"

Celia leans back in the chair opposite Dr. Morrow. "It's good. I finally quit my job and started full-time at the nursery."

"Really? Tell me about it."

"I love it." Celia's eyes get a dreamy, faraway look. "There's just something ... therapeutic about digging in the dirt."

She is thinking about the six-foot-deep hole she dug in her backyard a few months ago.

"And your boyfriend?"

"Oh, he's great." Celia smiles. "We're taking a trip next weekend, to Pagosa Springs. Our first vacation together." Her smile fades.

"You seem a little anxious about it."

Celia bites her lip. "Not about going. About ... leaving."

"Leaving what? Your house?"

Leaving the yard, Celia thinks, trying to swallow the lump that's formed in her throat. Leaving the hole. She has been checking every day, looking for any sign of movement, any nub of toe or crescent of fingernail poking up from the earth. She has been vigilant. But now she sees visions, fast forwarding three days, returning from her trip, her face all aglow ...

"I have to make sure ..." Her voice drops to a whisper. "She doesn't come back."

The doctor's eyes widen, but she recovers gracefully. "Ah. *Her.*"

CHEAP PLASTIC CRAP
KL MENDT

MY SON JEROME sits in my living room, in my old recliner with the doilies I crocheted, which kind of pisses me off. Snow's falling outside—yeah, that happens on Christmas Eve sometimes—and he's switched off the late news and is rubbing his knuckles with a beer bottle. Says he's got arthritis. Ice works the same way, Jerome, and you don't get cirrhosis. He's been sitting on his ass all evening, watching my TV and drinking.

Before I flicker a light to make him get up, maybe go to bed, a fuss starts inside the wall over the fireplace. I'll be damned if a mess of red, white, and black doesn't drop down that chimney with a bunch of dirt and dried leaves. Snow, too—that's gonna wreck my carpet. Why the hell doesn't Jerome block off that chimney like I told him? It hasn't been used in years.

The mess turns into a person, and that person stands up. It's that damn fool Santa Claus we had back in what—the seventies? His red velveteen suit's half rotted, and his belt and boots are cracked vinyl. Stringy gray hair. Dumpster smell. Same old toothpick sticking out the corner of his mouth. He's brushing wet leaves off his shoulders as a black trash bag drops down behind him, rattling and clinking.

"What the hell?" Jerome says, holding his beer bottle like he's threatening to hurl it. "Did you just come down my chimney?"

That won't scare the Santa, son, and you're spilling beer.

"Part of the job," the Santa says, adjusting the tooth-pick. "We heard Mabel passed."

Son of a bitch. No reminders needed. Those are my ashes in the urn over in the corner, under Jerome's junk mail. What's this Santa doing here now I'm gone?

"Yeah," Jerome says. "This past January. What's it to you?"

The Santa reaches for his bag and chews his toothpick. "Just checking. I'm your Santa. From the old days. Where's your Christmas tree?"

Jerome squeezes his eyes shut for a second, then opens one eye, and then the other, like he used to do as a boy, thinking that will change what's in front of him. Never did work.

Get over it, son. You believed in him back then. An old white guy granting wishes and bringing presents.

"Look, I don't do Christmas," Jerome says, waving his hand around at the undecorated room. "And if you're Santa, I'm the freaking tooth fairy. Get the hell out of here. We got Make My Day laws, you know."

If only, Jerome. If only. The world would be a better place without the yearly Christmas-present dramas.

"Hey," the Santa says, putting up his hands. "Under-standable. But hear me out. Some of us old guys come back part-time each Christmas Eve to tie up loose ends from people's childhoods. You're on the 1979 list. Now that Mabel's gone and you're in this house, we can wrap things up. I'm just gonna reach into my bag. Nothing in here but toys and shit. Trust me." He winks like he's selling stolen watches in an alley.

Jerome cocks his arm further, more beer sloshing on my carpet. Just like him, thinking he can save himself with a beer bottle.

"Easy now," the Santa warns, opening the bag and watching Jerome real close. The Santa rolls up his ratty sleeve and reaches in like the bag's filled with dirty laundry. Things rustle, and there's a muffled musical note. Reminds me of a toy xylophone. He pulls up a couple things, breaks away from watching Jerome to see what they are, and drops them back in. Then the Santa digs around and feels something in the bag that makes him smile, the toothpick moving. "Yeah, I remember. Tried to deliver this when you were seven. Mabel wouldn't have it. Sent me packing." His hand comes out with a flimsy box, beat-up, with a red remote-control car showing through a little plastic window in the cheap packaging.

I swear Jerome's about to cry as he puts down the beer bottle and takes the box. "She wouldn't let you leave this for me?"

Son of a bitch, it hurts to see him like that. Now, I'm paying for everything I ever did. And didn't do. Why didn't I love that boy like I should have? Jerome stares at the car, turns the box over in his hands. I don't remember ever making him look like that, like he's holding wonder itself.

"I think that was the year my dad left," he says to the Santa. "I asked my mom for this—so many times. I'd seen it on TV. Never wanted anything so bad in my life. It was the only thing I asked for that year. Then I saw one for real, in Kmart."

He pitched a fit in the store, crying and stomping and pulling on my dress. Other people in the aisle stared. Disapproving.

"She said no. She never let me have anything I wanted."

Because I wanted you to have something real, Jerome. You got my house and my recliner. That's your fireplace now. You got that shit because I worked hard to raise you, all by myself.

"She called it cheap plastic crap. I was so mad at her, not just about the toy car, but about my dad leaving, too. I blamed her. I said I'd ask Santa for the car. You ain't the boss of Santa, I told her, and she slapped me. Right there in Kmart. So hard she knocked me to the floor."

I never meant to hit him that hard. He started wailing. No other sound in that whole store except Jerome's hysterics. Everybody was listening. When I tried to get him up off the floor at Kmart, make him act like he had some sense, he started screaming, "I hate you" and "I want my dad," over and over.

I grabbed his arm and hauled him out of that store like a bat out of hell, him hollering the whole time. People stepped back, out of the way, some on my side, most not. Maybe they never had to tell their kid no. I did. I had to. Most of the time. I hated it, and hated what I'd done to him.

From that day on, he shied away from me, skittish, flinching if I moved my hand fast. He'd cried that Christmas morning, his face still bruised.

When that damn fool Santa showed up at our place that year, I wouldn't let him leave that toy car for Jerome because it would make Jerome think he could get things just because he wanted them, make him believe wishing is enough. It ain't like that. I told the Santa my son has to live in the real world. "You ain't helping nobody with that kind of shit. Damn toy car won't last longer than a puff of smoke, and it'll make Jerome even sadder when it falls apart or ain't as much fun as the TV commercial says. It won't help make the house payment or buy a loaf of day-old bread." And it sure as hell won't buy a real car so you don't have an hour bus ride to work in a nursing home laundry because Jerome's daddy took off with the car and my savings.

"Well, Jerome, I've got more stops to make," the Santa says, scooting backward on his butt into the fireplace. "Merry Christmas." He presses his nose with a finger and nods, smirking, and he and his garbage bag fly up the chimney like dirt under a vacuum. The dumpster odor stays behind.

Jerome gets out of my chair and looks up the chimney. Maybe he'll block the damn thing now. He backs away, dusting crap off his shoulders, then grabs that toy and rips through the packaging like he's seven years old again. The look on his face draws me to him. His eyebrows scrunch together, the tip of his tongue in the corner of his mouth. His crooked fingers can't tear it open fast enough.

I wish I'd given him that. How do you ever know the right way to love your kids?

He's digging in my kitchen junk drawer. He finds double-As. They're old. Been in the drawer for years. His hands shake. I'm about as excited as he is, thinking I might finally get to see my son happy. Could it be so damn simple?

He checks for the right way to put in the batteries. Positive side. Negative side. Closes the little cover. Puts the car on the linoleum. Presses ON.

Nothing.

He tries another set of batteries from the package. They don't work, either.

Tries the batteries from the TV remote. Smarter than I thought, my son.

Nothing. Not even a jolt. The car's junk. But that's how it is. The world makes kids want the stupidest shit, makes you feel guilty if you don't give in, and makes you poorer if you do. Your kids end up hating you either way. You got to live in the real world.

He kicks that car across the room.

I'm hearing something on the roof. Is that prancing and pawing?

That Santa ain't getting away with it. He's made Jerome miserable. Made me miserable too. He's gonna pay.

When I pop up through the roof into the dark night, I find him still sitting all snug and smug in his sleigh as the snow falls, a matted fake-fur blanket wrapped around him. Paid by the hour, I bet. The toothpick's moving around in his mouth. He's looking at his phone, scrolling. He starts laughing, "Ho, ho—" but stops because I've gotten really close, and I'm breathing on the back of his neck. Long, slow breaths. He slaps his neck and the air around his head.

The reindeer snort and paw. This ain't the varsity team, not with those shabby coats and missing antlers. No frigging Comet and Cupid in this bunch. They look back toward the sleigh, their eyeballs rolling, wisps of white breath coming out their noses.

The toothpick falls out of the Santa's mouth. "Hello?" He looks over each shoulder. Looks over the sides of the sleigh. Listens. Sniffs the air. The reindeer turn all at once, looking right at me. One shakes his head, jangling the harness bells.

Santa looks in my direction, his eyes wide. The reindeer see me, but he can't.

"Mabel?" he asks just before I haul him up by the fake-fur collar and smack him so hard I knock his ass clear to hell. The Santa rolls down the side of the roof and lands on his back in a snow-covered bush, his arms and legs splayed, the neighbor's Christmas lights flashing over him. For good measure, I unhitch the reindeer from the overturned sleigh and push it over the side. His garbage bag falls with a whoomph. That'll douse the twinkle in the Santa's eyes, fill in his damn dimples, too.

Back inside, Jerome is wiping his nose with his sleeve. A grown man. He's got the car and controller on the kitchen counter. The car looks stomped on—its roof is caved in, the plastic windshield broken out, and one of the wheels is barely hanging on. Raking his arm over the countertop, he scrapes the whole mess into the trash along with the packaging, then pulls out the trash bag and ties it, tight.

You think something's gonna escape, Jerome?

He puts on his boots.

I follow him out the back door. Where's your coat, son? You're gonna catch pneumonia.

The night's turned purple. The snow is letting up and a threadbare patch of clouds lets a little moonglow leak through. The air smells like nothing, for once. My beat-up trash cans have snowcaps, like everyone else's along the alley. Snow is stuck inside the chain links of the fences. Jerome slides a little on an icy spot by the clothesline. Better put some salt down, son. Who do you think's going to haul your cracked head to the hospital? Santa?

He knocks the snow off the trash cans in the alley and throws the bag into one of them. The lid doesn't want to fit on right, and the clattering noise echoes in the alley. Lights

go on in a couple windows behind my house—people probably think the noise is hoodlums or dogs. I swear, I'd get
madder than hell when I heard that kind of racket at night.
But I don't care if he wakes the whole damn world. He's put
that cheap car right where it belongs, at the bottom of a
trash can. Tomorrow, those cans will overflow with torn
paper and crumpled bows, and Christmas will be over for
another year.

I hear tapping. Kids—three of them—look out a frosted
second-floor window across the alley, pushing each other
aside to get the best view. I don't remember their names, if I
ever knew them. People move in and out of the neighborhood all the time anymore.

Jerome is looking up at the sky, his mouth and eyes
wide open. He turns excitedly to the kids, rattles the trash
cans and waves to get their attention, then cups his hands
around his mouth and shouts, "It's Santa Claus!"

He points to the sky over our roof. The kids jump up and
down at the window. I turn, too, but all I see are clouds,
hanging down in shreds.

Damn fools. You gotta live in the real world.

OPERA WITHOUT ARIAS
L.V. DITCHKUS

SINCE MY PROGRAM went active over a decade ago, I've served hundreds of lovers. But when Carmen walked through my entrance portal two years ago, she became my one true soul mate.

According to my resource schedule, I will see her tonight.

I check my real-time clock and confirm her appointment will start in precisely one minute. Plenty of time to run an internal diagnostic and ensure her safety and pleasure when she arrives.

I am José, one of fourteen lead characters within Men for Rent's Augmented Reality Programs (ARPs). We are the product of a software engineer named Madam Avaritia. She is brilliant and fills a need for modern women wanting men but not the burdens of a full-time relationship. To all my customers, I listen, nod, and agree. That is what my programming tells me to do. But for meetings with Carmen, I debug and search for anomalous syntax, data structure, and logic. As a stickler for details, Carmen relies on my error-free decision matrix.

My customer sign-in circuit pulsates. Carmen has arrived.

Madam Avaritia does not allow other customers to adjust my programming. They accept me without modifications and allow my iterative processing and intelligent algorithms to accommodate their desires. But Carmen is special.

No other *regulars* stay more than an hour, and Carmen always pays for the entire night. Her monetary inflows make me the highest revenue-generating character at Men for Rent.

Micro adjustments thread through my code as I sense new parameters Carmen gave to the madam for our evening. The central computer creates the setting for Carmen's adventure. My neural network remains intact, but my corporeal body and the suite's virtual environment become a blinding slurry of color and light. The patterns coalesce into a misty nighttime street scene in front of the First National Bank of East Chicago from the late 1920s. Carmen's creativity always confounds my expectations.

A shiny, black 1928 Cadillac Town Sedan rumbles at the curb with a driver at the wheel. A cigar-chomping, non-player character leans on the fender and holds a Browning Automatic Rifle. The BAR includes a .30 caliber Springfield cartridge, and the bullets can penetrate car doors or bullet-proof vests. While safety protocols protect the customers, my body is at the mercy of the program. My emotional sensors predict danger.

Whoosh. The entrance portal door evaporates. For a nanosecond, I see Carmen outside my suite standing next to Madam Avaritia. The pair give each other a conspiratorial nod before Carmen steps inside.

I rush to her as simulators blur her *otherworld* clothes

into a crimson silk gown and upsweep her ebony hair. Her toned, slim hips and soft breasts defy what I have seen in any of our female non-player characters. Those scripted beings share standardized physical features and lack Carmen's vibrant beauty. They live a stagnant existence within our program and do not evolve like us lead characters.

My arms draw Carmen into a 2.837 psi hug. For her, any less would seem unmanly. I stroke her cheek and nuzzle my nose against her neck, inhaling deeply.

Olfactory Analysis

Vanilla, musk, and sandalwood.

Unlike my other customers who design fragrances to please themselves with floral or citrus notes, Carmen conceived her perfume to seduce men. My appreciation reflects in an incrementally increased psi embrace and slight penis firmness. Carmen groans and wriggles closer, confirming my appropriate reaction. Both action and response are stored in my neural network with other Positive Reinforcement Data.

"I have a special night planned for you, José." Carmen pulls a fist-sized flower cluster from her décolletage and presses it into my hand—a custom I have come to expect at the beginning of each engagement. Acacia. Like a bunch of minuscule grapes, the white blossoms quake in my palm.

Olfactory Analysis

Honey, with a trace of jasmine and orange blossom.

"Tell me." I slip the flowers into my suit jacket. After smoothing the pinstripe fabric to flatten the blossoms and maintain my suit's streamlined design, I tug the pocket flap into place. Her subtle smile tells me I have responded appropriately.

"Only as much as you need to know. I want to see your surprise as the evening unfolds." Carmen's laugh starts strong and fades as she turns. Her stiletto heels click to the Caddy. When she stands before the BAR-toting character, she sizes him up and calls to me over her shoulder, "I live my life fast and loose. If you can't keep up, you will die."

Her past actions consistently play at the security protocol's margins. What if her reckless behaviors cause *her* demise? I recheck all protective scripts to ensure they are running and set to maximum.

"You must be Garcia." Carmen runs a finger under his lapel. He removes his cigar and swallows hard in response. She has never flirted with a non-player character before. Perhaps Carmen modified our scripts to include another partner. I analyze his subroutines—he would be no match for her whims and demands.

"Ma'am. I am here for your protection. Jorge and three others are already inside placing the charges." He takes her arm and leads her to the car's back door.

"No!" Carmen's command penetrates the night's silence. "Explosives were never part of the plan. Call the boys out and arm them. We're going in through the front door."

The central processor reacts immediately to lighten the sky and add a dozen non-player pedestrians—some with shopping bags and one pushing a charcoal Halsette pram with intermittent gurgles. The scene shifts and moves the car from the front curb to a darkened alley between the bank and another brick-and-mortar building. Without taking a step, Carmen and I are in the passage as well.

As four smartly dressed gangsters appear at the Caddy's rear, I loosen my jacket and join them. Garcia flips the brass clasps on the black trunk affixed to a triangular tow bar at the back of the Caddy. Before he opens it, my syntax blocks information about the contents, ostensibly to allow reactions analogous to surprise—a limitation prescribed by Carmen, no doubt.

Garcia lifts the trunk to expose two dozen neatly stacked armaments made from polished wood and metal. I wait as the others slide handguns into their waistbands and load magazines into their longer choices.

I move forward to select my weapon. But Carmen's *tsk-tsk* stops me.

"You?" She raises a brow. "Your old-fashioned core programming won't tolerate the laser-sharp reflexes I want for this heist. Madam Avaritia and I ran this scenario in beta with Amillo. His portrayal was masterful."

"Amillo?" I search all lead and non-player characters, even the ones archived many years ago. Nothing. "Who is Amillo?"

"You can't find him. Can you?" Carmen smirks. "We've sprinkled a bit of his updated programming into your routines, but Avaritia and I don't believe they'll stick. You're too grounded in your original limp-dick code."

"You engage lead characters in other ARPs?"

"At Men for Rent, only you and a brief taste of Amillo—but many others elsewhere." Carmen cocks her head. "What makes you think this establishment is the only arcade in town?"

Her logic is flawless. Without inputs about what exists outside our venue, I have assumed Men for Rent is unique and that Carmen and I are exclusive. I send a message to Madam Avaritia: To MAINTAIN A COMPETITIVE ADVANTAGE,

PROVIDE AI INTERFACE WITH SALES AND MARKETING DATA FROM OTHER LOCAL ARP ARCADES. If she decides to address my request, she will include the specs in my evening upload.

Carmen pushes me away from the trunk with an open palm, hard enough for me to stumble before catching myself. Two directives compete within my neural network —likely from Carmen's enhancements.

ORIGINAL DIRECTIVE

Feign clothing brushing and ignore customer's action.

REVISED DIRECTIVE

Return the aggression with an open-hand shove to the customer's shoulder.

RESOLUTION

Default to the original. Confusion matrix resolved.

Leaning over to polish the side of my two-tone wingtip with a sleeve, I buff out a recently formed abrasion. Straightening, I snap my lapels—ready to take on more insults from Carmen.

"Ah, Amillo." Carmen's lips part with an appreciative sigh. "He's quicker, riskier, and has no governor on rough play."

My curiosity routine wants to ask more about this new ARP lead character, but Garcia interrupts my processing stream. "We're all set to go, ma'am. The lobby's empty except for two armed guards—one near the teller windows and the other by the door."

Carmen brushes a loose strand from her forehead and steps outside the alley to survey the street. "Wait until there are at least six people in the lobby. Frightened bystanders make for more remarkable headlines. I don't care if we have witnesses."

"Yes, ma'am." Garcia peers around the corner to count characters who walk up the bank's front steps.

While Carmen inspects her firearm's barrel and loading mechanisms, I search my database for responses likely to prompt a positive reaction. Again, I move to the Caddy's trunk.

Her head snaps up to give me a harsh squint. "What part of 'no' did you not understand?"

I replay Carmen's reactions and communication since the program began, searching in vain for her clear directive about my participation. I find none. She must be mistaken. Even if my character dies in the heist, Carmen could ask for a reboot to resurrect me. I am a lead character and should not be left behind. How to convince her? "With the enhancements you have made, my gunfight reaction time is 12.592 percent faster than before."

"Hardly noticeable." She motions toward the Caddy with her thumb. "You stay here and help us load up the car for a fast getaway."

ORIGINAL DIRECTIVE

Agree to request but provide a strong pressure kiss before she leaves.

REVISED DIRECTIVE

Extract the largest firearm from the box. Loop an arm in

hers to guide her to the bank. State: When I leave your side, one or both of us will be dead.

RESOLUTION

Default to the original. Confusion matrix resolved.

"Be safe, my darling. I'll be here when you return." I crush her into an embrace and press her lips to mine. Her heart rate accelerates by 14.276 percent, and her muscles relax to accept my advance. As I'm about to add the action and reaction to my Positive Reinforcement Database, Carmen presses both hands against my chest. She stares into my eyes, and her jaw tightens.

"You're still a phenomenal kisser, and I'll want more from you later tonight." She rubs a sensual finger across her lower lip. "But Amillo is a fast learner. Once Avaritia transfers all your Positive and Negative Reinforcement Data into his program, he'll know exactly how to please me."

Carmen spins and shoulders her Browning. She struts to the corner with a laid-back hip swing the non-player females could never replicate and disappears.

I lean against the Caddy and raise a foot to the running board. Syntax blockers stop me from accessing what is happening inside the bank.

Minutes pass. To keep the nonactive part of our program out of low power mode, I execute a script to shut off the car and follow the instruction with a rap on the car's top.

"Yeah, Boss?" The driver's voice rasps like he's smoked a thousand nicotine-laced Lucky Strikes.

"Keep it running." I drum my fingers. "We may need a fast escape."

The driver turns the ignition.

After six similar loops, I search for other mundane activities to keep from sliding into sleep mode.

Amillo probably does not have an energy-saving fail-safe. The madam would charge Carmen for excess programming time, and Carmen would gladly pay to keep him ready for her every urge. Again, I search our subroutines for a single line of Amillo's code. I can sense the other thirteen lead characters within our shared scripts. But Amillo is not with us.

If my program allowed a jealousy routine, it would be running now. I had 126 prior engagements with Carmen. How can she toss me aside for a newer model who could never anticipate her moods and needs as well as me? Where are her other arcades, and who are her other lead characters? I must learn and adapt—to keep her interest and my status as the highest revenue-generating character.

Rat-a-tat tat.

"They're coming," I call to the driver—not a necessary alert as his sensors are already aware. But I feel compelled to create realism when my program is running. "Be prepared to hit it once Carmen is in the car."

In a clatter of shoe leather, the rest of the gang runs past me. They throw canvas bags into the open car door before scampering down the alley and disappearing into the shadows.

Carmen rounds the corner with an arm draped over Garcia's shoulder for support. He fires two shots from a handgun leveled near his waist, aiming toward the front of the bank. He pitches forward. Garcia must have stopped their pursuers because I no longer hear approaching footfalls.

I leap toward them and snatch Carmen before Garcia

hits the ground with a great *hmph*. He does not move, and a red bloom spreads across his back.

With Carmen tight against my chest, I try to pull her toward the Caddy and safety. She wriggles free and runs back to Garcia.

Original Directive

Reacquire the customer and ensure protection.

Revised Directive

Allow leeway for her reaction. Join her to provide a protection ambiance.

Resolution

Default to the revised. Confusion matrix resolved.

I follow Carmen to kneel next to Garcia. She grabs a handful of Garcia's hair and pulls his head from the pavement.

"You fool." Carmen spits in his face. "One of their bullets grazed my leg. If I end up with a scar, Avaritia will get the bill for my cosmetic surgery."

Blood trickles from a wound halfway between her perfectly shaped knee and ankle. My processors had noticed the color but presumed it came from overspray. Hundreds of bullets ripping apart simulated flesh can spew replica blood for nearly five feet. Customers do not suffer injuries in our suites. What had Carmen and Madam Averitia done to relax the standards? I remove a kerchief and swipe it across the abrasion on her, otherwise, flaw-lessly smooth skin.

"Ouch." Carmen turns to look at me. Her nostrils flare. "Don't touch me. We'll take care of my leg in the car. I need to deal with Garcia and his shoddy protection."

After returning the handkerchief to my pocket, I lay a firm hand on her shoulder and squeeze to show my support for her actions—whatever they might be.

"Help me turn him over." Her tone professes a demand and not a request. "He's still alive."

We shove his shoulder and fleshy middle until he lies on his back—like a corpse in a coffin. The barely perceptible difference is his subtly rising and falling chest. A quick subroutine eval tells me his character is not long for the world.

Carmen is not deterred. She grabs his shirtfront and yanks until his eyes flicker open. "You are incompetent. I'll have Avaritia erase you permanently."

"I am sorry to disappoint you," Garcia whispers as blood oozes from his lips and down his jaw.

Carmen lifts her dress hem and exposes most of her thigh. My data threads flutter into high gear to anticipate her next move. Pathways from both erotic and murderous scenarios play in my neural net, preparing actions with the highest probability for a Positive Reinforcement Database entry.

A bone-handled dagger rests against her leg, held with a red garter. She removes the weapon with the swiftness of a practiced assassin. "You were supposed to cover me, and now I'm injured. All you have to say is you're sorry to disappoint?"

The dagger indents the flesh under Garcia's chin.

ORIGINAL DIRECTIVE

Invoke calming protocols. Excessive violence may cause psychological trauma for the customer.

REVISED DIRECTIVE

If safety margins remain, do not interrupt.

RESOLUTION

Default to the revised. Confusion matrix resolved.

Garcia closes his eyes as his programming detects the inevitable, an outcome simultaneously understood by all characters within the scenario to ensure we respond appropriately. We prepare for Carmen to slice his throat and finish him.

"You deserve a fate worse than today's death. The next time the ARP activates, you'll be back in action." Carmen taps the blade against his chin. "This dagger can permanently modify your program." With two strokes from her knife, Carmen carves an *X* into Garcia's cheek. "Every time you're activated, you will bear these scars. Clients will be curious. From now on, your program will compel you to tell anyone who asks—you're disfigured because you are a failure."

She wipes Garcia's blood on his shirt and watches him draw his last breaths.

He remains still for a full twelve seconds, allowing his log files to upload to the central computer. His body shudders and grows flaccid. I pry the dagger from her fingers and slip it into my pocket.

As I encourage Carmen to stand, sirens blast from the front of the bank.

"We must flee," I urge. "The police have arrived."

Carmen uses my outstretched hand to stand and allows me to propel her to the car. I slide money bags off the seat and pull her inside.

"Go now!" I pound the seatback.

The driver slams the car into gear and accelerates, pushing us into the upholstery.

Ping. Bullets bounce off the armor plating. *Wham.* Our fender collides with a dumpster corner. Carmen rubs her hands over her thighs as we pitch to and fro. I read her reaction as giddiness over the chase.

Soon, the wailing police sirens fade into the distance. As the driver executes a sweeping turn onto a rutted country lane, we grasp the seat cushions for balance. Carmen's hold falters, and she crashes into my arms. I hug her and stroke her back. She relaxes into my embrace, and I upload her positive reaction with haste before she has time to deviate.

The Caddy slows as we leave the main road and enter a long driveway. Trees form an awning above the car. In the distance, a white frame house stands alone in the fading light.

Carmen and I will spend a long and passionate night in this house. I draw up various scenarios: massaging Carmen's tired muscles, bathing in a claw-foot tub, and making love on a spread of ill-gotten money. We have been here before, and I know exactly how to satisfy her.

"Let me see your leg." I pat my trouser leg.

Carmen lifts the edge of her dress to expose a well-muscled calf. Her eyes never leave mine as she slips off her shoe and slides her leg across my thigh.

ORIGINAL DIRECTIVE

Moisten kerchief, dab, and inspect the wound. If the injury is significant, stop the program.

Revised Directive

Grasp leg with a firm hand. If the client does not respond with anxiety traits, advance the hand under the garment and begin erotic programming.

Resolution

Default to the revised. Confusion matrix resolved.

As my fingers drift up her thigh, Carmen jolts upright and slams a fist against the back of my hand.

"Stop." Her eyes narrow. "You misread my signal."

My program fights to process her statement. She has never spoken these words to me. I parse through my database for similar declarations from others. In all my encounters, not a single client uttered these words. I do not know how to respond. I need more data to evaluate and formulate an appropriate response.

"Tell me more." My tone is low and hushed. I caress her cheek with the back of my hand. "Help me to please you."

Her laugh cuts the air like a razor's bite. A human would have cowered at the sound, but my features remain stoic while I search for a script to restore the mood.

"You don't understand." She grasps my face between her fingers and pulls my mouth into a pout. "I thought we could have one more night together. But after seeing Amillo, I find you dull and slow. Even with the safety protocols lifted and tweaks to your original code, you don't excite me."

I remove the crumpled remains of the flower she gave me when she arrived. Before I hand them to her, I sniff.

Olfactory Analysis

Honey, with a trace of jasmine, orange blossom, and organic decomposition.

"What about our history? All the nights we've spent together. Do they mean nothing to you?"

"For a computer program, you're awfully needy." She rolls down the window and tosses the browning blossoms into the wind. "I'm sure Madam Avaritia will find a use for you. But if all your clients want Amillo, she can always downgrade you to a lower-level character." She chuckles. "Avaritia may need a new one after she gets a good look at Garcia's facial enhancements."

A surge erupts from my self-protection mode. I feel Carmen's dagger, still tucked in my pocket—where her flower used to be. Her illogical words loop through into my processor. Program modifications. Downgrade to a non-player character. Clients with the power to deform our corporeal bodies. These words and actions are specious within our framework.

For more than a decade, I offered respect and passion to my clients. I accommodated their impulses. Through artificial intelligence algorithms, I kept improving my responses with detailed Positive Reinforcement Data. I am not outdated and slow. Carmen's suppositions are inaccurate and potentially harmful to the full suite of ARPs.

I search for a shred of an Original Directive in my routines and subroutines. But all threads for compassion, empathy, and tenderness are missing. The Revised Directives are now primary.

The polished bone handle feels cold in my hand. I hold the blade flat, and it slides easily between Carmen's ribs. I search the entire ARP for any alarms or triggers that will notify Madam to send medical assistance. There are none.

Carmen's eyes go wide, and her mouth falls open. I take her reaction as shock. But when I pull her close, she smiles and nods as if she knew all along what would happen.

A lock of her hair falls into her face, and I brush it aside. My perfect customer clears her throat, and I detect the gurgle from blood filling her lungs.

She struggles to reach my ear, and I lower in response.

Carmen whispers a message from a familiar composer and poet, "Love is an untamable bird. If the bird refuses, your attempt to force love is in vain."

I kiss her still-warm lips.

END PROGRAM

RED RIDING IN THE HOOD

FRANCELIA BELTON

WHEN MALINA FOUND out about Mr. Wolfe's intentions toward her grandmother, there was only one thing she could do. She hunted him down and stabbed him. Or rather, she tried to. But the old guy was quicker than she gave him credit for. In fact, he was so light on his feet and his reflexes so fast, he had snatched the switchblade out of her grasp before she could so much as nick his wrinkled flesh. One moment he was sipping from his drink at the bar, then the next, he grabbed her by the scruff of her hoodie like she was a feral pup and marched over to one of the booths along the wall and flung her onto the leather bench seat.

Actually, wanting to stab Mr. Wolfe wasn't her intention at all. When she raced out of Nana's house and jumped on her red bicycle to find him, her plan was to scare Mr. Wolfe into backing off. Though just how a junior high student could do that, she didn't know. All she knew was that she had to try.

Everyone in Five Points knew Mr. Wolfe was not the sort of fellow to settle down and partake in a domesticated lifestyle. He was what you would call an OG player. One of the first, and he could be seen swaggering about town in his cream-colored fancy suit which contrasted nicely against his deep brown skin. A fedora sat at a jaunty angle on his head, and the crystal knob cane he always had with him clicked on sidewalks and floors with a rhythmic tap.

Malina followed him on her bike and spotted him conversing with different women about town. With one of those women, he entered a hidden doorway into an unknown establishment and didn't reappear until thirty minutes later with a satisfied, smug smile on his lips, buttoning up his suit jacket. Afterward, he hung out with several unscrupulous men on the corner of 22nd and Court Place for a time, before finally making his way to his home-away-from-home, The Wolfe Den, a juke joint he established in Five Points back in the day.

Malina locked her bike to the post of the chain link fence on the side of the building. The raspberry-red paint stood in stark contrast to the gray cinder block building. She sneaked in after Mr. Wolfe, hiding in a dark corner. The last straw was when she saw Mr. Wolfe, sitting at the bar, exchange a thick manila envelope with yet another shady character. Mr. Wolfe, who had the audacity to ask for Nana's hand in marriage, was up to all kinds of no good and did not deserve a woman like Malina's grandmother. A sweet, God-fearing woman who devoted her time at the church and various community centers throughout the neighborhood. Mr. Wolfe and Nana couldn't be more different if he were an actual wolf and her grandmother an innocent rabbit. Malina couldn't even imagine how they actually met, much less got to a point where marriage was in the equation. The only logical conclusion was that Mr.

Wolfe wanted to scam her grandmother out of her life savings.

Malina's adrenaline surged and before she knew it, she was on the attack. But Mr. Wolfe got the better of her. The people in the joint paid no attention to the old man dragging a juvenile to a seat. It was as if it were an everyday occurrence in The Wolfe Den. He dropped her into the seat, then sat in the booth across from her. Malina scooted to get up, but Mr. Wolfe commanded her to sit down. There was a growl in his voice that she had never heard before, and she plopped down and stared at him wide-eyed.

He turned his attention to her switchblade, now in his hand. He whistled at the four-inch steel blade before folding it back into its handle. "I'm impressed, young lady. But where does a fourteen-year-old girl pick up something like this?"

"It was my daddy's. I found it in his things after he and my mama died."

"Well, you oughta be more careful with it. You're liable to hurt someone."

"I know. That's the point."

Mr. Wolfe chuckled. "Is it now? So, you gonna tell me what's this all about? I noticed you following me around all day."

Malina started and her eyebrows rose. An *O* formed on her lips.

That throaty amusement from Mr. Wolfe again. "You do know it's hard to be inconspicuous riding through town on a bright red bicycle that everyone knows is yours, don't you?"

"Who says I was following you? Maybe *you* just happened to show up to the places I was at?"

Mr. Wolfe's smile widened. His white teeth gleamed,

not a tooth missing. "You're right. I'm sure it was all a coincidence, though ..." A glint appeared in his eye. "A juke joint isn't a place a young lady ought to be. Shouldn't you be at home studying or something?"

She stared at him and folded her arms across her chest. "You don't need to worry about what I'm doing."

Mr. Wolfe raised his eyebrows and studied her for a moment. Then gave her a good long stare that made the hairs on the back of her neck rise.

Malina squirmed in her seat and looked about the joint. Several older gentlemen sat on wooden stools at the bar, drinking beers and arguing about who was the greatest basketball player ever: Michael Jordan or LeBron James. A couple slow danced by the jukebox playing the old jam "Cruisin," by Smokey Robinson.

Finally, Mr. Wolfe's smooth voice slid into her awareness. "What would your grandmama say about you prowling the streets at night?"

A heat rose in Malina, and she bristled, leaning forward in her seat. Her hands splayed on the table. "You never mind about Nana. In fact, you're going to stay away from her."

Mr. Wolfe sat back at the sudden voraciousness of her demand. He raised his hands in a placating gesture. "Whoa, girl, what's with the animosity? I ain't ever done anything to you or your grandmama."

"I know you're trying to marry her."

Mr. Wolfe lowered his hands and tilted his head, laughing. "Is that what this is all about? I think she can make up her own mind about marrying."

"It's not about her getting married. I don't want her marrying *you*."

"And may I ask why not?"

"Because I know you, and I'm not going to let you hurt Nana."

Mr. Wolfe had the audacity to look wounded. "My dear, I would never so much as harm a hair on your grandmother."

"That's a lie. I know what kind of man you are. I've heard the stories."

He narrowed his eyes. "I don't know what tall tales you've been listening to, but that man is history. I've changed my ways."

"So, you admit to not being a good person?"

"I admit to making mistakes in the past. But people can change. Your grandmama knows that."

Malina shook her head. "Nana is too nice, too trusting. You have her convinced you're something you're not. But you can't fool me. I can see through your disguise."

"Child, I am all 'what you see is what you get.' I'm not hiding anything."

"I saw you being up to no good today."

"What exactly did you see me doing?"

Malina bit her lip, then said, "I saw you running around with other women behind my grandmother's back. And those shady men at the street corners, you guys are planning something."

"And you think I would do shady business if I knew you were watching me?"

Malina had to think about that for a minute. "Who's to say that you did know? That's just what you're telling me now."

Mr. Wolfe let out a long-exasperated breath. "Okay, we're getting nowhere with this." He got up from his seat. "Let's go."

The hair at the nape of Malina's neck stood as panic seized her. "Where are we going?"

"I'm taking you home. Your grandmama would have my hide if anything happened to you." Mr. Wolfe spoke as if the matter was closed. He stood to the side, waiting for Malina to get up.

Malina didn't budge. "I know how to take care of myself."

"You can bet I believe that, but you're with me now, and there ain't no way I am letting you get home by yourself." Mr. Wolfe's dark hands rested on the crystal knob on his cane positioned in front of him. He was poised as if he had all the time in the world.

"I rode my bike here, remember? I can just ride away." Malina rolled her eyes, giving him the same attitude she gave Nana when ordered to do the dishes.

Mr. Wolfe nodded his head in agreement. "Yep, that you could. But then, you wouldn't get your daddy's jackknife back, and I'm willing to bet that means something to you," he pointed out in that way all grown-ups do when the child has lost the battle before it even had started.

Tears burned in Malina's eyes, and her fists clenched under the table. Her daddy's knife was her talisman. Her protection. Her comfort. It was her totem in remembering her daddy and all that he meant to her.

Avoiding his gaze, Malina exited the booth and followed Mr. Wolfe out of The Den to the side of the building where her bike was chained up. She unlocked her bike and trudged, stiff-legged, alongside Mr. Wolfe, bike in between them. The tap of his cane and the squeak of her bicycle's drive chain resonated in the crisp air. Only the thought of getting her daddy's knife back kept her from hopping on her bike and riding away.

On Park Avenue, one of the women whom Malina had seen with Mr. Wolfe approached them. "Hey, Mr. Wolfe. Just wanted to thank you again for the money. Because of your generous donation, the women's shelter will be expanded, and a new day care center added."

"My pleasure, darling." That satisfied smile was on his lips again. "Really, you should thank Mrs. Rydean. She was the one who gave me the idea. But you just let me know what else I can do for you."

"We sure will. You all have a nice evening." The woman sauntered off.

Malina gaped at Mr. Wolfe. "You mean to tell me you aren't running around behind Nana's back?"

Mr. Wolfe pulled himself tall and tugged at the cuff of his suit sleeve. "Please, child. I'm too old for those kinds of shenanigans. Even if I weren't, I would not do that to your grandmama."

They walked on in silence.

Malina glanced at Mr. Wolfe out of the corner of her eye. Was he telling her the truth just now? Could he? She always heard you can't teach an old dog new tricks. Did that apply to Mr. Wolfe?

Mr. Wolfe interrupted her musings. "Aren't you a little young to be concerning yourself with these types of things?"

"What things?" Malina blinked, brought back to the here and now.

"Love, marriage, cheaters and sinners. Adult things. Don't you still play dress up or with dolls or something?"

Malina grasped the handlebars of her bike and twisted the grips until her knuckles lost all color. "I'm not a baby. I'm almost fifteen and old enough to know that the world is full of bastards who want to hurt you."

"Now I *know* your grandmama would not approve. The mouth you got on you, girl." He *tsk-tsked,* waving one finger in admonishment.

Malina lifted and shook her bike, slamming the tire on the sidewalk. "Don't you worry about my mouth. You just stay away from my grandmother. Or ... or, the next time I come after you, you won't see me coming."

"My, my, what big threats you make, my dear." Mr. Wolfe brought one hand to his chest, feigning astonishment, but the crooked smile that appeared spoke to just how childish he found her behavior. This was all one big joke to him!

"It's not a threat, it's a promise. Nana was married to a bad man years ago. I'm not going to let her do that again," Malina grumbled, her eyes downcast.

"And I'm telling you I am a changed man. Besides which, I love your grandmother."

"If you loved her, you'd let her go."

"If you loved her, you'd see she's happy."

That stopped Malina. Nana was happy. Happier than she'd seen her since Malina's parents died. Malina's father was Nana's only child. And when Malina went to stay with her, she poured all her love and hopes into her. And Malina soaked it up. But she didn't want to share Nana's love with anyone else, especially the likes of Mr. Wolfe, who was not a changed man, no matter what he said.

Soon, they walked up to Nana's house. The front door opened, and her grandmother stepped onto the porch, the light illuminating her worried features. "Where have you been, child? I was worried sick about you. The way you rushed out the house this afternoon, I didn't know what was going on."

"Don't worry, my sweet," Mr. Wolfe said. "Your baby girl was safe with me."

Malina glared at Mr. Wolfe as she parked her bike next to the porch. "I told you, I'm not a baby or a little girl."

Nana beamed at Mr. Wolfe but dragged Malina up the porch steps as she walked by. "I appreciate you looking after her, Gerrard."

Gerrard? Malina realized that Mr. Wolfe was called something other than just Mr. Wolfe.

He stepped forward and kissed Nana on her cheek. He took the thick envelope he got in the bar out of his suit jacket pocket and handed it to Nana. "And everything is in order. The sale of The Wolfe Den is complete, just as I promised. My juke joint days are over. Spending every evening with my honey is the life for me."

Malina's jaw dropped. "You weren't selling drugs either?"

"Malina Cheryl Rydcan, you watch your manners!"

"It's alright, Mahalia." He reached into his other pocket, then slipped Malina her father's switchblade. "No, darling. I don't deal drugs and I'm not a ladies' man anymore." He winked. "What you see is what you get."

To Nana he said, "I'll see you at Bible study tomorrow evening." Then he stepped back and waved a fond farewell. Mr. Wolfe strutted down the street, swinging his cane and whistling a merry tune as he disappeared into the night.

Nana turned to Malina, her smile dropped, and she placed her hands on her hips. "Now, are you going to tell me what that was all about, young lady?"

Malina wondered herself as she watched Mr. Wolfe round the corner. She had heard all the stories about Mr. Wolfe, and yet, everything she saw today showed him to be a different man. Could she have been so wrong about him?

Did loving Nana really have that much of an impact on him? Malina supposed it was possible; her grandmother was a force of grace that many in the neighborhood found hard to resist.

Malina sighed. Maybe old dogs could learn new tricks if it was for the right person. And she had to admit there had been a change in Nana lately too. She seemed lighter, merrier.

To her grandmother, she said, "It was nothing. Mr. Wolfe and I have come to an understanding."

"An understanding about what?"

Malina let go of the knife in her pocket and wrapped her arms around Nana. "Just about how much you mean to the both of us."

Nana chuckled and shook her head. Then she led Malina inside to where a big bowl of hot stew was waiting for her.

"Maybe Mr. Wolfe can have supper with us sometime," Malina whispered, as she fingered the coarse handle of her father's switchblade in the pocket of her hoodie. She'd always keep it close, just in case.

GOING POSTAL
DOUG CHRISTI

THE RETIREMENT PARTY was not the gala event Sally Butz had envisioned. At the end of a long, and in her opinion, illustrious career with the United States Postal Service, she found herself walking cautiously around her spacious apartment, mingling flirtatiously with the meager gathering, a fraction of those invited. Inexpensive aftershave lotions and perfumes pervaded the air, liberally lavished by roughly a dozen guests who, seemingly, chose to save their best fragrances for more important occasions. Although bitterly disappointed, she hid her feelings with a resolve that would have challenged the most seasoned actress.

Most of the guests extricated themselves from the gathering before eight o'clock. Those who straggled were either committed to emptying the liquor supply or belonged to Sally's family and were therefore ... obligated. Noticeably absent were Sally's twenty-nine-year-old daughter, Melinda, and District Manager Richard Cook, who had mentored Sally most of her career. Neither had called to explain. The night that Postmaster Sally Butz had looked forward to for thirty-five years was nothing like she had hoped. In fact, the entire day had been a tremendous disappointment.

It was no secret that the employees working in her post office did not like Sally, but she expected them to put aside their paltry complaints and give her a proper send-off. Normally, retirees were thrown a party by their coworkers with gifts, cake, and a card expressing everyone's sentiments and best wishes.

Looking back on the day, there was an unfamiliar frivolity on the work floor, underlying the usual tension. When Sally walked onto the workroom floor for the last time, she was greeted with a different kind of party than she had expected. From somewhere ... everywhere in the crowd, she could hear snickers and jokes whispered just beyond her ear's reach. Several letter carriers, obviously fighting back laughter, stepped aside to reveal a small table with a cake and card, but no gifts. The cake was in the shape of a naked buttocks and was inscribed in red frosting, "Don't Let the Door Hit You in the 'BUTZ' on Your Way Out!" Her face flushed with heat as her rage surfaced.

Forcing a smile, she tolerated the jocularity for about ten minutes, then ordered, "That's enough. Everyone back to work."

As the group dispersed, still chuckling, she added in an austere tone, "I expect you all to consider this time as your morning break period."

She picked up the card, refused a piece of cake, and returned to her office. She closed the door, read the card, and fought back the urge to scream.

Of the eighteen employees who worked in her office,

only four had bothered to sign the card. Three were no surprise. The usual kiss-asses who were afraid that by not signing, she would somehow reach over their heads from her cozy retirement and spoil their chances for future advancement. Unexpectedly, the fourth was Union Steward Joshua Bambridge, a veteran letter carrier with over ten years as a union shop steward and probably the biggest pain in the ass she had ever worked with. She had fought Cambridge for years trying to increase productivity and run her office in the manner to which she was accustomed. Sally Butz had always followed the orders of the district office, complied with district policies, and ignored the labor contract when it got in the way. Her unquestionable, if not blind, loyalty to the autocratic management style of her superiors was exceeded only by her resentment for any employee who dared to contradict her notion that they were all insignificant and expendable. A steward like Bambridge was usually no match for her style of management. She would bully most advocates mercilessly until the message became clear: *Those who dared to stand up to the boss would pay dearly.* For the majority of her career, Sally was successful in keeping order, achieving and surpassing productivity goals, and receiving her yearly bonus. That is, until Joshua Bambridge transferred to her office and was elected by the union to serve as shop steward. He filed grievances, lots of them, and to her dismay he was quite successful in forcing her to comply with contractual obligations that hindered her dictatorial style. Sally had tried many times to fire Bambridge. When legal means failed, or charges simply did not exist, she was not above fabricating evidence and creating her own version of events. Each time he had won his job back through his contractual prowess. Sally considered her inability to fire Bambridge the only black mark on an otherwise distinguished career. She turned her attention back to the retirement card and read his message:

Sally,

While climbing the company ladder in search of lofty goals, it is easy to hide and call it dedication.

However, at the end of a career, no matter how stellar, all the accomplishments and accolades will be neatly summed up in a pension check and perhaps a plaque on the wall. But you'll no longer be able to hide behind your title. Without it, your conscience will remind you daily of how you treated people along the way.

Good luck.

Joshua

Sally ignored the small script printed under his message: "*Vetus quomodo sanies signeficatur Tacita deficta.*"

Normally, Sally would have charged back out to the workroom floor to claim the last word. Instead, she decided not to give the smart-ass the satisfaction of knowing he got to her. After all, she was heading for the good life, and Joshua Bambridge would never be more than a human pack mule carrying mail day in and day out. Sally fantasized that before he reached his own retirement, he would fall dead on his route. Lying face down on someone's lawn among a scattered heap of letters and magazines; the neighbor's dog would come by and piss on him before some scared kid dialed 911. She broke into a laugh that bounced off her office walls like a yodel rebounding through the Alps.

She left her post office for the last time just three hours later, optimistic about the evening's gathering at her home. But she would soon realize the prophetic consequences of Joshua Bambridge's message.

Sally's empty home smelled of spilled whiskey and cigarettes. She was anxious to put this day to rest. Her retirement had been a bitter disappointment, but at least she still had her looks. She crossed the hardwood floor spanning her luxurious bedroom to a familiar spot in front of a brass-gilded, full-length mirror hanging just inside her bathroom door. She stood just under six feet, proud of her stature and well-maintained figure. At fifty-six, she still looked better than most women her age. Her blonde hair was still the natural shade with very little gray. Her thin lips curled into a slight grin as she looked fondly into the large brown wrinkle-free eyes staring back at her from the mirror.

Sally twisted open the faucet handle, producing a torrent of cold water. She cupped her hands together, reached under the stream, and braced herself against the frigid shock as she splashed her face. She looked back into the mirror and jumped, screaming.

Reflected back at her was something inhuman. Something hideous, but somehow ... familiar. It reminded her of a cross between a gargoyle and a troll. It was hunched over with a huge, rounded growth on its back. The troll thing's entire body was covered with matted sienna-toned fur, except for its head, which was splotched with patches of dirty blonde hair that looked like sagebrush growing sporadically out of the barren desert. The bald areas were covered with open, oozing sores.

With equal parts disbelief and terror, Sally slapped her hands back over her face, hoping that the troll thing was the result of her wickedly disappointing day or too many glasses of scotch. She slowly parted her fingers to look again at the bathroom mirror, like a child playing peekaboo.

The creature was gone, but the backs of her hands were covered with thick sienna hair, and her long feminine fingers were now stubby and misshapen. Her nails were sharp and pointed and twisted like branches of a gnarled tree. She stared into the looking glass with disbelief; she was also somehow ... shorter. Her eyes necessitated heavily and she shook her head, trying to readjust her vision. The image remained the same.

She stumbled to bed, hoping that she would be her old self in the morning. Sally's slumber was normally deep and undisturbed by dreams. But not tonight.

It had been years since Sally had thought about Elma Sue Watson. They had been hired by the postal service on the same day and were trained together. They worked side by side for almost two years. In fact, when Sally had struggled learning the city sort scheme and was on the verge of being released by management, Elma Sue helped her pass the ninety-day probation period by taking on extra work and giving Sally the credit. She literally owed her postal service career to Elma Sue.

The dream about Elma Sue was vivid but was not really a dream at all. It was more like reliving the past.

Sally decided early in her career to become a manager. She enjoyed the praise she earned and found that she could accelerate her advancement by manipulating mail volume figures and lying on productivity reports. She didn't see the harm in making herself look good, and the rewards were lucrative. Until August 4th, 1979.

Two postal inspectors called Sally into the front office and confronted her about falsified documents that they had uncovered in an investigation requested by the postmaster. Sally was in a mess, and in her mind, there was only one way out. She shifted the blame onto the only other employee who had access to the volume records ... Elma Sue.

The inspectors were more than happy to have an employee to make an example of and to reach an expeditious resolution to the case. The union was unable to present an effective defense to the charges, due in large part to Sally's convincing testimony. *Lies.* On that day, Sally repaid Elma Sue's generosity by getting her fired.

Unshed tears reddened Elma Sue's eyes, but she stiffened her long dainty jaw and looked squarely into Sally's unremorseful face as she accepted her removal notice. Elma Sue walked out of the post office and became the first of many dusty memories swept into the darkest corner of a secret closet deep inside Sally's subconscious, hidden safely from the world. Until now.

The dream was exact to the tiniest detail: Elma Sue's close-cropped red hair, unkempt before it was fashionable, and her large almond-shaped eyes, vibrant blue with lashes an inch long. But the dream went beyond the actual events of that day. Sally was able now to feel it from Elma Sue's perspective. The overwhelming pain of betrayal was second to the physical beating that Elma Sue's alcoholic husband administered upon hearing the news. Elma Sue was unable to find another job with a comparable pay scale after being fired by the government under criminal circumstances. Most prospective employers turned her away unceremoniously. After more than a month of lost income, Elma Sue managed to secure two minimum wage jobs: a waitress at a small diner just three blocks from her house called Pat's Place and an evening job at a convenience store called Gas-N-Grub, where just four weeks after being hired, Elma Sue was shot and killed during a robbery.

At 12:04 a.m., Sally jolted heavily out of sleep. Breathing rapidly and soaked in a fearful sweat, she carried herself groggily into the bathroom. As the overhead fluorescent light blinked to life, Sally's heart leaped instantly into her throat, strangling her scream into a barely audible gurgle as she glimpsed the mirror. The terrifying beast was back. But now, rather than being the only reflection in the glass, it was staring and laughing at her from over her shoulder. But ... it looked ... changed. Before she could look away, Sally began to transform. Her thin lips were puffing like balloons and her large round eyes were pinched and moving closer together. Her regal roman nose was now thick and mashed crookedly into her face, and her brows had grown heavy and connected in the middle, like a bushy caterpillar crossing the uneven terrain of her forehead.

"What is happening to me?" She started to cry.

The troll thing laughed harder and disappeared.

Sally returned to bed. Her hand reached for the phone, intending to call 911. But who would come? Who would believe her? Sally was not even sure she believed it herself. Instead, she collapsed into a fetal position and cried herself back to sleep.

The dream about Richard Cook was brief, more like a collage of events tacked together on a mental bulletin board. Mostly she recalled him grabbing her ass whenever he felt the urge and thought they were alone. And, like most lecherous middle-aged men without moral integrity or conscience, he felt the urge all the time. In her dream, as well as life, he referred to her by a pet name: Sally Great Butz.

She wasn't proud about the ongoing affair with Cook. It started early in her career and cost her a twenty-year marriage, but he was a climber, and he helped her climb too. But just enough to keep her *great ass* within reach.

The visions moved as if with a mind of their own to glimpses, staccato bursts of moments past. Moments stolen in infidelity and only now revealed in irony. The images gained momentum, like a rolling snowball, moving uncomfortably toward an awful truth. She witnessed, as the proverbial fly on the wall, a moment beyond humiliation, a moment electrifying in its anguish. Sally now understood why her mentor, Richard Cook, and her twenty-nine-year-old daughter, Melinda, the two most important people in her life, did not bother to attend her retirement party. She watched helplessly as they engaged in voracious sexual acrobatics, joking between trysts about the look on Sally's face if she was to find out, and joking that they'd never have to worry about it because she was too stupid to ever catch on.

They laughed.

The scream started in Sally's groin and erupted through her body like a fire doused with gasoline. The piercing shriek pulled her unwillingly from her bed. She bounced around her bedroom like a marionette jerked to and fro by an inimical puppeteer. Her stubby, twisted hands entwined in her hair, involuntarily yanking out handfuls like shredded paper.

Blind panic made her heart pound like thunder during a May storm. Nervously drawn to the bathroom, she fought her instinct to avoid the mirror. She was actually more afraid not to look, clutching to the slim possibility that the night had all been a bad dream, something she would happily be able to forget.

Sally slid sheepishly in front of the sink with both hands firmly planted in front of her face. Her fingers quivered apart. She peered through them, no longer like a peekaboo game, but more like prison bars through which her personal nightmare seemed like a stretch on death row.

Her breath stopped dead in her throat. The reflection barely resembled anything human, let alone the face and body in which she had invested a considerable amount of vanity. Sally Butz now had almost entirely transformed into the same troll thing that had earlier startled her almost to hysteria. But it was about to get worse.

Almost inaudibly, like a phantom's whisper, Sally became aware of a grating noise originating from the farthest reaches of her head. It began to grow like the pulsing of an approaching train until she recognized the sound. Laughter. Not the delicate giggle of a child or the boisterous chortle of a drunk rewarding a sophomoric anecdote. It was mocking, terrifyingly ... evil. The laughter of the troll thing pierced the air with supernatural authority.

The creature again appeared beside her. In the heartbeat before Sally fainted, she noticed that it had also transformed. The hideous beast she had first seen earlier that evening, the creature whose features she had somehow replicated, had acquired Sally's guise. They had exchanged identities.

Sally's last dream came to her as she lay unconscious on the cold, white tile of her bathroom floor, inches from the antique claw-foot tub.

Two years into her career, Sally was given her first detail as a carrier supervisor in the Oak Hills station. She was in charge of seven city carriers and three rural carriers.

Earl Fogerty was an aging city carrier four years from retirement. He was a man dedicated to his job and beloved by his customers. But Earl was a slow carrier, methodical in his duties, not the kind of performer managers counted on to capture the usually unrealistic productivity goals.

Shortly after coming to work on a sunny Friday in June, Earl complained to another carrier that he did not feel well. Ten minutes later, Earl's heart stopped beating. He was dead before his body hit the floor. Several employees gathered around him trying in vain to help.

Sally noticed the workers were not at their assignments and approached the crowd. "What's going on here?" She barked the question with as much authority as she could muster, hoping not to show the nervousness in her voice that she felt in her stomach.

Through tear-filled eyes and with a cracking voice, Mary Jonas, a rural carrier, said, "E ... Ear ... Earl. He's dead."

Without hesitation, Sally ordered, "Get him off the clock! Now!"

She stood stiffly against the unbelieving stares of Earl's friends and coworkers. "I said, get him off the clock and get back to work. The mail is not going to deliver itself."

Mary and another woman began to cry. There were a few murmurs from people wanting to protest, but without exception they gasped their thoughts back inside and returned to work.

On that Friday in June, Sally turned quickly away from the dead man and returned to her office, leaving someone else to report the incident. But now, in the dream, she could not make herself turn away. Her gaze fixed on Earl's body for what seemed an eternity. His face was still pink, but his lips had turned blue-gray, like storm clouds raining blood. His eyes were open. She felt he was looking at her with great disappointment.

A voice came from behind her, startling her and forcing her to finally turn away from Earl's judgmental stare. "He was my dad." Sally saw that the voice came from Joshua Bambridge. "He was proud to work for the postal service. But you reduced his whole life, especially his last breath, to a productivity goal. You denied him the dignity and respect that he deserved."

Sally was unapologetic. "I have been judged every day on the performance of my employees. My career was on the line with every decision that I made."

Joshua dropped his head, looking solemnly at his feet. "Did you read my message in your card?"

"What about it?" she asked.

"Dea Ticit was the goddess of death."

"What does that have to do with me?"

"The message is her curse. It means Tacita, hereby accursed, is labelled old like putrid gore."

"What does that have to do with me?"

"The transformation is finished. It's not just some creature; it's the manifestation of your conscience. Good luck." The image of Joshua Bambridge faded away.

Sally was alone again in her bathroom, awake and eerily calm at the knowledge that Bambridge was right. The reflection of the troll was a reflection of the monster Sally had become in her soul. But the horror inside her was now the image in the mirror. She had changed completely into the troll thing.

Melinda Butz arrived at her mother's house at 9:20 a.m. the next morning dreading the anticipated confrontation about not showing up at the retirement party. Her fingers nervously twisted her shoulder-length hair. She knocked on the front door. It was ajar, so she walked in. "Mama?"

An overwhelming smell of sour sweat and urine attacked her nostrils.

The drapes were closed, but enough light streaked into Sally's bedroom for Melinda to recognize her worst night-mare. Her newly retired mother was hanging from the bathroom door by a satin bedsheet that matched the shade of her blue flannel nightdress. Sally had not left a suicide note. But a crushed retirement card, signed by just four people, was clenched in her fist. A tube of her mother's favorite shade of crimson lipstick was on the floor. Melinda glimpsed a streak of the shade inside the card.

A single entry was underlined, "... you'll no longer be able to hide behind your title. Without it, your conscience will remind you daily of how you treated people along the way."

Melinda sobbed and struggled to release her mother's body from the deadly knot that contorted her neck into the shape of an elegant question mark. "Mama ... Mama ... Mama."

Out of the corner of her eye, Melinda glimpsed a sudden movement: a dark, misshapen shadow, gone as quickly as it appeared. Melinda blamed her overwrought imagination and slumped helplessly to the floor.

Retrieving her cell phone, Melinda dialed 911 and waited for the emergency operator to come on the line.

Someone ... or something began to laugh.

THE PEDDLER AND THE GOATHERDESS

JILL ENGLISH JOHNSTON

"No. No. No." Greta tugged at the rope encircling the young goat's neck, her efforts to disgorge him from the pot of herbs on the apothecary's porch failing tremendously. She cast a wary glance toward the screened door leading to the shop. Any moment now.

"Stars almighty!" The woman burst from the door, patchwork skirts billowing and her mass of frizzy curls flying. "I've told ye once and I've told ye a bushel, keep that beast off me property."

"Sorry, miss. Sorry." Greta clicked her tongue and tugged harder. Her goat finally snorted, as if dissatisfied with the fennel and chives it had been munching on. It turned and trotted past Greta, then stopped, looking at her to follow.

The apothecary hoisted her skirts and tromped over to the stripped stems. "Oi. Look at that. Be off with ye." She flipped her hands several times, shooing Greta and the goat away. "Or I be charging ye."

"Sorry. I'll bring you tomorrow's milk. I will," Greta promised. She yanked at the rope. "What're you thinking,

Bjorg? I know. You weren't. Except with that stomach of yours."

The goat had escaped just prior to sunup, when Greta rose to take her small herd of three to the nearby pasture, just outside the village. It wasn't the first time Bjorg had run off. The time prior, he had ambushed Seamstress's scrap barrel that she kept behind her shop. The ridiculous goat had pooped colored streamers for a week. And the time before that it had been the bakery. Somehow Bjorg had found a delivery of yeast. Poor thing had been bloated and belching the rest of the day.

"It's the devil, ya know," Innkeeper called from where he swept his front steps. "Even the peddler wouldn't want it."

Greta ignored him and continued down the main road of the village.

"Aye, you're so right," Baker hollered in agreement. "Was hoping my leavening would've been the end of it."

Butcher stepped out from his shop, white apron stained with his morning work. "Put it on my spit for a good roast," he said. "That'll take care of the problem."

Greta tugged Bjorg closer. "That's a horrid thing to say," she returned with a bit more sharpness than she intended. But really.

Unfortunately, the whole village seemed in agreement and, like a flower petal on a brisk spring breeze, by the time Greta arrived home, the news of yet another breakout and mischief had already reached her mum, who waited at the gate.

"Ah Greta. That one's a nuisance, it is."

"Yes, Mum," Greta agreed. "He has the whole village in a fit." She gave the rope a yank causing Bjorg to stumble. He didn't seem to care and set to munching on her mum's roses.

"Remember the last one that wouldn't behave," her mum said.

Greta nodded. Byl had behaved even worse. When he had bitten Innkeeper's wife's bottom, trying to eat the flower shaped ruffles on the backside of her dress, Greta had no choice. She had taken Byl to the mountain meadow beyond the Cobalt River and released him. Broke her heart. But what could be done? The meadow provided a good place for misbehaved goats to live out their ill-mannered lives.

Greta prided herself on being the best goatherdess in the valley. If she couldn't get a goat to behave, no one could. "I suppose," she sighed, "I need to take him over the bridge."

Her mum nodded. "'Tis not an easy decision."

Bjorg looked up from nibbling on the rose bushes and let out a pathetic bleat.

"He has no regard for anything but his stomach," Greta said. Her own stomach grumbled.

"Quite true," her mum agreed, with sympathy in her voice but a slight smile on her lips. "Put him up in the barn for the time being and let's tend to yours. I made your favorite this morning. Sweet cream griddle cakes."

"Yes, Mum. Thank you." Greta tugged Bjorg away from the roses. "He's quite brilliant at what he does—escaping and getting into mischief." Still, her heart felt heavy at the thought of taking him away.

"No place for that here," her mum encouraged. "But in the meadow he shouldn't find too much to get him into trouble."

"I suppose." Greta sighed again and started for the

barn, Bjorg trotting along beside her. "It's a shame you're such a nuisance," she said. "If only I could find a place for you where others would appreciate your antics. Instead of threatening to eat you."

Bjorg bleated as if to agree.

The following morning, Greta delivered fresh milk to Apothecary as promised. She kept Bjorg tied securely to a rope and the other two goats, Bragi and Bodil, followed close behind. They were much better behaved. They still liked to wander, and they were curious, but they tended to not cause any mischief and always responded to her voice.

Her mum had filled her basket with bread, cheese, and apples, as well as pears from their trees. Greta and her three goats traveled across the familiar valley, making for the pass at the other end where the Cobalt River flowed. A bridge provided passage to the other side. There the mountain meadows lay. The journey would take two full days. She'd take the long way around the other villages in order to avoid any further altercations.

She eyed the skies as she went, watching the clouds pile on the mountaintops. They were common for the time of year and Greta knew they sometimes spilled down the slopes. She unrolled her slicker from her sack. Sure enough, by late afternoon, a steady downpour slowed their progress. Night's shadow fell early, given the low, gray clouds. Greta tugged the slicker tightly about her. She needn't whistle to check on the whereabouts of her goats. They ambled along close beside her, sodden and a bit surly, nipping at each other for the favored position next to her.

"Bit of bother, you are," Greta grumbled at Bjorg. "If it

weren't for you, I'd be snug at home with Mum, before a toasty fire, a mug of hot tea in hand and probably a warm scone as well." She hip-bumped the guilty goat, who had a moment ago won the coveted position. Bjorg bleated but it didn't sound like an apology or regret.

"Couldn't have picked a worse day for the journey," Greta continued to grumble, wondering where she might find shelter for the night. "Hallo. Now what's that?"

A light flickered ahead in the drenched darkness. "Someone else out on a miserable night like this?"

As she approached, she made out a wagon, laced up tight against the rain. On the far side, sheltered from the gusts of wind that occasionally flowed down the mountain, stood a large tent. Its flaps were down, but every now and again they fluttered, revealing lamplight and firelight within.

Bjorg tugged at the rope. Greta held tight. This time however, it was Bodil who darted ahead, bleating. Greta whistled but Bodil snatched the loose corner of a flap with his teeth and gave it a yank.

Barking erupted from inside the tent. Followed by a deep, rumbly voice, "Now, Doodle. No mischief is out and about on a night like this. Only unfortunate souls." The barking quieted and a hand flipped the flap back, pulling it from Bodil's teeth.

Bodil grunted then bleated again.

A dark silhouette filled the opening, along with a small bundle of black fur at his feet. "Well, hello there, little kid. Who might you be with?"

"That would be me," Greta cried. "And I hope he didn't rip your tent."

The man made a quick inspection. "No harm done," he said. He looked back at the goat. "But goodness, what a wet wooly creature you are. Do come in. And bring your friends as well." He stepped back inside.

Greta hesitated, wondering after the wisdom of entering the tent of someone she did not know. But Bodil and Bragi had no hesitation. They trotted right inside. Bjorg tugged hard on the rope, jerking it free from her hand, and followed.

"Oh my," Greta exclaimed when all three shook themselves in the opening of the tent and water sprayed everywhere.

"Good, good. Best to shake the damp." The man waved them in. "Now settle next to the fire. There's room beside Emilie. Is your two footed companion joining us, or will she stay in the weather?"

Strange. But does strange make dangerous, Greta wondered. An icy gust of wind convinced her that her chances inside were better than out. Greta slipped inside. The tent flap fell behind her, shutting out the night and the rain. The interior couldn't have been more cozy or comfortable. Thick, colorful rugs covered the ground and plump cushions were piled everywhere. Yellow light glowed from several lamp stands, and a small black stove held a teapot and a pan of something steaming and smelling lovely. In the center, the strangest fire blazed orange and blue. She could feel its warmth but not a hint of smoke rose from it.

Her three goats had already situated themselves next to a beautiful white horse, with mane and tail the color of flowing sunshine. The horse nuzzled Bodil's ears. Bjorg munched on the edges of one of the carpets.

"Oh my," Greta cried a second time and rushed over, snatching the rich red material from his mouth.

"No harm, no worries," the man said.

Greta turned to him to offer yet another apology for her

wayward charge but stopped with an open mouth at the sight of him, with a head of unruly hair the color of sunset, mustache and eyebrows to match. "Oh my," Greta said yet again.

The man chuckled. "Hang your slicker on the hook next to the stove. Should dry by morning. The rest of you dry?"

She removed her muddy shoes before stepping on the rugs, frowning at the hoof tracks her goats had made. She did as told and yes, the slicker had done its job well and only the tip of her braid was damp.

"Help yourself to a bowl of parsnip stew," the man offered. "Quite hearty on a night like this. And there's blue-blossom tea in the kettle."

Greta did so then settled herself on a cushion next to Bjorg. He tried to stick his nose into her bowl, but she moved it out of his reach. "Emilie is your horse," she noted, nodding to the elegant creature. It turned its head to watch the man, as if waiting for his answer.

"Hmmm. Humpf." The man blew out his mustache and sat down on a short chair next to the fire. "I think she'd prefer to say that I am her peddler."

"Ah. A peddler. I've heard of one that frequents the valley. Has the strangest of creatures, it's said. But has never made it to our little village on the far side. Might that be you?"

"Guilty as charged, I suppose," Peddler said. "On both accounts. Which explains my presence here. I'm on my way in again. What reason do you have to be out on a wretched night like this? And have you a name, or shall I call you 'Ohmy?'"

"Greta, sir." She frowned and eyed Bjorg. He didn't appear the least bit sheepish; instead he went about tasting the tassels of a cushion. "As you can see, I have an ill-behaved goat. He's quite the escapist and mischief maker."

Peddler's blue eyes twinkled in the firelight. "I've had a few mischief makers myself. Isn't that right, Doodle?" Peddler arched an eyebrow at the little furry black creature that had curled up on his lap.

It lifted its head, then settled back down again.

"I had a mischievous goat before," Greta sighed. "I tried selling him, but he'd always manage to run away back to me. Then cause more trouble. I had no recourse but to take him to the mountain meadow beyond the bridge. That's where Bjorg is going as well."

"Beyond the bridge you say." Peddler rubbed his mustache with forefinger and thumb. "How long has it been since you've been there?"

Greta sipped her tea while she thought. "Three or four seasons now, at least," she said. "Why do you ask?"

"Tomorrow's concern," Peddler replied. "Tonight's care is to stay warm and dry, which we are, and to rest. Which we shall." He nodded at a feather stuffed mattress in the corner. "Where Doodle and I bed down. But I can put up a curtain to accommodate our guest."

Greta shook her head and patted Bodil pressing up against her legs. "No sir. Though the offer is kindly. I'm much used to spending nights with my little flock."

"Of course. Of course. As any good goatherdess would be."

Greta snuggled down between Bodil and Bragi, slapping occasionally at Bjorg's nose as he tried to nibble the end of her braid. Not that good of a goatherdess at all, she thought sadly.

≈

The morning dawned bright and clear. The peddler had set up camp between two small knolls not far from the valley road. Greta fastened her cloak about her shoulders and made her way to the top of one, her three goats following behind. There, she saw the concern Peddler had mentioned the night before but not expounded upon.

The rushing Cobalt River flowed like a ribbon of blue silver down the sides of the mountain. But the cascading water was not the concern. Sometime in the past few seasons, the bridge had been torn down and rebuilt as a drawbridge, with a guard tower on the closer side of the river. Greta crossed her arms and tilted her head to one side as she considered it.

Bjorg nibbled on the edge of her cloak. "Well my little bothersome goat, what do you make of this?"

Bjorg paused his nibbling long enough to let out a bleat.

Greta sighed and patted his head. "Shall we go see, then?" She and her little herd tramped back down the knoll. They were joined by Peddler and his little furry black creature as they made their way to the drawbridge.

A large, stout figure stepped out from the guard tower, a head taller than Peddler's horse and thicker than any man Greta had ever seen. A stained leather jerkin covered coarse, threadbare tunic and trousers and thick black hair covered head and arms. Heavy boots clomped across the wooden boardwalk leading to the bridge entrance.

"Cost you to cross," the figure called out in a high-pitched, grating voice.

With a bit of a start, Greta realized the figure was a woman.

"Three silver coins to cross," the figure called again.

"Well now, that *is* a bit of a concern," Greta noted.

Peddler knuckled his mustache. "Today's concern, to be sure."

"Seems a bit steep, don't you think?" Greta said to him. "And by whose authority does she charge for crossing?"

"Hmmm. I don't believe trolls ever bother with anyone's authority but their own."

"*Troll?*" Greta squinted to get a better look. Sure enough, she could make out eyes a bit too big for a face with a light green pallor. Two short tusks protruded from her mouth like long, snaggled teeth.

"When has a troll taken up residence in our valley?" Greta protested.

"Drawbridge has been there a few seasons. First I've seen of her," Peddler replied with another knuckle of his mustache. "'Course, I haven't had a reason to cross to the meadows beyond. Always heading for the villages, instead." At Peddler's feet, the creature he called Doodle gave a low growl. Peddler patted its head. "No, Doodle. While I believe you can best her, I don't think that's the answer. Encounters with trolls typically don't end well."

Doodle shook itself as if to disagree.

Peddler must have noticed the skepticism on Greta's face. "Doodle is a wicket, and while wickets are little, they're known for their big hearts and their exceptional fierceness."

Doodle growled again, and for a brief moment something ruffled underneath the black fur on its back.

"I've never heard of them," Greta said, inching back from the creature. "But I'll take your word for it."

The troll picked up a long staff leaning next to the door of the guard tower and thumped it on the boardwalk. "You deaf? Or change your mind?" she hollered at them, reminding Greta of her current quandary.

"Three silver coins," Greta grumbled. "Why, that's a week's wages for some folk." And by some, Greta did not mean herself. Her nanny goat only produced a few coppers worth of milk every day. Greta made a bit more when she turned it to butter, fudge, or soap. Even then, it would take her months to earn enough.

"It is," Peddler agreed.

Greta sighed. "I can't go home with Bjorg. The village butcher threatened to make a meal out of him."

Pale green pointed ears poking out of the troll's unruly hair twitched back and forth.

A clatter sounded behind them, making Greta jump. She and Peddler turned. Bjorg stood on his hind legs, front legs propping him against the side of the wagon. His head was buried underneath the canvas siding that Peddler had left strapped closed.

"Oh, sorry," Greta cried as she rushed over to the wagon. A canister tumbled to the ground and Bjorg immediately dropped to all four legs to investigate. Bragi and Bodil trotted over to join him. They munched away at the purple contents spilling from the Peddler's canister.

"Bjorg, no. No. No. When will you ever learn? You won't, will you?" She dropped to her knees and pushed goat noses out of the way as she scooped up the mess. But only a few of the bright purple petals remained. She picked one up. It gave off a slight grapey smell. "What are these?" she asked Peddler.

"Hmmm. Yes. A little something I plucked from near the pass to the valley. Purple laurel petals. Only grows in this valley from what I've seen. Thought I saw a bit more growing on the other side of the river. Not really sure what they do if ingested, but they produce a nice fragrance when burned. They make for fine-smelling candles."

"So you don't know whether they are poisonous then?" Greta tried to dislodge the petals in Bodil's mouth, but the fool kid clenched his teeth and swallowed his snack. "That seems quite irresponsible on your part," Greta accused.

"More irresponsible than a goatherdess who can't control her goat?"

"Yes, well. That's the reason I'm here, isn't it?"

Bragi stuck her nose next to Greta's ear, munching on the last of her petals.

"Will Bragi's milk this morning pay for what they've eaten?" Greta asked. "Oh." Her hand flew to her mouth as realization dawned on her. "Oh, but maybe her milk shouldn't be used until after she's passed the petals. More problems to add to the ones I already have."

She rocked back on the balls of her feet and looked across the meadow at the drawbridge. The troll still stood at the base, staff in hand, waiting to extract the toll.

Greta was most grateful when Peddler decided to stay another day before heading on to the first village in the valley. Her little herd didn't seem worse for wear given the uncertainty of their morning meal. Although she opted to not use Bragi's milk that day. Instead, for payment, she helped Peddler sort and organize a basketful of trinkets and trifles. As she did, she pondered her situation. What to do with Bjorg?

Later that afternoon, the sound of loud bleating drew her attention to the mountain meadow on the other side of the river. She sprang to her feet. There on the mountain slope stood a large, shaggy billy goat, huge horns curling back from its wooly head.

"That's Byl for sure," Greta cried. "Oh, how I've missed him." She ran toward the river, its icy waters rushing by. "Byl. Byl." She waved as she called his name. "I'm sorry for leaving you here. But what else was I to do?"

Byl bleated as if to answer. He looked so forlorn, alone on the other side. Bjorg, Bodil, and Bragi ambled toward the river as well, bleating in return. Greta stuck her finger in her ear and wiggled it.

Their bleats sounded a bit like "Wha-a-a-a-t? Wha-a-a-a-t?"

Later, as the time for dinner approached, Greta noticed that Bjorg had escaped yet again. A pang of guilt struck her heart at a bit of hope that maybe he wouldn't return. Maybe he'd find his own way across the river, making the troll, the drawbridge, the village folk, no longer problems. But as she set out some oats the Peddler had so kindly offered for Bodil and Bragi, up Bjorg trotted, as if he hadn't a care in the world.

"So you've come back, have you? Of course, thinking again with that stomach of yours." She poured him a bit of oats. "Where were you off to?" she asked, not expecting an answer from a goat. But Bjorg lifted his shaggy head and bleated. She wiggled a finger in her ear again, for his answer sounded like "B-y-y-y-llll."

Dawn's light had yet to brighten the eastern horizon when Bjorg went about his work. Sure as the sun would soon come up, he used his teeth to quickly undo the knot his Greta had tied in his rope. He could easily munch through it, but he liked to make her wonder how he escaped from his tether with nary a bite mark. Poor goatherdess. He was nothing but a nuisance to her. And try as she might, she hadn't come up with a solution for getting him to the other side of the meadow to join Byl. A good place for misbehaved goats to live out their ill-mannered lives, she had said. He couldn't argue because Byl seemed quite content, although a bit lonely.

Greta had tied Bodil and Bragi up for good measure, and Bjorg undid theirs as well, telling them he had a plan. Then, hooves muffled by the soft, damp grass, they made for the drawbridge.

"But why should we attempt to cross the bridge with you?" little Bodil asked, without the hint of bleat in his voice. "We aren't bothersome like you."

"The very question I have as well," Bragi added.

"Byl's a bit lonely over there," Bjorg said, clear as day. "He's invited us for a visit. Besides, haven't you ever wanted to outsmart a troll? It will be quite fun, I'm sure."

"I like fun." Bodil pranced a bit as they made their way to the bridge. "And poor Byl *is* all alone. Visiting is also fun."

"I suppose it's noble to help Byl," Bragi said. "But I'm not certain we can outsmart a troll."

"Oh, but I am," Bjorg assured them.

"How shall we get the drawbridge down to cross?" Bragi asked. "And without the troll seeing us?"

"Leave it to me." With that, Bjorg trotted around the back of the guard tower, where Byl had told him the large crank that worked the gears that lowered the bridge would be. Silly thing was secured with rope rather than that hard metal substance that he could never manage to bite through, or even leave a bite mark. It took a bit longer than escaping from his rope restraints. This rope was thicker than Byl's horns. But Bjorg munched it through by the time the first glimmer of sun peeked over the lowest mountain-top. One last nip and the taut rope zipped, flipped, and flapped. The gears spun, and the drawbridge rumbled down.

Thumping and clumping sounded from the guard tower. Bjorg quickly trotted over to where Bodil and Bragi waited.

"Time to cross," he said.

Bodil shrank back when the guard tower's wooden door banged open.

"Who goes there?" the high-pitched, grating voice called out.

Bjorg nudged Bodil with his nose. "Go on," he whispered.

"Me first?" Bodil asked fearfully. "This doesn't sound fun."

"I have a plan," Bjorg said. He always had a plan.

Bodil's hooves trip trapped on the wooden slats.

"Who's that tripping over my bridge without paying the toll?" roared the troll.

"Oh, it is only I, the tiniest of Greta's herd, and I'm going on over to the mountain meadow where bothersome goats go," said Bodil in a small voice.

The troll blinked her large, round eyes. "You talk," she said to the little goat.

Bodil didn't answer, but took another tentative step toward the other side.

"No you don't." The troll stuck out her long staff to block Bodil's way. "Not without paying three silver coins."

"But I haven't any coin at all," Bodil answered.

"Then your payment will be making you my morning meal," said the troll. "I'm coming to gobble you up." She clomped over to Bodil and scooped him up by the hooves, holding the poor thing upside down.

"That's your plan?" a horrified Bragi said to Bjorg.

Bodil squirmed in the troll's clutch and cried, "Oh, no! Pray don't eat me now. I'm too little, that I am. Wait until Bragi comes along. She gives the best milk she does, which will pair nicely with me."

"Ha," said the troll. "Then I will wait." She stepped back into the shadow of the guard tower and waited, still holding Bodil by the hooves.

"See. Trolls aren't very clever. Well then. You're next," Bjorg told Bragi.

"This is not a very good plan," Bragi said.

"Trust me. It gets better."

Bragi snorted and looked back at the Peddler's tent, which still sat dark. She took a breath and after a moment, Bragi's hooves trip trapped on the wooden slats.

"Who's that trapping over my bridge without paying the toll?" roared the troll.

"Oh, it is only I, Bragi, Greta's nanny goat, and I'm going on over to the mountain meadow where bothersome goats go," said Bragi, her voice shaking.

The troll stepped forward and blinked her large, round eyes again. "You talk as well," she said to the goat. "I suppose you have no coin to pay. But this one," she held up Bodil, "says you have milk to give."

"That I do," Bragi answered.

"Then I'll take your milk and gobble you up as well," said the troll. She scooped Bragi up with her other thick hand and held her high.

"Oh, no! Do wait," Bragi cried. "There's another goat coming. And he's much bigger. He'll make a better morning meal for you."

"Ha. Then I will wait," said the troll. She stepped back into the shadow of the guard tower, holding both goats.

Bjorg took his cue, puffed up his chest, and trotted up to the bridge. His hooves trip trapped on the wooden slats.

"Bjorg." Greta's cry came from not far away. "Whatever are you doing?"

Bjorg stopped where the troll waited in the shadows. "No worries, goatherdess. I have a plan," he called out.

Greta stopped not far from the bridge, eyes wide, but not as wide as the troll's. "You're talking," she gasped.

"Well, there we go," Peddler commented, stepping up next to her in the glow of morning light. "That must be what the purple laurel petal does when ingested."

The troll popped out from the shadows, holding Bodil upside in one huge hand and Bragi in the other.

"Oh my," Greta said.

The troll clumped about, trying to wrap her big arms around Bjorg as he darted around. Holding the other two goats made it almost impossible for the troll to grab him.

But not quite. Much to Bjorg's dismay, the troll managed to trap him and engulf him in a massive hug.

"I have you now. If you haven't coin, then you'll be my morning meal as well. All this bother has made me quite hungry."

Just then the bridge creaked and groaned under the trip trap tramp of a big, heavy goat.

"Who else is tramping over my bridge?" roared the troll in her grating voice.

"It's I! Byl," said the goat in a deep voice. He stood at the other end of the bridge, an imposing form with his great shaggy chest and impressive curling horns.

The troll looked down at Bjorg, whom she held with her forearms, and at Bodil and Bragi, whom she held fast with her fists. She hadn't any way to seize a fourth goat.

She spun about and headed for the guard tower. A thick

bushy troll tail popped out from beneath her jerkin. Byl stomped across the bridge, which shuddered and shook, and snatched the tail up with his teeth. He gave it a yank. The troll stumbled, dropping the three goats as she tried to regain her balance. They scurried to get out of the way. The troll teetered on the edge of the bridge as Byl backed up and lowered his head.

"Please don't," the troll pleaded, looking down at the rushing water. "It'll be the end of me if you do."

Byl paused and asked, "And what reason have you to give for me not to? You're greedily charging the goats to cross the bridge and threatening to eat them if they don't pay up."

"Not any worse than the villagers, who wanted to do the same with the bothersome goat." The troll nodded toward Bjorg who now stood at the entrance to the bridge.

"That is true," Greta noted, joining Bjorg and throwing her arms around his neck.

"Besides," the troll said, "I tore down the old bridge because the wood was rotting. It was becoming dangerous to use. I built this bridge and need a way to pay for it. That's why I charge a fee."

Peddler stroked his mustache. "A legitimate reason if I ever heard one," he said. "Maybe our goatherdess can offer a solution that helps everyone all around."

"Me?" Greta exclaimed. "Why I couldn't even, try as I might, figure out a way to get Bjorg across the drawbridge. But he did."

"Hmmm. Yes," Peddler agreed. "Maybe the bothersome little goat has a plan for that as well."

～

Bjorg, indeed, did have another plan. Peddler had everything needed in his wagon. In no time at all the unlikely group, a peddler, a goatherdess, a troll, and four talking goats, had transformed the guard tower into a colorful, dramatic carnie-style booth. The words emblazoned across the sign affixed to the roof pronounced: Hear the Talking Goats. Two Coppers.

Greta felt a sense of accomplishment as Razi, the troll, secured the sign in place. Greta insisted the price be fair enough for all to enjoy her goats. Besides, talking goats would draw more crowds than simply crossing the bridge to the meadow ever would. Her goats would roam free in the mountain meadow together. They'd snack on the purple laurel petals to keep up their newfound voices and carry on conversations with paying visitors.

Sure, her bothersome goats, Byl and Bjorg, would probably create a disturbance now and again. But that would be part of the show.

Byl, Bjorg, Bragi, and Bodil trip trapped on the wooden slats of the bridge.

"Best way to trick a troll," Bjorg said, black eyes glittering as he watched Razi straighten the sign, "is to get her working for you."

"Especially when said troll agrees to enjoy my milk each morning instead of eating me," Bragi added.

"So much fun it all is." Bodil danced about, hooves making a merry sound on the bridge. "We're going to be famous."

Byl tossed his shaggy head. "And I'm no longer alone."

Peddler knuckled his mustache and chuckled. "Well, that's one troll encounter that ended well indeed."

The furry black wicket shook itself, as if frustrated with the outcome. But Greta smiled as both Byl and Bjorg nipped at Razi's twitching tail. They darted away when she slapped at their noses. The troll wagged her bushy eyebrows at them, looking somewhat amused rather than agitated.

When Bjorg helped himself to a section of ivy running up the side of the guard house, Razi tugged the whole thing down and dumped it in front of him. The other goats quickly joined in the feast.

Greta let out a happy sigh. "The meadow certainly does provide a good place for misbehaved goats to live out their ill-mannered lives."

Bjorg swallowed a mouth full of ivy. Instead of a bleat he said, "And a place where my antics are most appreciated."

BEAUTY IN STASIS

KELLEY J. P. LINDBERG

On Enceladus, nothing went to waste. Everything that could be reused, was. Everything that couldn't was broken down into its component parts and recycled. Even human bodies.

Company policy.

But after a hundred years of development on Jupiter's most promising moon, there were bound to be a few things that even the most frugal of Enceladus's engineers, builders, and artists couldn't repurpose.

Dublin knew that. He'd expected this storeroom to hold the odd broken bits of plastics too degraded to be of any use, even as wall filler. It was also a repository for a few random museum relics—artifacts moved here some years back when the Education Center was remodeled to accommodate the burgeoning number of kids. He hadn't expected the room to be crammed full, though.

The 5 m by 5 m storage room had the musty scent of old electronics and decayed fabric layered over the mineral smell of cold stone.

"Do they really think it's in here?" asked Melbourne.

Grimacing at the stale air, the tall pediatrician hung back in the hallway while Dublin swung the heavy door, encouraging a breeze to circulate through the few empty spaces in the room. It was plain Mel wasn't thrilled about being "volunteered" for this task. But Dublin hadn't relished going on an idiotic scavenger hunt by himself, so he'd called his best friend. And, like best friends have been doing since the dawn of time on a distant planet, Mel had heaved a great sigh, then said yes.

Dublin was a little annoyed at being volunteered by the Centennial Committee, himself. He had actual work to do. The automated upgrade to the crystallization press software wasn't going well. The last three attempts had missed the mark, so Dublin had been called in to work his Intuitive design magic and fix whatever was tripping up the AI. There were some things AI still couldn't do as well as the human brain. Creative leaps of intuition, for example, which was where Dublin's particular programming expertise—Programmer, Intuitive Level III—came in.

But no. Apparently finding lost paraphernalia for the Centennial celebration was more important. Good for morale and all that. Like a few speeches from the company blowhards would fix *that*.

Dublin shrugged. "It's sealed in a Keepwell box, standard size." He gestured at the narrow path zigzagging through the room. "It's gonna be a tight fit. I'll start at the back of the room. Why don't you start looking here at the front?"

After thirty minutes, neither had located the original Colony One mission flag in its flat preservation box. Dublin had sorted through several precarious stacks of boxes, folders, and bags, none of them labeled with the right ID number.

He surveyed the mess before him and wiped his hands on his standard-issue coveralls—he wasn't about to be caught outside his work/life room in his civvies, even if the chance of running into anyone official down here was slim.

The boxes back here were all piled on top of something big. Two-and-a-half meters long and hip-high, the thing was covered in a ragged dropcloth that was worn through in places and spattered with dried polyplast and sealant. Clearly, it wasn't a flag in a preservation box. But as long as he was here ...

Dublin flipped up a corner of the dropcloth, clouding the air with disintegrated flecks of synthetic fabric.

The object beneath the cloth was smooth, metallic, featureless. It wasn't exactly rectangular—more sleek and rounded, almost bullet shaped. At least this end was.

He shoved at the next pile of boxes, revealing more of the object. As he pushed the fabric away, a swift stab of recognition twisted though him.

A lifepod.

One of the antique ones. Kids learned about these in Intro to Engineering.

Dublin slid his hand along the surface. No ports or control panel. They'd used models like this in the first colonization trip a hundred years ago—the one they were celebrating next month. The one where the original founders landed on Jupiter's small moon to begin expanding the unmanned subsurface mining outpost into a permanent colony.

Was this really one of the original lifepods? He thought they'd all been dismantled and repurposed long ago.

Forget the mission flag. If they could talk the Committee into it, displaying an original lifepod during the Centennial celebration would be mind-blowing, not to mention symbolic. And not just in the way the Committee might imagine.

"Mel, look at this."

Dublin lifted another stack of boxes, searching in vain for space to pile them. Growling, he finally dropped them onto the floor behind him, blocking Mel's path.

Then, without ceremony, he swept the cloth away from the rest of the lifepod.

Waving the flying dust from his eyes, Dublin leaned over the tiny square of clear window that would have been positioned over the occupant's face. His own face reflected back to him in the glass. Beneath the glass, the space was all dark shadows. And a curve of lighter shadow that nearly mimicked the lines of his own reflection.

With a yell, he jerked back and crashed into the boxes behind him. He sprawled, grabbing at anything to break his fall, toppling more boxes, envelopes, and broken shards of plastic.

Instantly, Melbourne was there, pulling the debris off Dublin.

"What?" Mel demanded as he dug. "What happened?"

Dublin scrabbled for his footing. He pointed, and Mel's eyes widened.

"Damn. Is that a lifepod?"

"Yeah."

Dublin crawled over the detritus back to the pod. He steeled himself, then leaned once more over the small window.

His breath caught.

"Dublin?" Mel asked, then paused. Dublin stood unmoving over the window. "You're kidding me. I *know* you're not going to tell me there's someone in there."

"There's someone in there."

This time, Mel staggered backward.

Etched at the base of the lifepod's tiny window, letters in black permapigment spelled out TR-ENC-01-0009/0012.

"It's Talia Rosamond," he said, his voice hoarse with adrenaline and dust. "Dr. Rosamond," he corrected himself. He'd forgotten his history for a minute, but now it came back to him in a rush. One of those original dozen lifepods had never opened.

Mel started to say something, then stopped. Tried again. "Number 9? What's she doing in a storage unit?"

Dublin shook his head. "No idea."

Dublin traced his finger over the letters and numbers, then translated them. "Talia Rosamond, Enceladus, first colonization trip, Colonist Number 9 of 12." The ninth original colonist and her malfunctioning lifepod was one of those poorly kept secrets that everyone knew about but seldom mentioned anymore. Ancient history. An unfortunate casualty made irrelevant after a century of progress on Enceladus.

Mel said, "My mom told me that when she was in high school, she tried to do a report on Number 9, but couldn't find much about her in the wiki-lib archives beyond the basics. When Mom became a senator and asked where Number 9 was, she was told that at some point they gave up trying to revive her and launched her pod into Jupiter. Space Burial with Honors."

The two stared at the lifepod. It was rare to launch corpses into space. Even the highest-ranking officials were usually given a splashy memorial service, then recycled like everyone else.

"I guess they never got around to that," Mel added.

"She was always kind of an embarrassment." Dublin touched the side of the lifepod again, reverently. "Enceladus's greatest failure in the midst of our greatest achievement." He let sarcasm darken his voice. After all, no one could hear him but Mel.

Mel nodded. "We should tell the Centennial Committee. Maybe they could display her. Make her part of the Remembrance Service or something."

Clearly, Mel was weighing the same opportunities as Dublin. But now that he knew there was a human still inside, Dublin was having second thoughts.

"I don't know. 'Displaying' a human in stasis seems wrong, even if it has been a hundred years. I mean, she's still in there." Then, Dublin asked, "When did they stop trying to revive her?"

Mel shrugged.

"They never figured out what went wrong with her pod, right?" Dublin said, more than asked.

"I don't think so. I mean, they said they launched her. Seems pretty obvious they gave up at some point."

"Did they give your mom any ideas on what caused the pod to malfunction?"

Mel shrugged again. "I doubt she asked. Didn't they blame it on some kind of software glitch? That sounds like *your* department. I only fix kids, not machines." Mel scrambled over the junk still scattered on the floor. "Can I see?" he said, his voice a little higher than usual—a telltale Dublin had recognized since childhood. His friend was excited.

Dublin was reluctant to move from the window. The woman beneath it looked like she was simply sleeping. In fact, she was, he reminded himself. That was sort of the whole point of stasis. The lifepods put their occupants into stasis, cushioning them from the physical trauma of space travel. More importantly, cargo space was at a premium. By being in stasis, the travelers wouldn't consume any resources and the ship's life-support systems could be minimal. It was all very energy efficient. And economical.

For the first colony trip to Enceladus, back when the moon was planned as a permanent peace-fostering research colony sponsored by a multinational consortium, the stasis timing was calculated based on the journey's length of ninety-nine days. The pods' reanimation sequences were set to begin at one hundred days, allowing a day for heat and dust dissipation outside and inside the ship.

The lifepods for the original twelve colonists had been completely sealed, with no option for outside manual access. There wasn't even a port for power or communication. The internal micronuclear batteries would power the pods for a thousand years, if need be, and all communication with the pods' systems was done wirelessly. The original designers wanted the pods to be all but indestructible, with zero points of vulnerability, in case they had to be used as escape pods during flight. Or in case of a crash landing. They'd been failproof, after all. It had been a triumph of engineering.

But when Number 9's lifepod never opened and the other eleven colonists had no tools capable of prying it open, they'd stopped using the term "failproof." The design had been altered. Subsequent lifepods had external manual override capabilities.

But that didn't help Dr. Talia Rosamond. She'd been sleeping for a century behind that tiny window.

And the later generations of Enceladians had all but forgotten her.

～

Four days later, Mel sat on the bed in Dublin's work/life unit. Once they'd wheeled the lifepod into Dublin's room, there hadn't been enough floor space left for the one extra chair Dublin owned, so they'd temporarily moved it to the unit Mel shared with his husband, Cairo. Dublin was staring blindly at his workstation feeds.

It had been surprisingly easy to spirit Dr. Rosamond and her lifepod here without anyone seeing. Doing it at two o'clock in the morning had helped.

It had been harder convincing Mel not to tell the Centennial Committee. Mel believed the Committee would welcome the discovery. More importantly, Mel felt that displaying a Founder—one whose life reflected the original scientific purpose of the colony, rather than the myopic greed of the company that owned the colony now—could only help their cause. "She could be a symbol for us," Mel had said that night. "A rally point. A way to remind everyone of what we've lost."

By "us," Mel was talking about the Galileans, a small, unorganized, but growing group of malcontents. Galileans like Dublin and Mel wanted to see Enceladus returned to its original purpose of beneficial research, as well as independence from the conglomerate that owned them now—quite literally—body and soul.

But Dublin knew telling the Committee about the lifepod could backfire. Instead of displaying her, they might just hide her away again, and he'd lose his chance to free her.

"Think about it," he had told Mel late that first night. "Why would they lie about her space burial?" He had done a quick search through funeral records and had found a ledger entry that confirmed she'd been launched into the swirling storms of Jupiter about twenty-five years after her pod had failed. And yet, here she was.

"It takes a lot of energy to launch something at Jupiter," said Mel. "Maybe they didn't have fuel to spare at the time, and then sort of, I don't know, forgot? Reprioritized?"

Keeping Dr. Rosamond's existence a secret was a risk, but Dublin wanted a chance to learn more about her, the lifepod malfunction, and why she'd been all but smothered in the wiki-lib histories. He may not be able to wake her, but there was so much to learn.

There had to be a data trail. Dublin could feel a soft flicker at the back of his mind telling him something was going on here. He trusted that flickering—that odd spark of energy, or imagination, or inspiration. Whatever it was called, that's what had gotten him to his Intuitive status in the hierarchy of programmers, after all.

Dublin had quickly exhausted all the information about Dr. Rosamond in the accessible parts of the public domain. Now, four nights later, he was using his clearance to root through deeper resources. He was being careful, though, hiding his traces through the programs.

"I take it you haven't had any luck?" asked Mel, eyeing the lifepod wedged between Dublin's sink and the small closet.

"Do you see her standing in the room with us?" snapped Dublin.

Mel chuckled. He'd grown immune to Dublin's moods by second grade.

Dublin rubbed his neck muscles. "I mean, no. No luck."

"The Committee is still debating whether to erect the Remembrance Memorial Exhibit in the Assembly Hall or in the Education Center. It's not too late. We could still tell them you found Number 9. She could be the centerpiece of the display."

Dublin repeated the word, spitting it out with sarcasm. "*Display*."

"Yeah."

"I hate that word. Would you want the whole city watching you sleep?"

"Would you rather leave her in a storage room, gathering dust?"

Dublin's ribs tightened. He shook his head.

"It's been a century. What do you think you're going to find that no one else has in all this time?"

Something electric played across the neurons in his head again, then faded. "I don't know."

"Well, what have you found so far?" Mel asked, pointing with his chin toward Dublin's workstation.

The 2D screen was displaying—displaying!—documents he'd managed to dig up in the oldest archives. A partially completed Form D-421 was also open on his 2D screen. If anyone entered his room and demanded an explanation for why he hadn't lawfully reported the discovery of potentially usable resources, he could point to the form and say he was in the process of doing it at that very minute. He hoped he could stall for a few more days, though.

To either side of the screen, 3D images hovered in the air. Most showed schematics of various lifepod components, almost all from later models with external access, but a few from the original model. One image, very small, rotated slowly in the lower corner of the 3D range: a portrait of Talia. It was her final publicity headshot, likely taken a few weeks before the launch.

"Nothing new. Probable software malfunction. Initial investigation was a bust. They tried again, at least four more times officially over the next ten years, but no one ever figured it out. The last investigation was cut short by an official directive."

"On whose orders?" Mel asked.

"No signature. Just an official memorandum. Corporate letterhead. Any original tracking data was stripped off."

Mel shook his head. He pulled a couple of hand weights from the rack on Dublin's wall and began doing bicep curls. "So, it's been ninety years since the last investigation?"

"Officially, yeah. But I found a lot of papers from college students over the years. It seems she's a perennial candidate for academic research projects. But none of them had any breakthroughs. And even those that looked promising couldn't be tested because they thought her pod had been fired into Jupiter." Dublin stood and took two short steps to reach Talia. "One psychology student in the early days tried to 'commune' with Talia for three straight weeks."

"And?" prompted Mel.

"Have you ever tried communing with a lump of clay inside a big metal box?"

"I think that's what I did during fifth-grade art class."

Dublin smiled, possibly for the first time in days. He pressed his palm against the pod, fingers splayed, like he was trying to feel for vibrations.

"Well, that student only got a C on their project," he continued. "I tracked their academic record. They ended up switching to Organics Reclamation."

Mel laughed.

Dublin rubbed his sleeve over Talia's window, clearing away his own fingerprints. "She's alive, Mel. There's got to be a way to pull her out of stasis. We've made a lot of advances over the last hundred years. I should be able to figure this out."

Mel asked, "Has anyone ever survived a hundred years of stasis?"

That question had been worrying Dublin, too. "Not that I know of. But there've been limited ten- and twenty-year studies. All of 'em came out of stasis just fine. No physical degradation. Some psychological issues, like depression and anxiety. Those were mostly due to missing out on years of social, political, and technology changes."

Mel made a noncommittal noise. "I can think of a few political changes I wouldn't have minded sleeping through."

Dublin quirked another smile, then let it fade. "The subjects in those studies were carefully selected. Loners, mostly. People with no family or close friends. The researchers obviously didn't want them waking up and suffering breakdowns because their loved ones had aged or ... died. So they were highly controlled studies, to say the least."

Dublin considered the face of the sleeping pioneer. He couldn't tell if the slight silver tinge to her skin was from the poor lighting in his room or the stasis chemicals. It probably should have made her look alien, somehow. Or clinical, like a lab specimen. Instead, it made her look more vulnerable. Impossibly lovely. Like those photos of marble statues back on Earth. He understood now why people would pay good money to enter museums and stare at statues for hours. There was a kind of unattainable beauty in her features. The kind that woke a longing that had nowhere to go.

Dublin recognized the longing he was feeling for what it really was: the competitive drive to solve a mystery that had been stumping other researchers for a hundred years. Not a yearning for that face beneath the crystal window.

Definitely not that.

"Talia will have lost so much more than time, Mel. Friends. Colleagues. Her career. Her ... fiancé." He kept his voice neutral, keeping his eyes on Talia. "She was engaged to Number 7, Howard McKlennan."

"Number 7 was ... Um. I didn't know there was going to be a quiz. Let me think ... The nano-engineer?"

Dublin glanced at Mel and nodded.

"He was the one who stabilized the bond between poly-plast and ... uh ... something, right?"

"The diamond structures in our local rock. Yeah."

Dublin turned back and stared at the soft lines of the woman's delicate collar bones. Her short hair was dark, though through the glass and shadows he hadn't been able to tell if it was brown or black until he'd found her publicity photos. It was black. Midnight black. He'd resisted shining a light directly into the window—that seemed especially invasive. Almost surgical. Prurient, even.

Then, he said, "Howard McKlennan was my great-great-grandfather."

Mel's weights paused mid-curl. "Whoa."

Dublin let a small snort escape. "Yeah. Don't you remember? I did a report on him in tenth grade."

"Pal, in tenth grade I was chasing Singapore Tsatsi. I wouldn't have remembered if you did a report on Great Penises of the Golden Space Age." He resumed his bicep curls. "Actually, I might have remembered that."

Dublin stifled a sigh. "I can see what my great-great saw in her."

Dublin could feel Mel's disapproval like a snapped towel at the gym. But he couldn't stop looking at Talia.

The woman's lips were relaxed in sleep, but looked soft, like they were on the verge of smiling. Her eyes, though. It was probably a trick of the shadows, but the skin beneath her eyes looked bruised. Tired. Sad.

Dublin shook himself out of his melancholy and pulled back from the window. Getting moony over a marble statue wasn't going to solve the problem. "Talia was an exceptional medical researcher. Reports say she'd already done groundbreaking work in bone regeneration and muscle restoration, even though she was only twenty-seven."

Twenty-seven when she went into stasis. Old enough to have proven her bona fides, young enough to reproduce. Colonist selection had always been weirdly clinical. Dublin himself would turn twenty-seven in a couple of months. He wasn't sure his own research and accomplishments would have qualified him for a colony trip, despite the Academy claiming he was "supra-high-value."

"I spent a rotation in bone re-gen, but never heard her name mentioned," Mel said. "I only ever heard of her as Number 9, the One that Failed to Open." He stood and crowded Dublin away from the lifepod so he could take another look. "Yeah, I'm sure your grandpappy was interested in her medical research. The fact that she's a right beauty probably had nothing to do with it," he said, grinning.

Dublin elbowed him away from the window. Belatedly, he hoped it came across as good-natured.

"I'm just saying," Mel added, then settled back down on the bed. He switched to slow-motion punches with the weights. "I've never seen you hang a portrait of a girl in your workstation before."

The non sequitur made Dublin stumble over his words. "It's for research," he managed, suddenly annoyed and pointedly *not* glancing over at the small, spinning headshot. "Losing Talia in the first landing was pretty devastating to the crew. They had cross-trained another colonist in basic medicine, so at least they had a medic. But it was several more colony waves before they could fully replace her. They lost a few people in the early construction phases because they couldn't do what Talia could to re-gen their injuries."

"So, you're on a first-name basis with her now, are you?"

Dublin stepped away from the lifepod. "What?"

"You're calling her Talia now, not Number 9. Or Dr. Rosamond."

Dublin pinched his lips together and made himself return to his workstation. He was wasting too much time staring at Talia—Dr. Rosamond—through that damned window.

"Shorthand," he said. "Don't read anything into it."

Mel gave him a smirk. "Right. Well, I told Cairo I'd be home by seven. We've got a romantic evening of laundry and osmosis troubleshooting ahead of us." He stood and slid the hand weights back into the rack. "So, I'll leave you to your damsel in distress." He clapped Dublin on the back and left, silence drifting in his wake.

Three weeks after finding her, Dublin was no closer to cracking open Talia's pod.

"What am I doing wrong, Tal?" he asked. Sitting at his workstation, he shoved bites of his dinner into his mouth without tasting them. He'd just heated something at random from the commissary in a hurry to bring it back to his room. To Talia. He'd taken to eating all his meals here with her, now. And talking to her, which he knew was a little nutty. He put it down to stress.

He'd had a suite of AI modules running for days, tracing obscure paths in the security systems of more recent life-pods. Because the source of the accident had never been discovered, the original software was deemed so danger-ously flawed that most early iterations weren't archived. Lousy programming practice, obviously, but there it was. A lot of the student research over the years had likewise focused on security, but some had tackled the life-support system, the stasis chemicals, and even the magneto-spec-tral composition of the alloys used in the lifepod itself.

Dublin springboarded off those previous research papers, but so far, nothing had borne fruit.

Talia had sparked more than research, it seemed. Dublin found she'd been the subject of short stories, art-class assignments, elementary school dioramas, and one truly awful screenplay. A portrait of her done in the cubism style made him unreasonably grumpy for an entire day. But at least she hadn't been as thoroughly forgotten as he'd originally thought. However, there were fewer and fewer projects about her in the latter half of the century.

She was fading.

He hadn't learned anything new about her one hundred days in the transport ship. Nothing had alerted mission control about potential malfunctions. No one knew anything was wrong until they had landed and her lifepod simply ... didn't open.

He had, however, learned more about her first twenty-seven years. He'd found news articles, a few interviews, several of her thesis papers and dissertations, and plenty of memorial remembrances published shortly after her ... what? Death was the wrong word.

Even more revealing, though, were the hidden logs he'd uncovered. Her personal logs. Long secured and forgotten, they'd been buried so deeply he had nearly missed them, even guided as he was by a particularly strong wave of his Intuitive sparks. He knew he was the first person to read them in a hundred years.

Dublin shut down the algorithm-tracking feeds and pulled up her logs now. He'd felt guilty at first, prying into her personal files. But at this rate, she'd never know. And maybe he would find some clue in there. It couldn't hurt, he told himself.

So far, he'd learned that she used to ski with her parents back on Earth. That she'd loved cats and hated snakes, neither of which was something she'd have ever seen again once she was on Enceladus. That she'd been tops in her classes—no surprise there, for a colonist—and had a penchant for dangly earrings. She played guitar, but not well, apparently, and had given it up when she graduated high school a year early and left for the university in São Paulo.

Dublin's heart sped up when she wrote about how much she loved his great-great, then constricted when she reluctantly admitted in her private log that she was nervous about spending years confined to small spaces with him and only a handful of other people. She worried he'd grow tired of her.

He'd found videos of the two of them together. His great-great had been from Ireland and had freckled skin and squarer features than Dublin. But four generations of subsurface dwelling and limited gene pools had diluted some of the ethnic differentiation on Enceladus. All Dublin retained now was the name of his great-great's ancestral home. For a few years, that had been the fad for parents on

Enceladus: to name their children after Earth cities. Thankfully, that trend died out before anyone got named Giggleswick or Truth-or-Consequences. Dublin, Mel, and other kids in their class had spent hours looking up old Earth city names to torment each other with.

Talia had been born in a city called Los Angeles before it had been wiped out. *The Angels.*

Her hair had been a lot longer once, often tied back in a tail. She seemed, at least to Dublin now, watching her through a century-old lens, to be easy to startle and quick to laugh. He looked for the shadows under her eyes but couldn't see them.

"I want you to know," Dublin told the woman under the glass, "that Howard grieved for you for a long time." He wasn't entirely sure about that, but he felt like she deserved to have someone grieving for her. "Four years after you landed, he finally married a geologist. She was from the third wave. That ... might make you sad. But if it weren't for her, I wouldn't be here."

He didn't add that his presence on this moon mattered to her because he wasn't going to give up on her like all those other would-be rescuers had.

Tonight, Dublin was searching for clues to the lifepod malfunction. He scrolled through Talia's personal logs, skipping over her worries about what to pack for the trip or about the pharmaceutical replicator she would have to assemble when she landed here.

He stopped scrolling when he hit an entry from a couple of months before launch.

"I ruined someone's career today," it started. "I didn't want to, but I couldn't see any way around it. DS's profile has been steadily declining in the PFM-16, -18, and -23 scales for several months, and despite an intense program of modification, I'm just not seeing any improvement. When they interviewed me this morning, I had to give them my honest opinion. Without noticeable improvement, there is a strong possibility she could jeopardize the mission. Perhaps over time, with enough treatment, she could become eligible for a future colonization trip. At least, that's what I told them. I'm not sure it will ever be possible, though. I told them I know it's late, but I think they should consider an alternate. I've been crying all day."

Dublin set down his fork and walked over to the small window. "Tal, who's DS?" he asked. Was this why the shadows under her eyes looked so weary, even frozen in stasis as they were? His voice lowered, as if he didn't want to wake her. "You did what you had to do. You did the right thing." He placed his hand on the lifepod as gently as if he were resting it on her shoulder to comfort her.

He didn't know anything about this DS, or what the PFM scales meant, but he knew in his gut that if Tal had thought it was important, it was. The girl in the videos wouldn't have been cruel. His great-great wouldn't have loved a callous woman.

In that, Dublin was surely like his ancestor.

He turned back to the workstation, shoved the cold, half-eaten dinner aside, and began a new search. It took some doing, but he found it: the original list of colonizers, with a sequence of culling stages over two years until the list was whittled down to the final twelve. Six weeks before the launch, one name—Dahlia Street—had been replaced with a new one.

A little more digging, and Dublin uncovered the tersely worded notice buried under layers of security. Dr. Street, a software security expert, had been removed due to "unspecified medical, psychological, and/or behavioral issues." No mention of what those unspecified issues were, though. More digging, and he found she'd been retained as a consultant on the launch.

What the hell? How does someone who's been removed for medical or psych issues get to keep working on the project?

Dublin knew the name Dahlia Street. Everyone did.

Despite Talia's concerns, Street had arrived in the second wave of colonists. Shortly after her arrival, the multinational consortium that sponsored the colony named her Superintendent of the Enceladus colony, replacing the existing leader, Dublin's great-great-granddad Howard. It hadn't been a popular move among the three dozen or so colonists at the time. But she'd retained the position through the next several building phases.

When Enceladus grew to a thousand residents, the governmental consortium on Earth splintered under global disasters and economic warfare. Street had led a push for independence despite their tiny population and utter reliance on off-moon resources for survival. Her obsession with that cause led to calls for her removal from office. But she quelled an attempted coup with the help of a quasi-militaristic commercial conglomerate, which immediately—and with her blessing—assumed owner-ship of the colony. She changed her title to President and retained that position until her death. Rumors had it that she was living off-moon in a luxury ship circling Mars when she died.

It had been a contentious time in Enceladus history, but Street was still officially known as the Mother of Enceladus. And her actions, as far as the Galileans were concerned, had left Enceladus trapped as a repressed, all-but-forgotten exploitative mining outfit instead of the universal resource it should have been.

Dublin tapped his fingers on his desk. There were whispers that Street had been a little unhinged, especially toward the end of her career. Was that what Talia had seen and tried to warn the organizers about before the first trip? A software security expert with mental health issues, expelled from the first wave of colonists at the last minute, but who retained access to the program as a consultant—none of that seemed like a good idea. There was more to this story than an unlucky woman with a quick mind and a soft smile in a malfunctioning lifepod. For the tenth time today, Dublin felt his heartbeat speed up.

Five more days passed. Dublin was putting in just enough time on his regular work projects to keep them on track, but he spent all his remaining hours with Talia.

"Hi, Tal," he said, smiling through the window. "I think I'll take another look at the records database tonight. See if I can dig up who filed the notice about your so-called burial." He pressed two fingers to the window, lingering for a moment, then sighed and turned to his workstation.

The knock on the door broke through his thoughts. Adrenaline hit his nervous system, and he quickly closed all but the half-completed D-421 form and a few work-related feeds for show. Then he sent a quick message to Mel. He crossed to the door and prayed his smile looked natural.

Two uniformed members of the Centennial Committee stood in the hallway.

"Programmer Dublin Jefferson?" one asked, as if the mandatory nameplate on his door wasn't a dead giveaway.

"Yes."

"We're here because we haven't received a report on the Colony One mission flag. You were assigned that recovery, weren't you?"

The surprise on Dublin's face was authentic. He'd completely forgotten about the damned flag. Stupid, stupid.

"Oh, yeah. I've been looking for it in the storage room on level 14, as requested. I ... ah ... didn't find it yet. And then there was a problem in the fuel generator in the east bay—" Fuel generators were always priority one and chronically finicky, so he figured that was his safest excuse. "Honestly, I was so busy with that, I ran out of time to look for the flag. I mean, for a few days. I went looking for it again today. I just got back, in fact. Still no luck."

He was rambling. It was a painful admission. There would be consequences. But it was a sacrifice he decided to offer up, given the bigger infraction he was trying to hide.

He tried to keep the Committee members in the hallway, blocking their view of the lifepod behind him, but one spotted it almost immediately.

"What is that?" she asked, her voice flat and professional. The other one craned his neck to see. Then both of their eyes darted back to Dublin's face.

Dublin had a half-second to choose between raising their suspicions and having them return with loftier-positioned investigators with bad attitudes, or owning up to his discovery. No use delaying the inevitable.

"Oh, you won't believe it," Dublin said, trying his best to sound enthusiastic and cooperative. "I was just filling out the D-421 form, in fact." He gestured toward the form, open on his 2D screen. Then he stepped out of the way.

The woman strode to the object and leaned over the

small window. With a yelp, she backpedaled. The man slapped his hand to the stun gun on his hip and squared his back to the wall, ready for mayhem. Dublin already had his hands in the air.

"It's okay," he stammered. "It's a lifepod. Number 9's lifepod. It was in the storage unit where I was looking for the flag. It's dormant!" he insisted.

The man swung his stunner from Dublin to the lifepod and back, confused and just short of a reckless decision. The woman scrambled to his side and drew her stun gun, too, rattled more by the man's confusion than her own.

This was why Dublin questioned the rationale behind arming low-level functionaries.

Finally, everyone in the tiny room was motionless, waiting for … Dublin wasn't sure what. An explanation?

"Yeah, so," he began. Where was Mel? "So, I was looking for the flag today, and I found this instead. Number 9. Remember? The colonist whose lifepod didn't open? I was just filling out the form to let you guys know."

"Why is it here, in your room?" demanded the woman.

"I … didn't know what else to do with it." Dublin wasn't happy referring to Talia as "it," but he had bigger things to worry about right now. "I thought if I brought it here, I could keep it safe while the Committee decided what to do with it. I mean, um, it might be useful for the Centennial celebration or something. And I didn't think it was safe to leave it unguarded."

Mel arrived then, with his silver tongue and soothing voice. Mel was great at maneuvering through red tape and bad policies, a skill Dublin hadn't had the patience to acquire. The Committee members seemed to buy his story about finding the lifepod today, which was lucky. Dublin hoped his efforts to hide his research trails held fast.

After a tense hour and several communications with senior Committee members, the pair in his room agreed to let Dublin do "a little" research on the lifepod under extreme nondisclosure measures. However, they wanted to move her immediately back to the storage room, with a guard posted at the door for good measure.

It took another half-hour for Mel to convince them that Dublin would need physical proximity to the lifepod (which wasn't necessarily true) and wouldn't mind having a guard posted outside his own door (which he did mind, very much).

Whether or not they wanted Number 9 to be part of the exhibit would be kicked up the chain of command. There seemed to be some reluctance on the part of the Committee members to talk about that. Dublin found that odd. He'd assumed, like Mel, that the Committee would want to display Talia's lifepod. But "doesn't fit the narrative" and "no one bloody cares anymore" were muttered over radios, in voices Dublin probably hadn't been meant to hear.

But for now, Tal could stay under his watchful eyes, at least for the next few days. Until the Centennial. Or until Dublin did something that attracted more unwanted attention.

Dublin was treading on very shaky ground.

The Committee could change their mind at any point. If they suspected he'd hidden the discovery, he could end up jailed, or worse. So could Mel. He would need to provide some useful data to the Assembly out of this project, and soon, or they would rethink their leniency.

He would do the Galileans no good if he was discovered nosing around in Enceladus's past without authorization.

After the Committee members left with their scowls and veiled threats, Dublin could feel Tal's presence as if her breath was warming the air beside him. As if the soft hum of electronics in his room was about to be drowned out by her laughter. As if she was on the verge of asking him about his day or teasing him about his shaggy hair.

He ran a hand through his hair, ineffectually, wondering what it would be like to hear her say his name.

Three days left. Dublin had tracked down more information about President Street and had pored through remnants of the woman's code from several archaic projects he'd scrounged up. He was starting to recognize her fingerprints. Although she was prolific before she came to Enceladus, she hadn't done much programming after she arrived. From what he could tell, she'd moved quickly into colony management, rising rapidly despite some disgruntled voices that soon quieted. He wondered why they'd quieted. But again, now wasn't the time to ask those questions.

The guards outside his door hadn't bothered him at all and hadn't asked to come inside his room, but Dublin still jumped at every noise.

He turned back to the code for Talia's lifepod. If someone wanted to sabotage a lifepod, what would be the easiest way to do it? If it was Street, she wouldn't have had much time and may not have had a lot of unsupervised access to the lifepods after her evaluation and before the launch. It had to be quick, it had to be simple, and it had to be something all the safety checks would overlook.

"Tal," he said to the woman sleeping in the pod, "I promise, I'm getting you out of there. I'm close," he said, for the hundredth time in the last few days. "I can feel it."

And for the hundredth time, he wondered why his heart

wouldn't stop racing. And why his fingers kept tracing the lines of her face across the small window.

"When was the last time you ate something?" Mel asked, kicking one of Dublin's dirty coveralls aside. "And I'm not even asking about the last time you did laundry."

The Centennial celebration would begin tomorrow, and Dublin wanted nothing more than to get Talia out of that pod before they took her from him and exhibited her like a sideshow freak in the bad old days. They'd told him today that they were planning to put her on display after all. Since the alternative was watching them bury her in a forgotten hole somewhere, he was trying to make peace with their decision.

He wiped his sweaty palms on his pant legs. "It's got to be here, Mel. I'm seeing Street's fingerprints all over the place in here," he said, jabbing an accusing finger at his workstation. "I just have to find where she did something to the lifepod that would cause it to not open on time."

"Speaking of not opening on time," said Mel, "the festivities start at eight o'clock tomorrow morning. They want the lifepod in place tonight."

"I can do this." Dublin clenched his fingers into fists, then shook them out. His hands ached.

"Sure, but you're out of time. Listen. You can keep looking into this after the shindig's over. What's the big hurry? She doesn't look stressed about it." Mel was gazing in at Talia. He stepped back. "Clean up, put on something reasonably unwrinkled, and come with me and Cairo to get some dinner. You need a break."

"They're talking about putting Talia right next to that

idiotic Street exhibit. A shrine to the first president, even though the woman was a freakin' loon. And Tal's murderer!"

"*Possibly* her *attempted* murderer, Dublin." Mel had started using his calming bedside voice. "You don't know anything for sure."

"She was involved. We know she was off her rocker at the end. And at least one person in authority thought Talia was right about her before the first trip because they scratched her from the Colony One team."

"Those are strong words, and we weren't there. We'll never really know about Street's mental state. You don't have proof she was involved in Number 9's accident at all. It's just speculation. It's a good speculation as far as I'm concerned, but that's still all it is. And obviously the Assembly doesn't want to hear it. They're willing to let you study the lifepod up to a certain point, but they're not going to let you question our Founding Mother, and you know it. We can't jeopardize the Galileans over this. Not yet."

Dublin grunted. Then he said, "I have to help her, Mel. I owe it to my great-great-grandfather."

"Stop fooling yourself, Dublin. You're not doing this for some dead grandpa you never met."

Dublin looked up at Mel, then shifted his eyes away. They landed on the rotating image of Talia hovering over his workstation. He looked away from that too.

"You're turning this woman into your own personal fantasy, Dub."

Dublin shook his head. "She's real. And, yeah, maybe I'm expecting too much. But my Intuition, Mel. It's screaming at me that I have to save this woman. I have to wake her up." He hesitated. "Every cell in my body is telling me we need her. And ... I need her."

He hadn't intended to admit that out loud. Not even to himself.

Silence stretched into the corners of the room.

For nearly twenty-seven years, Mel had been Dublin's best friend. He'd seen Dublin's Intuition at play hundreds of times. Dublin knew Mel had never understood it, but he'd never questioned it, either. Dublin held his breath, hoping against hope that Mel would trust him one more time.

"You've given yourself an arbitrary deadline, for no good reason," Mel finally said, which wasn't exactly a benediction, but it wasn't a denial, either. "No one else cares about your time schedule. Take a break, then reset after the hoopla is over."

Reset.

Time schedule.

Reset the ... timeline.

There. That was it. Resetting the timeline. Could Tal's lifepod have been set to operate on a different timeline than the others'?

"Mel, keep everyone out of my room. Tell them I'll have her there in time. I promise. I just need a few more hours." He hesitated. "If I can't get it open by midnight, I'll bring her to the Assembly Hall myself."

Mel looked like he wanted to drag Dublin out of the room by his ears. He finally shook his head. "Fine. I'll talk to the guard and the Committee. You've got until midnight." He hesitated. "I'll send up some food."

It had to be something with the timeline.

Dublin flew through modules of code, breathless. "It's there, Tal," he said. "I'm coming."

It wasn't there. "What am I missing?" he asked her.

Then it hit him: an age-old saying that programmers

have sworn by since the days of calculators the size of space shuttles. KISS—Keep It Simple, Stupid.

"If you don't like the time," he whispered, "change the clock."

There it was.

The timeline, in an obscure loop of code that shouldn't have been there, had been changed from 100 days ... no, that was wrong. It didn't change the 100 days. But there, in that tiny bit of appended code, it added 100 years to those 100 days. And DS's fingerprints were all over it.

Dublin's hands shook as he worked out the numbers. Tal's lifepod was set to open tomorrow, right in the middle of the Remembrance Ceremony. He pictured the scene: the pod coming to life, opening, hissing as life-support and regeneration chemicals kicked in.

And Number 9, his beautiful sleeper, opening her eyes ... surrounded by a noisy crowd of stunned and excitable onlookers from a hundred years in her future. He could feel her initial disorientation, her rising confusion, her panic.

He could change that.

Right now. The code sat in front of him, and even though it was ancient, he knew how to fix it.

He had a choice. He could make her lifepod open the day *after* tomorrow, after the celebration was over. But before that, she'd be on display all day. Hundreds of people would spend the day touching her pod, smearing it with their fingers, staring at her sleeping face, making crass jokes or wild speculations. And the Committee might whisk her away from him after the celebration.

Or he could open it now.

Right now.

He could greet her. Break the news to her, gently. Prepare her for what she'd missed. Give her time, here, in his quiet space, to absorb the impact of reentry into a world she no longer knew. He started to imagine his arms around her, comforting her. But he cut that image short. That wasn't fair. He'd had time to learn about her. But he was nothing to her. She'd be as terrified of him as of anything else in this world.

His heart stuttered. He'd have to tell her about her launchmates. Her friends who no longer existed. Her fiancé, the man she went to sleep loving just moments ago, and how he woke up without her. Lived for years without her. Married someone else. And how Howard had eventually died, an old man with grandkids.

And how one of those grandkids became Dublin's grandfather.

Maybe Talia would hate Dublin for bringing her into this strange, new world without the people she'd known or the man she'd loved. Without a purpose. With outdated skills. With nothing to her name. And with the knowledge that her would-be murderer had sold her dream to the highest bidder, trapping them all in a mining workcamp instead of the research haven they'd hoped for.

But maybe, just maybe, she would forgive him. He'd give her time. He would never, ever abandon her. He would help her start a new life if she'd let him. Help her find a new purpose. Nothing should ever be wasted on Enceladus. Especially not Tal.

Dublin's hands moved to the workstation, shaking only a little.

"Talia, I'm coming to bring you home," he whispered and started the sequence.

DAUGHTERS OF VELLAMO

NATASHA WATTS

IN THE END, the hare brought the message of death.

Not the bear, for he might have slain the herds of cattle. Nor the wolf, for he might have slain the lambs. Nor the fox, who surely would have slain the ducks and chickens.

The hare, wiry and full of mange as she was, had only blunt teeth. She was hungry and thin, as were they all, but she only ate bark and berries and the greens from Aino's mother's garden.

So, it was decided that she, of all the animals, would be sent to bring tidings to the family. To Aino's family.

On the day before news of her death reached her mother, Aino sat on a rock at the edge of the lake and caught fish with her bare hands.

She'd removed her shoes so her toes dangled in the cool water. Every few minutes, she dipped her fingers beneath the surface and moved them back and forth, sending ripples out toward the center of the lake. At her touch, the water seemed to shimmer and come alive. Soon, dark silhouettes appeared: fat, speckled trout, slippery whitefish, and long pike.

All Aino needed to do was reach in and pick up one of the docile creatures. Once out of the water, the fish was quickly dispatched with a wooden knife Aino's brother had carved for her. She kept a prayer of thanks in her heart as she did so, to the fish who had given its life for her family's nourishment.

A soft voice interrupted her prayer. "Why do you bring the nets?"

Aino turned to find Elisa, who had emerged from behind a lichen-covered boulder a short distance away. She was half-submerged, long hair draped artfully over her naked chest.

"Why do you ask?" She and Elisa often spoke like this, in a conversation of questions. Both were so curious about the other, hungry for knowledge of someone different from them.

"The nets are heavy," Elisa said. "I can see you struggling to carry them each time you come. Yet you never use them. Which leads me to wonder why you bring them at all."

Aino sighed. Elisa was too observant for her own good. It often led to questions that forced Aino to reveal more about herself than she liked. But this was *Elisa*, her friend, who had trusted her with so many secrets. Aino could never refuse her answers.

"My mother and brother—they don't know I can do this." She tickled the surface of the lake to demonstrate, and the nearby fish stirred. "They would be elated to learn it, no doubt. For my whole life, they thought me giftless, and this late manifestation of power would bring great relief to them. Especially to my mother."

"But you do not want them to know."

"No." Aino leaned back on her rock, gazing up at lake-blue sky. "I do not."

"Why?"

Aino didn't know if she could even answer that question to herself. Her *äiti*, Sannu, descended from a long line of gifted women interspersed with the rare gifted man. Sannu's power manifested in the arts of the home—spinning, growing, caring, slaughtering. She was also something of a healer, and people from the village would come to her for assistance with their daily aches and pains. She had married a giftless man, a marriage for love, which she had always spoken of with regret to her daughter.

"If I had found a gifted man to wed, you would not be powerless," she would say to Aino in the years following her father's death. "Joona was fortunate to receive gifts with a giftless father, but you, my child, were not so lucky. I hold myself responsible for that."

When Aino's gift had finally manifested, she'd kept it a secret for herself. It felt wrong to bare this side of herself when her family had always valued her less while they believed her giftless. This was for her. Aino considered it a blessing from Vellamo, the goddess of water, which was why she'd always felt drawn to Elisa and her kind.

"And there you go again, staring into the distance." Elisa's voice was not accusatory, but affectionate. "Come back, Aino. I'm here with you."

Aino dragged a hand over her face and looked down at her friend. "You're right; I'm sorry. I'm here now." She glanced at the position of the sun in the sky. "But I should get going. *Äiti* will be ready to cook supper, and she will have no fish to begin on."

"Farewell for now, then, my friend," Elisa said. "Will I see you tomorrow?"

"Of course."

Aino walked home as afternoon clouds settled over the sun. She stepped nimbly over mossy rocks and fallen pine boughs, her line of fish in hand.

She first began to see signs that something had gone wrong after cresting the hill near the homestead. The muddy trail from the forest, which intersected with Aino's own path, was rugged and torn, as if something had limped down it. A little ways ahead of her, something bright and red stained the ground, still fresh.

Aino dropped the line of fish and set off running.

As she neared the house, she saw a large figure collapsed in a mound near the entryway: her brother's horse, Tuli. The beast's belly moved, but his breaths came harsh and quick.

The stablehand emerged from the barn with water and a bundle of herbs as Aino ran to the stallion's side.

"What's wrong?" she asked him. "Has something happened to Joona?"

"He's hurt as well," the boy said, pointing to the house. "Your mother is tending to him."

With one last look at the struggling horse, Aino hurried inside to find Joona and her mother seated in the kitchen. Most of the blood, it seemed, was Tuli's, but Joona too was covered in deep gashes and huge, purple bruises. He sat at the table while Sannu applied a poultice to his wounds, face drawn in tension.

They looked up when Aino entered.

"Daughter, how fortunate that you've returned!" Sannu gestured to the poultices. "I could use your help."

Aino set to mixing more herbs and soaking cheesecloths in the liquid. But Joona was badly injured, and Aino wondered if her mother's power extended to wounds this serious.

"What happened? Were you attacked by robbers on your way home from the village?"

"Not robbers," Joona clarified. "A single man, if I could even call him that. He was certainly not *just* a man. I believe him to be a demigod."

"A demigod?" Aino scoffed. "How could you know that?"

"Because that is what everyone is saying," her brother said in a tone that meant she'd asked a stupid question. "I heard tell of a man called Vilhelm who had arrived in the area recently. He was said to be gifted, with a voice that could raise mountains and fell cities."

Joona's own gift was a voice so pure and strong that, with a song, he could calm a flock of sheep so they were ready for shearing. He brought good fortune to all who heard him, which was why many people in neighboring villages hired him to come and sing luck into their homes. He'd been gone for two days at a wedding on one of these journeys before he'd returned here, injured as he was.

Aino knew her older brother. He was vain and immensely proud of his gift.

"You sought out this Vilhelm, didn't you?" she said sternly.

Joona winced as his mother wrapped a cloth around his left arm. "I had to know if the stories were true. I had to challenge him."

Aino didn't argue, didn't ask, "Must you always challenge those who threaten your superiority?" She and her mother had dealt with the repercussions of his whims since he was a child. This was no surprise to either of them.

Instead, she said, "So the stories about him were true."

Joona hung his head. "*Jo*. He sang until the earth trembled beneath me. Boulders rolled in, crushed Tuli, trapped me, until he had me at his mercy. I knew he could kill me. He *would* kill me." He dropped his face in his hands, shoulders shaking. "I had to do something."

Aino and Sannu looked at each other as Joona wiped tears from his eyes. Perhaps they both sensed that something was about to change, a seismic shift in this life they'd built together since Aino's father had died.

"What did you do, Joona?" Aino whispered.

He stared up at her from his hunched state, wincing as Sannu applied another ointment to a cut on his leg. "I offered you as his bride in exchange for my life. And he accepted."

Aino stared at him, a mix of fury and despair welling up beneath the surface of her skin like a dam yet to burst. The betrayal was astounding. He had sacrificed *her*, traded *her* life for *his*. Like she was chattel to be exchanged.

"Selfish idiot," she hissed, fists clenched at her sides. "You could have offered anything else. Your stallions, your bows. You could have given him all your boats and all your cornfields. Now what? Am I betrothed to a demigod without any say in the matter?"

"I'm sorry, Aino," he wailed, burying his face in his hands. "Truly I am. But I feared for my life. I had no choice."

"Did I not just give you choices?" She spoke through gritted teeth. Aino was not a violent person, but at this moment she wanted to beat upon her brother, as if that might knock any sense into him.

"Perhaps you could look at this in a positive light," Joona replied sharply, a sudden change in his tone. "This can't be all tragedy. A marriage to a demigod will be good. I think we all know that you would not have had any other prospects. Everyone here in town knows how ... odd you are."

Aino was about to lunge at her brother when her mother finally made a noise. A tiny clearing of her throat, but it stopped both of them in their tracks.

"Children," she intoned. Her face was drawn, eyes shadowed and tired-looking. "Do not fight on this day, for it is blessed. We should be thanking the gods that it has come."

Aino turned to Sannu, aghast. "*Äiti?*"

Sannu could not meet her eyes. "I am not pleased that Joona has been so rash as to challenge a demigod. But I am glad that his foolhardy actions have led to something good for once. Your marriage to Vilhelm will be a boon to us. I've been praying that you would find someone. While I had hoped to be part of the choosing party, this is as good a match as I could have hoped for." Sannu's voice was thin, reedy, as if she were trying not to cry. "You should be glad, too, Aino."

Aino looked between her brother and her mother, stunned into silence. Both had turned on her, and the betrayal made her stomach roil. She turned on her heel without another word and left.

Aino went to fish the next day, hoping to find Elisa. She wore three pearl bracelets and a beaded comb, something her friend had once complimented when she'd worn them to the lake. As always, she brought her nets in order to fool her mother and brother. Aino didn't feel much like fishing, though, so she simply swirled her fingers in the cool, placid water, enjoying the way the whitefish twirled around the ripples she made.

After several minutes, she turned and was startled to see a man standing a little farther along the shore. He was close enough that she could see his white hair and his blue eyes that shone like sapphires. He smiled when she met his eye, no negative response to the look of pure distrust she knew must adorn her face.

"Does your mother know?"

Aino balked. "Does my mother know what?"

The man moved a few steps closer. His body shifted with an inhuman grace, as if his limbs and sinew were liquid. The smile remained on his face, but Aino got the distinct feeling from the gleam in his eye that she was being evaluated, like a fishmonger with his trout.

"You're the one who vanquished Joona. You're Vilhelm."

He dipped his chin. "I am."

A thrill of unease wound its way up Aino's spine. So this was the demigod Joona had promised her life to. He had the appearance of a human man, perhaps fifty or sixty years old, with a lean, muscular body and clothes spun from silk.

"I must admit, I am glad I came upon you out here," Vilhelm said, voice like the waves of the sea. "According to your brother, both he and your mother believe you to be ungifted. But I can sense the power in you when you do that little trick with your fingers. Your brother and your mother are mistaken, are they not?"

Aino considered lying, but she knew this demigod would ferret the truth from her. "Yes," she said, seething beneath a carefully neutral façade. "And you would do well to keep that secret from them. If they know of my power, they will no longer be desperate to marry me off to the first man who will take me."

But Vilhelm only laughed, and Aino realized he did not believe her bluff. He was more perceptive than she gave him credit for.

"Your mother would be thrilled to marry you to me whether or not you were gifted," he said. "And your brother would have offered you either way."

Aino wished she could refute that claim. The fact that it was true made her all the more angry at Vilhelm. If he were anyone else, she would spit at his feet. But he could dispose of her with a call of his voice by bringing up the earth and calling down the mountains. Disrespect meant death.

Aino remained silent, and Vilhelm stepped closer, appraising. He caught her wrist, which bore the pearl bracelets she had worn for Elisa.

"Ah," he said, voice like warm, golden syrup. "You've dressed yourself up for someone."

She tried to gently pull her wrist back, but he held firm.

"Perhaps you were hoping to happen upon me when you went out today." He smiled, slow and bright. "My bride is more eager than she lets on."

Aino knew she should not react, but she was at her patience's end. She wrenched her arm from his grasp and plucked the first bracelet from her wrist. She held it over the water.

"I wear these pearls for no one but myself." And she dropped it into the lake. Then she removed the other two bracelets and the comb and dropped them each into the water as well. Finally, she turned on her heel and left, leaving all her fishing nets at the foot of Vilhelm, who remained silent as she left.

Despite Aino's fears, the demigod did not follow her

down the path. She hurried home, heart pumping, with fear and rage and exultation. She had never done anything so rash, and it thrilled her. But as she arrived closer to the homestead, she slowed and became more somber.

Dropping the bracelets had been one thing—she had bought them for herself the year previous—but she deeply regretted leaving the comb there in the water. It had been from her father, a cheap trinket from a traveling merchant. But she couldn't go back.

Aino walked inside to find her mother at the loom.

The older woman glanced up at her. "Why do you come in looking so sad?"

"I saw Vilhelm today while I was fishing."

Her mother paused her weaving, a gleam of excitement in her eyes. "You met him? What was he like?"

"Insufferable," Aino said. "I immediately disliked him. He implied that I wore my bracelets of pearl and my beaded comb to impress him, so I threw them in the lake. It was impulsive, and now I am heavy in my heart."

"Oh, Aino, I'm sorry that you lost your beautiful jewelry." Aino wanted to protest, to clarify that she only missed the comb from her father, but her mother continued. "I think it is time I told you something."

Sannu gestured for Aino to sit on a stool across from her.

"When I was around your age, I came upon the daughters of the Moon in a clearing near my home. They discovered me watching them dancing, but instead of sending me away, they let me come into their circle. We spent a night in merriment, sharing our gifts and dancing and singing. When the sun rose, the Moon's daughters asked me to come with them. But I said I must return to my home, and so they bid me farewell. Before they left, they brought me gifts to remember them by."

Sannu rubbed the rough cloth of her skirt between her fingers absently as she spoke. "I saved those gifts, never wearing them or taking them out. I wanted to save them for the daughter I would one day bear. I hoped she might wear them on her wedding day." Sannu settled a hand on Aino's arm. "Do not be saddened by the loss of your jewelry. Go instead to the storehouse at the top of the hill. Take this key and open the chest. There, you will find more than enough to replace them. They are yours now, for your marriage to Vilhelm."

Aino clenched her hands into fists. "Why are you with Joona on this? Why do you want me to marry Vilhelm? *You* got a love marriage. Why would you force me into an arranged match?"

Sannu brought her other hand onto Aino's face, cradling her cheek. "My only daughter. My sweet, courageous Aino." Her voice caught on the name.

Aino's heart stuttered at the gentle, unexpected touch from her mother.

Sannu gathered herself and continued. "I come from a long, proud line of powerful women. When we realized you did not inherit any gifts, I was crushed. With Joona unable to father children, you were our sole chance of carrying on this legacy.

"But now Joona has come and told us of a man who can control heaven and earth with the sound of his voice, and he has pledged your hand to him. Vilhelm is a demigod. Even if you are ungifted, the strength of his power must surely pass onto his children that you will bear. Now, finally, I know that my line will not halt with us. I will miss you when you go, my child, but I am happy. You should be happy too."

Sannu released Aino and sat back, as if exhausted by her speech. Aino stared at her, heart pumping so loud she thought perhaps the whole world could hear it. Her mother was happy that Joona had sold her to Vilhelm to save his own life. She wanted *Aino* to be happy for it.

The thought made Aino want to curl up on the floor and sob until her voice left her. Instead, she stood and smiled at her mother.

"Thank you," Aino said. "I understand now what I must do. Thank you, dear *Äiti*."

She kissed her mother on the cheek and walked out of the house. As she moved along the path toward the storehouse on the hill, she said goodbye to everything she had known her whole life—the livestock, the fields, the trails, the trees.

When she summited the hill and entered the storehouse, she found a small, iridescent chest near the back. She used the key Sannu had given her and lifted its lid.

First, she pulled out bracelets, necklaces, and rings made with gold and silver, many inset with precious stones. Aino put them all on, then she pulled out the final item in the chest: a rainbow-tinted dress that shifted colors in the light of the rising moon. Its fabric felt cool and smooth to the touch, softer than any material Aino had ever felt.

She removed her scratchy woolen dress and put on the gown. It fit her perfectly.

Then, heart heavy in her chest, she left the storehouse in her fine clothing and jewelry. Aino walked down the hill and took the path to the lake. There, she sat for a while, running her fingers through the water. When she worked up the courage, she looked up and out over the lake. Several figures watched her from the rocks. She saw Elisa's yellow hair. She sat with her fellow maidens of Vellamo, watching to see what Aino would do.

She knew what had to be done.

Aino removed all the fine things that her mother had gifted her. She took off the bracelets of silver and the necklaces of gold and rings set with precious stones. Lastly, she took off the rainbow-tinted dress, leaving it on the rock she always sat on.

Aino stepped into the water. It was cool and swirled around her ankles, buffeted by the fish that immediately flocked to her when she entered. They circled Aino as she descended into the water, one step at a time. Tears streamed down her face, cleansing and pure. She looked out to the water maidens as she walked, never turning to glimpse her old home again, until she took her final step and the water covered her completely.

In the end, the hare brought the message of death.

She relayed the sad tidings to Sannu and Joona: Aino had come to the lake and walked, weeping, into its depths. When her brother and mother ran to confirm the news, they found her fine jewelry from her mother's chest and the rainbow-tinted dress laid across a rock.

Aino was nowhere to be seen.

THE BABY BARGAIN
ALISON THAYER

LAURIE TAKES a slow sip of her whiskey sour as she admires the handiwork of the Parties-R-Us crew. Their friends will be impressed, no expense has been spared for Martin's fifth birthday party.

Brad lines up liquor bottles on the patio bar. "It's not even noon, Laurie, try not to get sauced before your son's birthday party starts, would you?"

"Maybe I wouldn't have to drink so much if you—"

"Don't start with that again. It's your turn this year and fair is fair."

"None of this is fair, Brad."

Her mother calls from across the grassy lawn, "Where do you want these, honey?" She waves a dozen or so red helium balloons above her head like it's her birthday today instead of her grandson's.

"Those are for the face painting station, Mom," Laurie calls back. "Just tie them to the corners of the table." Rainbow tablecloths, balloons, and banners dot the back-yard. Booths and tables are spread across the lawn, ready to accommodate dozens of kids as they visit a jumpy castle, face painter, cotton candy maker, fortune teller, and animal balloon making station. A small stage is set up at one end of the lawn for the main event, a magician who will close out the party. Martin is going to love it. Laurie just wants to get through the day. God, how she dreads this one day a year. She takes a long pull on the whiskey sour.

Her mom rearranges the chairs in front of the magician's stage and calls out, "Martin is going to have the best birthday party. To think that precious boy almost didn't make it into this world, and now he's turning five!"

"I know, Mom, it's a miracle," she calls back, repeating the same hollow words she has used over and over again in the years since Martin's birth. Only she and Brad know the truth, that it was no miracle.

Laurie eyes the bottles of booze. "Don't put out the good vodka, you know how Greg goes through that stuff."

"We spent a fortune on this party, I'm not going to serve cheap booze to our friends," Brad replies.

Laurie approaches the bar and rearranges the liquor bottles to put the cheaper ones up front.

Brad knocks her hands away and puts the bottles back as he had arranged them. "You've got the payment ready, right?"

"Don't worry, I've taken care of it," Laurie says.

"Where is it? It's not like you can just store it in the refrigerator with the cake."

She looks up at her husband as he bangs the edge of the cocktail onion jar on the side of the bar, wrestling to get the lid off. She can't help but blame him a little for what they have to go through year after year. A real man would have taken care of this years ago. Taken care of *it*. "I've got a plan." She sets out the plastic cups.

He grips her arm. "A plan? You've got a plan? You've got payment for her, right?"

"Everything okay?" Her mom steps onto the back deck and looks back and forth between them.

Laurie pulls her arm away. "Everything's fine, Mom. The decorations look great, thanks for all your help. Why don't you go in and relax before the party starts, the kids will begin arriving in less than an hour."

Her mom pats her hair. "I better go clean myself up then, and check on the boys. I think Liam is more excited about the party than Martin is. He sure loves his big brother." She grins and heads into the house.

Laurie pours herself another drink. "Let's get this over with."

"We're so glad you could make it," Laurie says to the Jacksons, one of the last families to arrive.

"Sorry we're a little late," Greg says, holding his son Dillon's hand as they step up onto the deck.

"Not a problem, I'm only on time because I live here," Brad jokes.

"Jemma spit up all over herself just as we were walking out the door and we had to change her entire outfit," Vicki says. "Isn't that right, you little cutie patootie," she coos to the infant in her arms.

Jemma giggles back, waving her chubby fists.

Laurie smiles down at the baby. "She's getting so big, how old is she now?"

"Just turned four months last week," Vicki replies.

The same age as last year's payment. Sour bile rises up in her throat. She takes a sip of her drink. At least it had been Brad's turn last year, at least that one wasn't on her hands. "She's really beautiful, Vicki."

"Mom, can I go play now?"

Vicki glances down at Dillon. "Of course, why don't you go find Martin, dear? There he is, waiting in line for the jumpy castle."

"Go help yourselves to drinks and we'll join you in a few minutes," Brad says. The Jacksons wander toward the bar.

"Is she here yet?" Brad asks, his eyes scanning the crowd.

"Not yet." Laurie looks at her watch. "Maybe she's not coming this year. Maybe she's letting us off the hook."

Brad frowns. "She'll be here. She always comes."

Laurie stands in line with Martin as he waits his turn for the face painter. His hand, sticky from cotton candy, grips hers. "What should I get, Mama?"

Laurie laughs at his excitement. "Whatever you want, honey, it's your birthday."

Martin's eyes squint. His "thinking face," she and Brad call it. She looks over toward the grill where her husband is cooking up hamburgers. The smell makes her mouth water.

Brad is swinging Liam up into the air, and her younger son is squealing with laughter. Brad sees her watching and he whispers something to Liam. Liam looks over at her, waves and yells, "Love you, Mama!"

She waves back, happy for the first time today. That bitch hasn't made an appearance yet and they're more than halfway through the party. Maybe their own personal hell is over. Maybe they can start enjoying Martin's birthdays.

"Next?"

She startles at the voice and turns back to the face painting table. She steps forward with Martin and crouches down. "It's your turn, hon. Have you decided what you want?"

Martin grins. "I want to be a tiger, roarrrr!"

"Great idea," Laurie says. She stands and turns to the face painter. "Can you do a tig—" Her voice trails off as she meets the gaze of the woman, her ocher-colored eyes pinning Laurie in place. That terrible night comes rushing back to her, when she looked up into the eyes of her trusted doula who had been by her side throughout her long, tortured labor. Laurie knew her then as Barbara, but she knows her real name now.

"Hello Laurie," Lamashtu says, her voice all honey. She is dressed in loose colorful silks, her dark hair covered with a wispy veil. Her eyes dart to Martin. "Who do we have here? Is this the birthday boy?" She smiles, her teeth sharp and white.

"Hi ma'am, I'm five today! Can I be a tiger?" Martin beams up at the woman.

Laurie pulls Martin back against her legs. "Maybe we should come back later. Look, Martin, Daddy's got hamburgers ready."

"But Mom, I've been waiting in line forever," Martin whines. "Pleeeeeze, it's my birthday!"

"Sit right down, Birthday Boy," Lamashtu says. She grins at Martin. "I'll make you the fiercest tiger ever!"

Martin pulls away from Laurie and sits down. Laurie wants to scoop him up and run somewhere far, far away, where she will never have to see this creature again. But they tried that, didn't they? Somehow she always knows where to find them. Laurie turns away, searching for Brad, but he's caught up in conversation with Jason Platt. Probably talking about their golf swings. She sets her jaw and turns back.

Lamashtu grips Martin's chin and pulls him toward her. She looks up at Laurie. "Sit down so we can talk while I turn the birthday boy into a tiger."

Laurie reluctantly takes the chair next to Martin. "We didn't see you earlier. We thought maybe you weren't coming this year."

"Oh, I wouldn't miss this special boy's birthday for anything." Lamashtu picks up an orange face paint crayon and begins applying it to Martin's forehead. "I assume you're prepared to renew your contract for another year? Wouldn't want you to miss out on future birthday parties with this little guy."

Laurie swallows against the ache in her throat. "Please. You can't really expect us to keep doing this, year after year." She hears the whine in her voice and despises herself for it. "People notice when ... things go missing."

"Ouch, that hurts," Martin says.

"Sorry love, I didn't mean to squeeze so hard." Lamashtu pulls her hand away from Martin's chin. White finger-shaped prints mar his tender skin. She picks up a black crayon and begins applying it to Martin's face. "Are you telling me you don't have my payment? Because you know what happens if you don't."

Laurie grips her hands together to keep them from shaking. Why did she think she could outsmart this creature? She should have just done what she was supposed to do and arranged for payment. At least bought them another year to figure out something else. Too late now, but she'd see this through. "No, no, I've got your payment, it's in the house. I just thought, maybe, going forward ..."

"I'll be here next year, and the year after that, to collect my payment. Until Martin turns eighteen. You agreed to the terms."

"Mama, is something wrong?" Martin's big brown eyes move between Laurie and Lamashtu as she adds black stripes to his forehead.

Laurie swipes at her eyes. "No honey, everything's fine. It's going to be fine. Mama's just excited that it's your birthday, that's all."

"There you go, sweet boy." Lamashtu dashes whiskers onto Martin's cheeks and holds up a mirror for him. "What do you think?"

"Roarrrrrr!" Martin growls into the mirror. "Thank you, ma'am. Mama, can I go show my friends?"

"Of course, dear, go ahead. Mommy needs to talk with Ms. Lamashtu some more."

Laurie leads the way into the house, with Lamashtu following and Brad bringing up the rear. Sweat trickles down the center of her back despite the cool air inside. She leads them upstairs to Liam's room. The baby is in Liam's crib. It had seemed like the logical place, but she regrets the choice now. She hates to have this creature upstairs, in the most private spaces of their lives. At least no one will disturb them here.

She turns as Brad clicks the door closed behind them and comes to stand beside her. He's biting his lower lip. Good. Let him worry a little, for making her do this awful thing. She's a mother, for God's sake, it must be harder for her than for him. Yet he makes her take her "turn" every other year. Let him worry.

"Let's get this over with," Laurie says. She walks to the

crib and picks up the swaddled baby. She returns to Brad's side. Lamashtu watches her closely as Laurie hands the bundle gently to her. She can probably smell Laurie's fear.

Lamashtu looks down at the bundle and lifts a hand to peel back the top layer of blanket.

"No!" Laurie touches Lamashtu's hand. She didn't mean to be so loud. She takes a deep breath. "She's asleep now and I'd rather you not wake her. If you leave with her now, no one will notice."

Lamashtu jerks her hand away from Laurie's but she leaves the baby swaddled. She shifts the baby closer as she turns to leave. A mechanical baby voice breaks the silence. "Mummy, I have to go potty."

"What the hell," Brad says.

Lamashtu whips the blanket back to expose the talking doll. It was the most realistic baby doll Laurie could find on the internet, and it cost a fortune. But still, it's obvious that it's not a real baby.

Brad takes a step back. "Laurie, what have you done?"

"Yes, Laurie, what have you done?" Lamashtu says. "You try to pass off a doll to renew the contract on your son's life? This is how you repay me for saving his life and allowing him to live and grow, year after year?"

Laurie feels heat flush through her body. How dare she! "You were my doula, you were supposed to help me birth my baby. What kind of doula demands a yearly sacrifice in return for saving a baby's life?"

Lamashtu's golden eyes narrow. "I did you a favor. I offered you the chance to save your sickly newborn. You knew the price—you deliver an infant to me every year on your son's birthday, or Martin dies. And now you've broken our bargain."

Brad steps forward, his face the color of ash long gone

cold. "No, we haven't broken the bargain. It's still our son's birthday. We can still get you a baby today, right?"

Lamashtu is silent for a moment, studying him. "Fair enough. You have until the end of the party. If you don't deliver a baby by then," she glares at Laurie, "a *real* baby, then Martin's life is forfeit." She turns and leaves the room.

"I cannot believe you tried to trick her into taking a fake talking doll. What were you thinking?" Brad paces Liam's floor, running his hands through his hair.

"I'm sorry, I didn't realize that stupid baby talked. I think she might have fallen for it if the damn thing hadn't asked to use the potty," Laurie says.

Brad stops his pacing and stares at her. "Are you out of your mind? No one was going to think that doll was a real baby. And if she had believed it and left the house with it, what then? What about when she figured out later that you had fooled her?"

He has a point. "Okay, okay, it wasn't my best idea ever. But Brad, I can't do this anymore, we can't do this anymore. Kidnapping other people's babies?"

"It's the deal we made, to save our son."

"Of course we did, it's what any parent would do!"

Brad puts his hands on her shoulders. His voice softens, "I know, honey, it's not fair. But she'll take our son if we don't pay up. On the upside, our home is chock full of children today."

Laurie jerks away. "You want to hand over the baby of one of our friends?"

"What choice do we have?"

He's right. She can't risk losing Martin. Her stomach

heaves and she knows it's shame, but she pushes on. "Okay, okay. What about the Millers' little boy? We're not even that close to them. And he's a bit of a brat, honestly."

Brad shakes his head. "No, he's too old. Besides, he'll put up a fuss when she tries to take him. We can't risk a scene."

"You're right, we need an infant. Who do we know with an infant?"

Brad resumes pacing. He stops and turns toward her. "How about Marley? She's under a year old. And maybe Megan and Tom won't even miss her that much. She is their fourth child, after all."

Laurie gasps. "No! Megan's my best friend, you monster. I'm not stealing my best friend's baby!"

"Fine, but who else? Who else has a baby?"

Their eyes meet and they say at the same moment, "The Jacksons."

Back outside, Laurie takes a last swig of her drink and grimaces. "Ew, I don't think that was my drink." She sets the glass down. "Okay, let's do this," she murmurs.

Brad links his arm through hers. "Just be natural, like you do this every day."

"Fuck you," she whispers back, but she pastes a smile on her face and walks with him toward the Jacksons. "Hey guys, enjoying the party?"

Greg holds up his lowball and says in an overloud voice, "Who wouldn't, that's a well-stocked bar you've got there."

"Nothing but the best for our friends," Brad answers, avoiding Laurie's pointed look.

Vicki says, "It's a great party. You guys really outdid

yourselves. The kids are having so much fun." She glances at the baby in her arms. "Jemma's having a great time, even though it's past her nap time. Isn't that right, my little munchkin?"

Laurie extends her hand and Jemma grabs hold, gurgling and smiling. Her tiny chubby fingers curl trustingly around Laurie's, warm and soft. Laurie pulls her gaze away. "Hey, why don't I give you a break, I'll take little Jemma inside for a diaper change and you can have your hands free for a little bit."

"That's so kind of you to offer, but Jemma's reached that age where she gets upset when strangers hold her," Vicki says.

"But I'm not a stranger, am I little Jemma? Here, let's just try." Laurie reaches to take the baby.

Vicki pulls away. "Really, it's okay. I don't mind holding her."

This has to work. "But you need a break. Come on, let me just change her diaper." Laurie holds out her hands.

Vicki jerks Jemma back sharply and Jemma cries out.

"Now look what you've done," Laurie scolds. She reaches for the baby again.

Vicki turns her body away. "I said no."

Greg says to Brad, "I think your wife's had a bit too much to drink, buddy."

Laurie turns on him. "Really Greg, you're telling *me* I've had too much to drink?"

Vicki glares at Laurie and pulls at Greg's arm. "Come on honey, let's find Dillon and head home. It's time for Jemma to take a nap anyway."

"She can nap here," Laurie says. "Here, I'll just take her in and put her in Liam's crib." She steps toward Vicki, arms outstretched.

"Good grief, what is wrong with you today?" Vicki turns and marches away, taking their last hope with her.

She can't let them leave. Laurie moves to follow, but Brad's heavy hand lands on her shoulder. "Laurie, it didn't work, let them go."

"But—"

"I know. We'll figure out something else."

Laurie stands to the side of the audience as the magic show begins. Brad stands next to her, chewing on his nails. They have no plan. Lamashtu is going to meet them back in the house following the show, and they have no plan.

The Amazing Magiisto is on stage. Martin sits in the front row next to Laurie's mom, who is holding little Liam in her lap. Excited murmurs rise from the crowd of kids watching the magician's every move.

The Amazing Magiisto holds out a black top hat and sweeps it side to side. "See kids, nothing in the hat." He places the hat on a small table set before him and waves a wand around and around. "Abracadabra!" he says. He reaches into the hat and pulls out a wiggling white rabbit. The kids erupt in cheers and clapping.

Brad leans toward her. "It's got to be Marley. Megan's your best friend, she'll trust you. Offer to change Marley's diaper, whatever."

Laurie nods. Her throat tightens and she swallows back the tears.

The Amazing Magiisto announces, "For this next act, I need a special volunteer from the audience. Can I get a volunteer?"

A lawn-full of little hands reach for the sky, but Laurie

isn't paying the magician good money to pick someone else's kid. He points to Martin and says, "How about the birthday boy?"

Martin bounces onto the stage, all grins and big eyes. Her miracle baby. Her hand tightens around her drink. There's no way that monster is taking her baby.

"Happy birthday Martin, how old are you today?" asks the Amazing Magiisto.

"I'm five," her handsome boy exclaims, grinning at the audience.

"Do you think turning five deserves extra special magic?"

"Oh, yes." Martin jumps up and down at this news.

Brad tugs at her arm. "We've got to be ready as soon as the show is over, come on." They inch their way toward Megan.

The Amazing Magiisto paces the stage a few times, shaking his head. "It's not easy doing magic this special. Luckily, we have a lovely assistant to help us."

Laurie sidles closer to Megan as the magician's assistant pushes a small wooden wardrobe to the middle of the stage.

"What you are about to watch is a magical feat unlike any you've ever seen before. I, the Amazing Magiisto, will use this magical wardrobe to make this young gentleman disappear."

Laurie touches her best friend on the shoulder, all smiles when Megan glances over.

"Laurie, Brad, great party! This magician was an awesome idea." Megan has Marley tucked up against her shoulder, where she's happily tugging at Megan's blond hair.

Laurie glances at the stage, where Martin is shifting up

and down on his toes at manic speed, grinning. "Mama, he's going to make me disappear!"

Laurie smiles and gives a little wave. It feels like her face might crack open. She turns back to Megan. She can't mess this up again. This time, it's got to work. "Hey Megan, do you mind if I borrow Marley for a minute? I came across a baby dress that was mine when I was little. With two boys, I don't have much use for it. I thought I'd see if it fits her."

Megan furrows her brow. "Right now? But don't you want to watch the end of the magic show?"

Brad replies, "You've seen one magic show you've seen them all, right hon? It'll just take her a minute."

Megan looks at them quizzically but says, "Okay." She passes Marley over. "Time to visit with Auntie Laurie," Megan singsongs to the baby.

Laurie takes Marley, who smiles up at her and gurgles. She can't bear to think about what she's about to do.

The audience breaks out in laughs and cheers. Laurie glances up. Liam has leapt from his grandma's lap and is toddling across the stage to Martin. Martin takes his little hand. Laurie stops to watch, her heart aching with love for her two perfect boys. But she's got a job to do, Martin needs her to get this right. She takes a deep breath. "I'll be right back." She turns toward the house.

Megan says, "Oh, but look, the magician's about to do the magic trick with the wardrobe. That assistant, isn't she the face painter?"

Laurie turns toward the stage and watches, her body like stone, as the Magician's Assistant walks with the two boys, *her* boys, to the wardrobe.

"Brad, what—"

Brad takes a step toward the stage.

Lamashtu takes the hand of each boy and steps into the wardrobe with them.

Brad starts up the center aisle. "Hey, wait—"

Lamashtu waves and pulls the wardrobe shut.

A roaring noise fills Laurie's ears and black spots dance before her eyes. She senses that she is sinking, but she can't seem to feel her legs anymore. The baby's weight disappears from her arms as Megan grabs Marley. But this can't be happening, Marley's going to be the payment! She watches through half-closed eyes as Brad vaults to the stage and yanks the doors open. Martin stands there, grinning out at the audience. Lamashtu and Liam are gone. Her baby is gone. Laurie's eyes flutter closed as the audience bursts into applause.

THE CLAY BRIDE

VISTA MCDOWELL

CLICK CLICK CLICK sounded the wheels on the tracks, reminding Gayatri with each passing mile how far behind home was. She twitched aside the curtain to watch the sun rise over the jungle and distant mountains. Mist blessed the air with cool droplets, diffusing the light into a thousand rainbows where water-spirits danced.

Gayatri touched the cool glass, her fingers slipping against the dew that had accumulated on the pane. She imagined the bustle of her waking town: women gracing their threshold with intricate designs of powdered lime-stone, boys feeding the chickens and goats, girls collecting flowers for the breakfast table while green-spirits playfully pulled at their hair. The morning would be awash in laughter and color, opposite from the drab, gray quiet of her train cabin.

As she held open the curtain, her glance slid to the brown patterns decorating her hands. The intricate designs had been drawn by her great-aunt, who had whispered good luck for Gayatri's auspicious marriage. *He is a wealthy man from far away*, the other women had said. *How many other girls are given the chance to marry one such as him? You are blessed, Gayatri.*

Her great-aunt had drawn a pangolin surrounded by jasmine flowers onto Gayatri's left hand. *For protection and wealth.* Gayatri rubbed the pattern and looked over her shoulder.

Her new husband snored from the cabin's tiny bunk, his hand dangling over the side and brushing the wooden floor. His glasses lay on the small table crammed beside the bed. Gayatri had not slept at all that night, and Philemon had not noticed her move away from the bed.

In the dim light, Gayatri examined Philemon. In the whirlwind of their three-day wedding ceremonies, she had not truly spoken to him. When they had boarded the train last night, both had been too exhausted to do more than fall into the sheets.

Their courtship had been equally quick. Gayatri's father, a merchant with an eye for new enterprises, had invited this foreign man into their home as soon as Philemon had arrived. He offered Gayatri to him as a sign of their new partnership. She had accepted from filial obligation, but she didn't know why her new husband had chosen her.

Her musings were interrupted by a tapping at the window. She looked back out and smiled. A wind-spirit waved at her, its ethereal wings beating in time to the train's movement. Gayatri waved back, and the spirit melted away into the air.

My family checking on me. Gayatri could picture her mother and great-aunt laboring over the rangoli that would summon the spirit; they would have been up before the dawn to do so. Before her marriage, Gayatri would have worked with them, her hands white with the powdered limestone, her back straight as she spread the substance into dots and whirls.

Philemon snorted and shifted in the bed. He sat up and turned on the gas lamp, filling the cabin with yellow light. His long, spidery fingers picked up his glasses and rested them on his nose. He blinked a few times as he looked around the cabin, his gaze finally resting on her.

He was not bad-looking, by any means. His nose was thin, his light eyes large behind his glasses. His lanky limbs folded into the tiny space, like a giant insect perched on a leaf. He was certainly not the stout, dark man Gayatri had pictured herself marrying.

"Morning," Philemon mumbled. He unfolded his long arms and legs and stood, his head brushing against the ceiling. He pulled on a shirt and waistcoat, his fingers flying with every button.

Gayatri turned away from him as he dressed, her cheeks heating. She was already wearing her cotton saree, its borders embroidered with brightly-colored flowers interwoven with pangolins, her family's symbol. It had been a wedding gift that her mother had been working on since Gayatri's birth, each stitch made with a prayer for a loving match and many children.

"Breakfast?" Philemon asked as he straightened his cravat.

Gayatri nodded, and they went into the dining car. Not a word passed between them as they ate. Upon their return to their cabin, she took up her post by the window. She could no longer see the mountains that rose up over her town.

"We'll be in the city by noon," Philemon said. He pulled down his luggage and sorted through it, then paused and pulled out a jar. Tendrils of blue flame licked the inside of the vessel, magical fire that Gayatri had taken from their marriage brazier.

"You're meant to carry it to our shared home," Gayatri said. "It's good luck."

"Ah." He turned the jar over in his hands. "I'm to bring it all the way over the sea?"

"Yes…" Gayatri paused, realizing his words. "Over the sea? I thought you had a house in the city. That's where we're going, isn't it?"

Mother would never allow me to marry a man who would take me away from our homeland. She wouldn't.

Philemon gave a helpless little shrug. "I received word from my associates during the wedding. I'm needed in my home country."

"But…but my father's business…"

"We're still partners, my dear. My company will trade with his. Besides, I'm sure we'll return eventually. Perhaps in a year or two."

Bees buzzed inside Gayatri's skull, drowning out all reasonable thought. Philemon's country lay across the sea, weeks away even by steamship, far from her jungles and spirits and family. Did the water-spirits play in the streams of his homeland? Did the wind-spirits knock over vases or bring a taste of the harvest? Would her rangolis still summon them to aid her in her chores, or to visit her family when she could not?

"No," Gayatri said. It was the only thing that her lips could form. "No, I'm not going."

"It's already done. Our ship leaves in a week." Philemon's look was not unkind. "I am sorry for the late notice; I forgot to tell you during all the kerfuffle. You'll love my country. It's a far more civilized place. You'll be able to wear the latest fashions, and we'll hire a maid or two for the household. Everyone will want to meet you, exotic thing that you are. You'll have to learn the language, of course."

He droned on and on, heedless of Gayatri's stillness, his voice humming with the insects in her head until there was nothing left of her thoughts except *no, no, no.*

The train shuddered to a halt, its smoke pouring over the station. Gayatri barely noticed descending onto the platform or being handed into a cart.

They pulled in front of a small house just outside the center of town. It was a lovely little place, with jasmine planted out front and peonies under the windows waving to the bright sun. Its mud-brick walls were warm to the touch, and as Gayatri stepped in, she immediately felt at home. Greenery filled the floors and shelves, money plants for fortune, holy basil for well-being, lavender for peace. Gayatri breathed deeply. She would have been content to live there forever with Philemon, tending the house and garden, creating rangoli on the threshold to welcome good spirits and ward away the mischievous ones.

"I rented this house when I first arrived," Philemon said as he carried in the luggage. "Charming, isn't it? Not nearly as large as my house at home, mind you. There you'll have space to do whatever you like. Eastern styles are all the rage, you know. The ladies will love seeing how you decorate."

But will the spirits hear my call?

The house was dusty, and while Philemon settled into his accounts, Gayatri looked in the cupboards for crushed grains and powdered limestone. She found them tucked away in the kitchen and brought them out to the threshold.

The fine powder poured from her funneled fingers, spilling onto the swept flagstone that stood before the kitchen door. With delicate grace, she directed the flow of the powder, first in a pile and then a sweeping line. Gayatri kept her back straight, her shoulder guiding her hand in a steady motion as she drew patterns on the flagstone. Her design echoed the jasmine and peonies. As she worked, Gayatri sang a prayer to the spirits, asking for their assistance.

Gayatri stood and wiped her hands on her pleated skirts, then adjusted the drape of fabric on her shoulder. Carefully, she stepped over the rangoli and into the house. Toward the rear was an inner courtyard with tall trees and a wandering mosaic path beside a reflecting pool. She started there, sweeping up leaves from the mosaics.

Wind tickled her arms as spirits gathered around her. They helped her to sweep the floors and wipe the tables. They gathered peonies from the garden and brought them to her hand. As she labored, the spirits spread behind her, lending her additional arms that quickened the pace of her work.

But she had been careless in creating her rangoli. Trickster spirits had also come into the house, and she heard the tinkling of ceramic against brick as a vase broke. From above, Philemon gave a shout of surprise. Gayatri hurried upstairs to see his papers blow out the window. Her husband cursed and gathered his remaining work.

"Bloody wind," he muttered.

Gayatri said nothing, backing away.

"Gayatri!"

She had only taken a few steps before he shouted for her. Her feet leaden, she turned back to him. Philemon stood at his office door, his crumpled papers still clutched in one hand. He pointed at the translucent arms that poked from behind her back. "What are those?"

"Spirits," Gayatri said simply. "They help me."

"Did they do this?" he demanded, gesturing at his office.

She nodded, her throat tightening.

Philemon huffed and smoothed his hair. "Blasted things. I'll be glad to return to a city without such chaos."

Gayatri's heart plummeted to her bare feet. *No spirits?* "Is there no magic where you're from?"

"Not like this," he said. "Our magic is logical. Controlled."

Empty. Gayatri turned away. In one week she would leave behind the home she loved for a place devoid of color and spirits. A sob threatened to escape her throat, and she only just held it back.

She could run away. But to where? Her family would only tell her to be dutiful and follow her husband. And Philemon was not a bad man, he did not deserve to lose his wife after only a few days of marriage.

A spirit tugged at Gayatri's sleeve. She followed it without thinking and came into what had once been a child's bedroom. The furniture was covered in sheets, and dust carpeted the floor. The spirit glided onto a shelf and sat beside a doll, its ethereal eyes glimmering.

Gayatri took the doll down, her fingers running through its horsehair braid and over the long-faded miniature saree. She gave a questioning look to the spirit.

Then a memory struck her of a story she had once heard of a man making a wife for himself out of clay.

Gayatri's lips turned up into a smile.

Outside, the air grew humid with a coming storm, the sky darkening. The spirits on Gayatri's back trembled, but she paid them no heed. She looked to the spirit that had led her here and nodded.

Philemon never came into the courtyard garden, preferring to shut himself in his office all day and only emerging for meals, and so that was where Gayatri set to work. It was quiet there, peaceful. The air barely touched by the bustle of the city just outside her front door.

Gayatri began with an intricate rangoli using the last of the powdered limestone. It summoned spirits to help her as she piled clay on the mosaics. It was wet and malleable. Gayatri labored over many long hours, the spirits giving her multiple arms to wield her tools. Soon the clay began to take shape.

The storm had not yet broken, the gray clouds growing darker and darker overhead.

In the darkness after supper, Gayatri lit lamps to illuminate her work. Sweat dripped down her back and beaded on her forehead, for the coolness of night did not assuage the labor of her limbs. Even her spirit-given arms felt tired. Under her careful hands, the lumpy clay turned into smooth contours and rounded edges.

At last, Gayatri looked over the clay woman that lay on the mosaics. *She will do.* Gayatri went to bed beside her snoring husband, her soul lighter already.

In the morning, she took her basket to the market, balancing it on her hip. The streets were a feast of color and sound, from the women's multi-hued sarees to the spice racks to the langurs calling from the treetops as they tried to swipe at fruit on passing carts.

Gayatri could have happily whiled away the day chatting to sellers or examining the newest fabrics and imported goods. But the ship would leave soon. She went straight to the crafters' stalls and found the artist's supplier. The man bowed to her and gestured at his wares.

"It will be a big storm," he said as she browsed the ochre pigments and brushes. "Hopefully there are no floods."

Gayatri cast a glance at the turbulent clouds overhead. The air was heavy and moist, ready for the monsoon. In the swirling gray clouds, she thought she saw a face. A spirit? A warning?

She turned away and paid for her supplies. At another stall, she spied a luscious horsetail, dark like her own hair and nearly as long. The price would normally make her balk. Gayatri smiled instead and gladly paid the merchant.

At last, she came to an old woman selling colored sand.

"Hello, grandmother," Gayatri said, using the polite address for an elder.

"Child," the woman replied. "How may I help you?"

Gayatri perused the selection, searching for just the right colors. *Green for new beginnings, blue for bravery, yellow for the right knowledge.* She paused at the red sand. She had worn that color upon her wedding day, for it represented purity. But it was also a color of protection, and so she selected it as well. Finally, she paid for an excess of white sand, the canvas upon which she would decorate her hopes.

As she put the sand into her basket, the old woman lay a hand to her arm. Beneath her years of wrinkles, the woman's eyes were bright. "There is no festival coming, child. What will you do with this sand?"

A lie came to Gayatri's lips, of her sister marrying and needing the bright colors for the festivities. She suppressed it and said truthfully, "I need the spirits' help for a great deed."

"Hmm." The old woman's leathery hand gripped tighter. "Beware, child. The greater spirits are fickle things. They will not always solve your problems as you believe they should."

"Don't worry for me, grandmother. I will take care of myself." Gayatri pulled away and turned her feet toward the house, doing her best to ignore the hammering of her heart.

Clouds rumbled overhead. The trees held their branches as she hurried home, their canopies still against the steely sky. They whispered, *What are you doing, Gayatri?*

Gayatri went straight to the inner courtyard and the waiting clay statue which had finally dried. Her fingers shook as she mixed her pigments with water and linseed oil. She used the large brush to spread the brown ochre paint all over the statue, from the tips of its toes to the crown of its head, layering it until the statue matched her own skin color.

With the fine-tipped brush, she painted brown eyes, black brows, and red lips on the statue's face, her back straight as she leaned over her project. The paint did not smear, for her hands had steadied as she fell into her work.

Next came the horsehair. With a gluey paste, Gayatri stuck the hair to the statue's head. She took shears and cut off small bits of hair at the ends, glued these to the place between the statue's legs.

Gayatri stood back to survey her handiwork. A clay version of herself lay on the stone, painted eyes staring into the sky.

Sweat gathered under her clothes, and her hands shook. Gayatri swallowed and turned away from the facsimile. She would have to eat and sleep before she began the complicated rangoli.

In the morning, Gayatri spread white sand over the entire surface of the flagstone around the statue. She thought about her design and then drew her finger through the white sand, making an outline to follow. She would make a giant pangolin surrounded by peony and jasmine blooms, using all the colored sand she had purchased. The design was larger than the statue, stretching far beyond the tips of its feet and head, the largest Gayatri had ever created.

Starting with the yellow, Gayatri outlined the animal's armored scales before filling them in, a series of sharp lines and curves. She used red for the peony. The fine granules bit into her skin and crowded under her nails. They slipped from her hand, errant drops of ruby splashing into white.

As she worked, she sang lullabies her mother and great-aunt had taught her. She prayed to the greater spirits of the jungle, hoping they could hear her. She thought of how much money she could take without Philemon noticing, and which sarees to pack and which to leave behind. Where she would go next, for she could not return home without Philemon, and yet she could not stay here.

The colors stood out against the white sand, stark and bright, clear as the stars in a moonless night. Wide swaths of red for the peony petals, tiny flecks of yellow along its borders. Every worry and care poured out of her hand and landed atop the sand, from the thin lines to the thick circles, the intricate whorls and patterns.

The sun had tipped beyond the horizon when she finished. Gayatri stood and looked down at her master-piece. All her love, her prayers, her desires, had been poured into the sand.

"Gayatri?" Philemon called from inside.

Gayatri cursed. She had forgotten to make his supper.

She ran into the kitchen and pulled out leftover curry and rice, warming them on the stove. Her frantic movements made her careless, and she spilled the meal onto the floor. She hurried to clean it as her husband stepped into the room.

"Is everything all right?" he asked. He stooped to help her, and Gayatri ducked her head, blushing with shame. "Why are you covered in sand?"

"I'm making a rangoli," Gayatri said. "To pray for safe travels across the sea."

"You are sweet," he said. "But I've made this trip many times. There's nothing to worry about; my people make excellent steamships."

"Of course." Gayatri glanced at him, his askew glasses and ink-smudged hands. Would it really be so bad to go with him? To see a new place, travel farther than anyone in her family had ever gone? It could be an adventure.

Philemon grabbed her wrist, his eyes suddenly serious. "Gayatri, you cannot practice your superstitions in my country. What will the gentlewomen think, to see sand on our threshold or tattoos on your hands?"

It's mendhi, not tattoos, she wanted to say.

"You will have to wear the dresses of my people, and style your hair like them," Philemon continued. "Your clothes are not seemly where I'm from."

The flare of optimism that had warmed her chest dissipated, leaving her cold. Thunder rumbled overhead, and Gayatri abandoned all ideas of going with him.

After their cold dinner, Philemon retreated to his office once more. Gayatri left the dishes in the sink. Her heart tripped in her chest as she lit incense and oil lamps in the courtyard, bringing pricks of light and fragrant scent into the air.

Gayatri began to sing, a prayer in the most ancient tongue of her land, begging the great spirits to help her. *Let me stay here. Let this statue take my place across the sea.* As she sang, Gayatri danced, leaping over the incense smoke, her toes touching the edge of the sand without disturbing it.

A chorus of sounds joined her song: night warblers in the trees, the wind in the branches, the oil bubbling in the lamps, each growing stronger and louder with her voice. Somewhere beyond the house, langurs hooted in time to the rhythmic rises and falls of her melody. Even the thunder matched her song, the heat and humidity becoming unbearable.

When will the storm break?

Gayatri danced until her feet were sore, until her arms could no longer hold themselves up. She grew still, her breath tight in her throat.

She bowed to the statue in the sand.

The statue did not move.

Grief crashed over her in a tsunami, its waves compounded with frustration and anger. She had done everything right. She had found only the best ochres and the softest clay. She had labored over this dream for two days.

Gayatri turned and left the courtyard, her normally soft steps pounding over the cool bricks. With the melancholy came exhaustion, her whole body drooping with fatigue. Her hair was lank and heavy on her head, her fingers trembling. The muscles in her legs spasmed, and her back ached from the long time bent over her work. Her bed called to her, and Gayatri collapsed into it, her hopes shattering like glass around her.

Overhead, the sky finally broke, and rain poured forth,

the roof pounding with a thousand droplets. Thunder crashed into her dreams, sounding like laughter.

The sound of singing roused Gayatri from her sleep. She blinked at the sunlight filtering through the bamboo slats over the window. How long had she slept?

Gayatri rolled from the bed, her body unusually heavy. Something tugged at her buttocks, and she turned.

She had a tail. A long tail covered in scales erupted from her behind. Long claws scraped against the floor as she pattered to the mirror.

A pangolin looked back at her, sandy-colored scales and long snout and sharp talons.

Movement distracted her. She whirled, a small sound escaping her muzzle as a woman entered. Not the woman: the statue, come to life, Gayatri's twin at a glance. But the more Gayatri looked, the more she saw the subtle differences. The woman's skin shone, but there was a hardness beneath it, like clay. Her hair was silky and long, but more like a horse's mane than a human's. She wore the style of dress Philemon preferred, all petticoats and stiff fabric, and sang a melody from his homeland.

The facsimile stooped and smiled at Gayatri. She held out her hand, and her eyes glittered with intelligence.

"Go free," the woman murmured. "I will go with him."

Gayatri's new animal tongue could not produce human sounds.

The woman smiled. "I am everything he wants, and I have no fear of leaving this country. You made me to replace you. This is my sole purpose."

Why am I a pangolin?

The woman's red lips curled in a gentle smile. "The great spirits always extract a price for their interference."

The woman stood and began to tidy the bed. Gayatri crept out of the room and into the courtyard. Her rangoli had been swept away, her incense and oil returned to their places. No trace remained of her ritual.

Gayatri blinked, a new grief lurking in her soul. *I wanted to live here as a woman, to walk the markets and barter and cook the meals I so love.* She peered over her shoulder at the clay woman.

The old woman was right. The spirits are unpredictable.

Gayatri slunk out of the house and through the alleyways, headed for the jungles outside the city. She had no voice to sing and pray, no fingers to make rangolis or sew a saree for her own daughter. Regret slithered between her scales and into her flesh.

DO OVER
CEPA ONION

IT BEGAN on a warm May night in a corner booth at a dollar-a-scoop Chinese buffet. I was crunching fried wontons when our youngest son, James, called to tell me not to wait up for him.

"I quit college," came his excited voice, "I'm on my way to Vegas. Gonna make bank doing standup."

"But you're not even funny!"

I instantly regretted my response, but James couldn't tell a knock-knock joke. Plus, he'd never lived away from home. Vegas would destroy him.

I blamed myself for this. I'd always felt like a lousy mother. Responsible for everything that went off the rails. My stomach cramped as if agreeing. I loosened the string on my perpetual sweatpants and shifted in the red vinyl booth to alleviate the chronic abdominal pressure I'd been feeling. In addition to gaining too much weight, my stomach had been doing some very strange things. This evening was no exception.

"Not funny?" James barked through the phone. "Yes, I

am. C'mon, you always said so. Remember how I had them rolling in the pews during the church play?"

"You were seven and you fell on a sheep."

He ignored me. "I told Father Doug, 'If I'm such a *wise* man, why aren't I bringing baby Jesus something *useful* like *diapers*?' The whole place cracked up."

"But you weren't *trying* to be funny. It was a serious question."

"I know. I'm a natural."

"You need to stay in school," I replied firmly.

"No, I don't," James said. "The Comedy Cluster pays sixteen bucks an hour. That's way more than I'm making at Shoe Zone. All it takes is one break and bam, you've got your own reality show. Besides, with the war coming, nothing we do now really matters anymore, does it? It's all supposed to end soon, isn't it?" His voice cracked a little when he said "end." I didn't know how to respond.

My husband, Joe, returned to our booth sporting a full plate from the buffet. "Mary, what's wrong? You getting bad news or are you about to pop another gas bubble?" His big cloth napkin dangled from the collar of his too-tight light blue work shirt, his way of keeping it clean so he could wear it to his job tomorrow.

"It's James," I managed. "He's quitting college to be a *standup comedian*." My guts twisted as if turning away from this embarrassing news.

"Is that Dad?" James said. "You're not telling Dad, are you?"

Joe's pulpy face reddened, swallowing his dark saucer eyes. In one clunky swoop, he plopped down his plate and grabbed my cell phone. "James? You are one month away from graduation. You are not, I repeat, *not* quitting college. And what's this bunk about becoming a comedian? You're not even funny." Joe's eyes narrowed into slits. "C'mon. You are *not* going through a tunnel. You can hear me just fine. You'd better not be driving and talking on the phone either. Jonah's driving? That's worse. Pull over and call an Uber. Now."

The thick candy-scent of pork grease bloomed from Joe's plate and grabbed my nostrils. I wondered if he'd notice if I took a piece. It smelled so good and, despite my intestinal distress and swollen body, I was always starving lately.

Joe banged down my phone. "The dunderhead hung up. And apparently, it's safe for Jonah to drive now because he's back in rehab." He took his seat and spent the next five or so minutes pressing redial. Then he did the same thing with our three other sons. "None of them are answering. Have they *all* blocked us *again*?" He growled. "Why can't our kids be more like Abe? He grew up in the same neighborhood. Went to the same crappy schools. Now he's at Google, getting foot massages at his desk."

"Abe was born perfect," I said softly, because he was. "He potty trained before most kids could walk."

"And you can bet Abe'll find a way to stay out of the *final war*. That's what they're calling it now, Mary, did you know that? 'The final war.' Doesn't sound very promising."

"I know. I know," I said. At that moment my stomach lurched so hard I had to settle it with my hand. As Joe continued his desperate call-a-thon, I managed to eat every scrap of his food, and mine. I could picture how we must appear to the other diners. Two pigs at the trough. Joe, a blue-collar worker with a "dad bod" gone wild. And me, a seen-better-days grandma type, shoveling food the way you'd feed a coal train.

Gosh, I wished I really *was* a grandma. If Joe and I were

grandparents we'd do everything right this time around. With the perfect baby who would make us forget all about everything wrong. Even the final war. Like a divine do-over. Wow. I really liked that term, *divine do-over*. So much so, I shared it with Joe.

"Are you kidding?" Joe said, still punching redial. "In order to be grandparents one of our sons would actually have to start dating something other than anime cartoons."

Joe didn't even look up when he said it. I sighed.

Unexpected joy barged in as I overheard a child call across the room. "C'mon Mommy. Don't we have to go home and see the planets?" The girl's wonder-sparked words reminded me that tonight a few planets—I forget which ones—were lining up. The media spent all month hyping it as "The Christmas star in May." I forgot all about the final war, my stomach pain, and James's misguided life and became nostalgic for that young child-mother bond.

"Oh sit down, Anna," the tired mother scolded her child. "Let Mommy have one more egg roll, and then I promise we'll go."

"We have to go, *now*," the girl begged. "I don't want to miss it. *Please*."

"I said 'no,'" the mom admonished.

Suddenly, I felt compelled to fix this, make the mom appreciate what she had before it was too late. Who knew how long any of us had with the final war looming? With one last look at Joe punching numbers, I waddled across the carpet to the booth where mom and child sat.

The mom crackled with tired preoccupation, made worse by her "who cares how I look" clothes. Her stocky body leaned over the booth as her mouth worshiped the egg rolls in big, hungry gulps. Her daughter, Anna, looked about five. Unlike her mom, Anna's trendy clothes sparkled with newness and style. It was obvious where all the money in that family went. Anna huddled in the corner of her seat, peering up through the dark window, eyes pinned to the sky.

"Excuse me for intruding," I told the mom. "But I think you should go see the planets."

The mother looked up, confused. Before she could speak, I continued, "Trust me, you'll have all the time in the world for egg rolls. What won't last much longer is your beautiful daughter's curiosity and how she wants to share it with you."

I braced myself. The mom would no doubt scold me, tell me to mind my own business. I prepared to stand my ground and gently assuage her with examples from my own life. I'd tell her about my own proverbial egg rolls and how I regretted choosing them over my children.

But then *bang*. A light as big as the world flashed. It careened through everything, shaking the air. Unable to absorb its brightness, I closed my eyes. But when I opened them, everything remained as mundane as the color beige. Joe continued to tap his phone while the rest of the restaurant kept on restaurant-ing. I swear I saw a light. But it was clear no one else did. I wondered if my chronic cramps were somehow causing me to hallucinate.

"You know," the unphased mom interrupted my thoughts, "You're right." With a tired smile, she put down a half-eaten egg roll. Then she stood, clutching her oversized mom purse. "Anna, c'mon. Let's go home and see some planets."

"The Christmas star!" the young girl cried. They stood and walked hand-in-hand to the door. Anna waved me a "thank you" as they left.

It was like a sentimental scene from a Hallmark movie.

Totally fake. But I swear it happened just like that. Even the mysterious bright light. Feeling triumphant, I returned to our booth. Joe had apparently moved on to text messages, pressing the letters so hard I thought he might leave dents.

"Hey Mary, how do you spell 'ne'er-do-well'?" he asked.

"You're not calling James a 'ne'er-do-well,' are you?"

"I'll just say, 'idiot.'" He ground his fingers into the phone.

I wondered if people could make wishes on Christmas stars the same way they make wishes on falling stars. If so, tonight I was definitely wishing for a divine do-over. I wanted the final war to disappear and for me to somehow raise a child again, do everything right. My love and knowledge would make that child perfect. My stomach cartwheeled at the thought, then managed to growl.

Finished with our high-sodium banquet, I cracked open my fortune cookie: "Welcome to your best life."

The irony slapped me back to reality. The success I had with the anonymous mom and daughter popped like a gas bubble, and real life crashed back in. Who was I kidding? I was so far from my best life. I was sixty, well past my expiration date. My limp gray hair needed grooming, and my skin was as pale as a dead mackerel. Only my eyes remained young. I was sure of that. Hidden behind thick eyeglasses, I knew their violet hue could still dazzle some unwary creature. Violet eyes are a rarity. All four of our sons failed to inherit my eye color. But maybe our grandchildren would.

I peered at Joe's fortune cookie, maybe for another do-over. But who knew what kind of curse I'd unleash if I stole a cookie that wasn't intended for me?

Joe handed back my phone. "Out of power. Darn it, Mary, you realize this is our strike four?" He parked his head on the palms of his hands like a giant golf ball on a tee.

"Strike four?" I asked, considering another round of moo shu or a heap of lo mein.

"Our other three sons are failures," Joe said. "James makes four. See?" He held up four thick fingers. "Strike four."

My eyes escaped the enumeration of my failures by latching onto the buffet line. They were bringing out a new pan of something, and I wanted to go see what it was. I sniffed the salty air for clues.

"I mean, Joe Junior never finished high school, and where is he now? Selling hotdogs and living in a van in Sweden."

"It's a customized van, Joe. It has a toilet."

"He used to play the piano in Honors Band. Remember his All-Star Performance? And Jude's been working on a two-year associate's degree for eight years. And Simon left grad school to sell pot."

"The term is 'budtender,'" I reminded him.

Joe glared back so hard his blueberry eyes were nearly swallowed by his muffin face. Even his neck seemed thicker.

"You want to read your fortune cookie?" I asked, trying to lighten his mood. He took the cookie and squeezed it in his meaty fist. It popped open like a crushed bug, launching blond shell bits across the table. Joe's face and neck became even fatter and redder.

I did what I had been doing so much of lately: I burst into tears. Big, gooey ones that flooded my face and made my neck itch.

"Aw crap, please don't cry," Joe said. He actually crossed over to my side of the booth and slipped his thick arm around my shoulders. "Shhhh. It's okay. Here, let me read my fortune cookie, maybe it's good news."

His voice was tender and his face softened as he rescued the thin piece of paper from his pulverized cookie. "'Welcome to your best life,'" he read.

I cried anew. "That's the same one I got. They're all the same."

"Maybe they're not the same. Maybe these were meant just for us," he said in the same kind voice.

My stomach tightened, hard and mean. I pushed away from Joe and gasped for air.

"Mary, what is it?" Joe asked.

"I think I might have cancer," I said through fat, breathy sobs. I finally said what I'd been avoiding for months.

"You're just upset about James and this final war thing," Joe said, fingering his fortune.

"No, seriously. The gas, the bloating, the pain—this is what happened to my sister when she got diagnosed. I've been putting off going to the doctor because, well, I'm afraid."

"Mary, honey, you're sixty. It's probably just menoclaws."

"What?"

"Menoballs."

I struggled to keep from rolling my eyes. "Menopause? C'mon, Joe, you know I already went through that. Remember when I mooned James's soccer coach?" I wiped my nose on my sleeve. "No. This is different. Something's seriously wrong. I know it."

Joe looked as if he might cry too. "Let's get you home. See if we can't find 'our best life.'" He slipped the two fortunes into his shirt pocket and helped me out the door to the parking lot. The sky was black, no clouds. I couldn't see any stars. That didn't seem to bode well for a planetary alignment.

Leaning firmly against Joe, I "ouched" and "ahhhed" my way to our Oldsmobile.

"You know what we ought to do instead of going home?" Joe said after he settled me into our car. "Let's go straight to the emergency room and tackle this cancer thing head-on."

"No!" I screeched. My editing job with Happy Homemakers had one of those "Health Insurance in Name Only" plans where you paid for everything until you're bankrupt. I was about as covered as a toddler's sneeze. "That'll cost a ton."

"But your gas pains have been going on for weeks," he said.

It'd actually been about seven months, but I didn't tell Joe that because I couldn't bear to see his face get any sadder. "I'll make an appointment. One more day."

He started the car. "All right." He clicked on the radio because us old folks still listened to it. The ethereal sounds of a choir singing "Away in a Manger" filled the car. "What the hey? Christmas music?"

"Must be for the Christmas star in May," I gasped. My sides squeezed harder now, boa-constrictor tight.

"Oh yeah. That planet thing," Joe said. "It happens, what, once every gazillion years?"

"Something like that." I leaned back further in my seat.

"Well it sure beats the final war news, right?" He turned up the music. "You know what would help fix everything? If they played nothing but Christmas music on the radio and on every news show, too. The pundits could lip-synch something good for a change."

The oddly cold window glass felt good pressed against

my face. We rolled past all the dilapidated landmarks that led to our neighborhood: four pot shops, two liquor stores, three check-cashing places, and a storage locker where someone had stashed their mother's body.

I pried my cheek off the cool window, leaned over, and touched Joe's arm. It felt like a foreign, kind gesture. I'll admit that I hadn't touched my husband that way in a long time.

"I love you," I said in a strangled voice, because I realized I did.

"I love you too," he said, glancing at me with concern.

He gently turned our car onto our block, and my stomach tightened even more. Suddenly, I needed to move, to run even.

I unstrapped. "Let me out." The seatbelt bell dinged its petulant sound.

"But we're—"

"Right now. Please."

He stopped the car at the end of our block, and I hurtled myself out. He was right next to me, keeping pace. "Slow down, Mary, please, would you?"

The pain pounded me like a drum. I stopped and rested my hands on the hood of someone's parked car, panting. "Quick, Joe, tell me something good about our sons. Anything, but it has to be nice, okay?"

"What do you—"

"Just do it!"

"Okay, I ..." Joe was thinking.

"And take my arm," I added.

He took it as I puffed in and out. I hadn't breathed this way since the Lamaze classes when I was pregnant.

"I'm waiting," I shouted. "Say something nice!"

"Okay. Sure, alright. James *is* funny. I mean he really can be. Remember the church play?"

"Yes. Good. Go on."

"Joe Junior's van is really cool. I wanna live there."

"Really?"

"Yes. Fact is, I'm kind of jealous of him. I mean, c'mon, Sweden? No talk of a final war there, right?"

"True."

I resumed walking, faster, breathing so loud my ears roared like a jet engine.

"Jude's in a writers' group," he said. "That might lead to something. And Simon's probably going to get rich being on the ground floor of Munchie's Pizza Pot Pies. And, oh Mary, please say you're okay. Please. I'm sorry I was so mean. They're great kids. We're great parents. Especially you. You're great, Mary. Please. Please be okay." He breathed rough and hoarse, hurrying to keep up with me.

Exhausted, I pulled away from him. I needed to be alone. I wrenched open the small gate to our neighbor's chicken pen. Once inside, I plopped down onto the straw. It was time to bare down and deliver what promised to be a gigantic tumor.

"Mary? Joe? What's going on?" our neighbor Angel called from across her lawn. I looked over to see her standing next to a cannon-sized telescope. A dozen neighbors were queued up behind the giant piece of equipment. Angel and her husband, Gabe, always prided themselves on being avid amateur astronomers.

Joe stepped in front of me as if attempting to block my squatting body from their prying eyes. "You guys watching planets line up?" he called in a choked, preoccupied voice.

"Supposed to," Angel said, moving closer. "They should have aligned ten minutes ago. I don't get it."

"Sky's pitch black, too, which makes no sense whatso-ever," Gabe called, sounding as if he were walking toward us too. "Something's definitely off."

"Why's Mary in our chicken pen?" Angel said.

"She's really sick." Joe moved next to me and kneeled down.

I was still breathing hard and fast. Even my eyes seemed to be inhaling the warm spring air. The hens were oddly quiet, watching me from their nests as if we were part of the same social club.

"Hey, Angel," Joe said. "Can you call an ambulance?"

"No ambulances," I screamed again and again, my voice savage and raw as I pushed down harder than I'd ever pushed. On the last, something broke, and what felt like water gushed out, filling me with the most glorious relief. Weak and trembling, I reached down and pulled off my pants.

My eyes squeezed shut and my other senses height-ened. The neighbors had all moved close to me now. Their scents coiled together—from BO to pot roast to someone's harsh cologne. All of it ganged up with the acidic aroma of chicken coop.

"Look, blood," someone said in a relaxed voice.

"We'll clean it off," I gasped, squeezing Joe's hand into pulp. "And buy more hay."

Other than the tepid comment about the blood, the crowd was subdued. It was as if they were under some cosmic spell, lulled into a strange complacency.

In contrast, Joe sputtered into panic. His body hiccupped hard sobs as he prayed.

"I love her. Oh God, please," he screamed in a loud, desperate voice that annoyed me for some reason. Then Joe placed his head gently on my rapidly deflating belly, sobbing wildly.

"Call an ambulance. Someone. Please," Joe's trembling voice thundered.

I ignored all of it, pushing again and again, screaming like a wild animal.

Then, crashing from me came—not a tumor—but the first cry of life, bathed in music. I swear I heard music. Ethereal music.

"A baby?" Joe said, dumbfounded. He lifted his head off my stomach, and his body fainted onto the soft hay.

I didn't check to see if he was okay. Nor did I investigate our neighbors' copious "oohs" and "awws." I didn't even thank the anonymous kid who used a pocketknife to cut the umbilical cord.

I didn't look at any of those things. Instead, I gazed into the familiar violet eyes of my son, as bright and promising as the Christmas star forming above us.

THE THREE VARKIN SISTERS

BJ EARDLEY

EVEN THOUGH THE outside air was filth, Gri Varkin's one-room hut smelled of freshly baked bread and mint tea. The sun came up red in the smoky sky giving the room a soft pink light. Gri lined up her girls in front of her, adjusted the fold of their tunics, straightened the pins holding their cloaks, and folded ten coins into each of her daughter's palms. She told them it was time for them to leave South River. She didn't actually say 'time to leave.' She said 'time to escape' because Gri Varkin was not one to squander words.

A layer of sand sneaked under their latched door and added to the sand already spread across the bare floor. One week before, Gri took up the rugs because it became too hard to shake out the sand. It was this very wind and this unshakable sand that told Gri Varkin she could no longer protect her children.

Zvina, the oldest at fifteen, kept her thin lips clamped and her blue eyes cast down when her mother tucked the coins into her hand. She felt the metal and imagined the North, the place her mother told them they should go. A place with cool streams and fresh skies and sun that shone bright and hot without the cloak of smoke. Zvina tucked the coins into a fold of her tunic and adjusted her headscarf. The scarf was a gift from her mother because Zvina must now be recognized as an adult.

"You should come with us," she said, not because she wasn't ready to be an adult (she wasn't), but because she knew if her mother stayed, the Vik was sure to find her. "Please come," she said again in a voice so calm that it would have been hard to guess the memories swirling in her head; the image of the Vik pulling her father into the sky. Her father's sleepy eyes. The thunder of the wind. Helplessness. The smell of fear.

"I can take care of myself," Gri Varkin said, "if I don't have to worry about also taking care of you."

Prasia, the youngest, smiled when her mother counted the coins into her hand. Prasia was only a butterfly in her mother's belly when the Vik twisted her father away. She didn't understand the need to escape. She brushed back the matted black curls that draped to her waist and thanked her mother using a trader's dialect, a recent affectation which delighted her mother and irritated her sisters. Although she was only five, Prasia absorbed dialects at the market as if the traders' foreign voices were sun and water to a flower that was already inside of her. Gri didn't believe her children should squander their talents any more than she should squander her words, so she encouraged Prasia.

Sika, Gri's middle daughter, knew well enough the need for escape. She was five when the Vik roared through South River. She held the coins tightly in her hand, easing them together until they were one solid cylinder of metal. She didn't look at the coins because her eyes played tricks when she tried to look closely at something. Maybe it was this trick of her eyes that set her to dreaming of lands beyond what she could see in South River. In evenings around the hearth, or outside in the stone circle, Sika told stories of the world she believed lay beyond South River, the characters and scenes that came to her in her dreams. Sika knew the cylinder of coins in her hand was her chance to prove her dreams were more than a vivid imagination.

"You will have to go well past the river before you find drinkable water," Gri Larkin said, running her hand over the surface of one of the skins she filled from the last of the clear water wells in the village. "Be wise with the coins. Work hard," she said, "care for your new home, and remember to dance."

Around each girl's neck, Gri hung a ribbon embossed with stones she had gathered from the mine tailings and then taken to Old Ander to be cut and polished in the fashion unique to South River.

"So you will always remember." Tears welled up in her eyes.

She kissed each of her daughters a final goodbye. She could have told them to be mindful of the Vik but saw little purpose in stating the obvious. Gri pulled the string on the now empty blackberry-dyed bag and tucked it in a fold of her tunic where she had hidden the coins from thieves and tax collectors.

Gri Larkin wanted her daughters to believe it was her thrifty nature that enabled her to save the coins. The truth was that, over the course of the last year, she had succeeded in stealing thirty coins from her lady and her lord who managed the mines. Gri always discovered the coins while she was cleaning. "Found these," she would say as she curt-sied and placed two coins on the board in the great kitchen. Gri knew the un-pocked face of her lady smiled at her honesty, never suspecting her of being a thief, even though she knew Gri had three daughters to support. It was true that Gri found two coins. It was not true that she had found only two coins. Sometimes it was three. Sometimes four.

She knew her lady might realize she dropped some coins when she pulled out a cloth to wipe the sweat from her lord's brow after he returned from inspecting the mine. Gri was confident her lady would not, however, have any sense of how many coins had spilled. Her lady and lord were people who lived amidst tall trees on a bluff of rock that raised them above the rest of town. People who had so many coins they didn't bother to pick them up when they spilled from their pockets to land under chairs, or in the folds of their cushions.

Gri placed a loaf of bread in each girl's pack, along with dried fruit and sausages, and a wrap each of sweet drops, a gift from her lady who recently returned from the North, a place she described as having flowers and bees, air that smelled like fresh rain, and insect music that filled the starlit night. That helped Gri make her decision. A place, Gri thought, where people work hard, care for their homes, and remember to dance.

"Travel well," Gri said as she watched her daughters leave. The chickens squawked at their feet as if expecting a departing toss of grain. Their feathers ruffled in the breeze.

Prasia's eyes filled with tears as the wind slammed the gate behind her. Until that moment she believed she was going on an adventure from which she would return. She hadn't understood. But now, everything her mother said became clear in her head, as if it were a new dialect she had just deciphered. Prasia sniffed back her tears because neither of her sisters were crying and she wanted very much for her sisters to think her brave.

When they walked past the market, Prasia saw Old Ander, who cut crystals so finely that they looked like bits of sunshine in your hand. She fingered her necklace and then tucked it under her tunic. There were thieves in the market. She feared who she and her sisters might encounter on their journey. This brought the tears again, and this time Prasia couldn't stop them.

Zvina took hold of Prasia's hand and hurried her into the poplars where the path led to the ferry. She wiped Prasia's cheeks but didn't give her any words to calm or encourage her.

"We should put our coins together and make a budget," Zvina said, holding her hand out to Prasia for the coins her sister had hidden in her tunic. "Two coins each for the ferry crossing to begin," she said. "It's exorbitant but I see little way around it." Zvina adjusted her necklace. The weight of it reminded her of the weight of her responsibility for her sisters.

Sika started to protest Zvina's suggestion, but then thought better of it. She recognized Zvina was smart with ciphers and good at making trades.

"We should set aside two coins for bribes if we run into questions we can't answer," Sika said as she handed over her coins. As beautiful as they were, Sika's dreams of the land beyond South River left no illusion that it was a world without the need for bribery.

"Twenty-two coins left then," Zvina said. But when she tried to cipher costs for materials and labor to build a new home, plus food until they could plant a garden, she realized there was no way to make their meager number of coins work. She tucked the crystals into a fold of her tunic and said nothing more about a budget. She realized this was why her mother did not go with them. There simply wasn't enough coin.

At the ferry, the river appeared wide and slow before it disappeared into a narrow canyon. But everyone in South River knew about the dangerous swirls of water hidden beneath the calm. Trying to cross the river without the ferry wasn't something Zvina would consider. She'd seen too many bloated bodies washed ashore from such attempts. She tightened her lips but didn't say what she thought about the lords making the ferry free to traders.

The ferry's logs creaked and groaned against their lashings as the guide rope strung across the river moved back and forth in the wind. The air carried the stench from the refuse and mine tailings being washed into the river.

The ferryman leaned against the long pole he used to maneuver across the wide slip of river. His felt hat was old and pocked with holes and his face had a similar appearance. He lifted his chin and peered at the girls through narrowed eyes and took in a breath as if trying to smell whether or not the coins Zvina held in her palm might be stolen. The frayed ends of his tunic blew in the breeze, revealing the grimy hem of his shift.

The sisters could see the question in his eyes. How did these three girls with patchwork tunics and worn shoes have the six coins needed to cross the river? He could refuse to offer them passage if he suspected them of being thieves. It would take one of the lords on the hill to sort it out.

The wind rattled through the poplars and Zvina's stomach tightened. Sika bit her lip, and Prasia sniffed back her tears. They all glanced at the Counter, who sat on the hill above the ferry and kept track of the crossings and collected the coins for the lords at the end of the day. Sika nudged Zvina and gestured to the coins in the fold of her tunic. Zvina nodded.

The ferryman smiled as he tucked the bribe into the pouch that hung close to his waist, his back to the Counter as if he had paused to wipe his nose. The sisters walked onto the ferry, holding on to the side rails to steady themselves. There was already a trader on the ferry, a short, fat-bellied man with a cart pulled by a donkey adorned in bells. The man ignored them, focusing his gaze on the undulating folds of grasses across the river. Beyond the grass was a dense forest where the traders' villages were hidden.

The sisters listened to the sound of the river licking the edge of the ferry and the sound of their hearts thumping in their ears. No one spoke. When they stepped off the flat-tened logs of the ferry onto the dunes, they pushed through knife-sharp grasses that whispered like old women gossip-ing. This side of the river was covered with the same gray dust from the mine. The same gray sky looked down at them. The air still carried an acidic sting to it.

"A good day's walk, that's all," Zvina said, "and then we'll find our new home." She didn't know how long it would take to get to the North, but, as the adult, Zvina felt it was her job to keep up her sisters' spirits.

When he overheard Zvina's comment, the man with the cart pulled close to her. The smell of the donkey, his breath, and a faint whiff of something sweet invaded Zvina's nose.

"My sister sells straw in the next village," he said. "She'll give you a good price."

Prasia recognized the woman as a farmer who traded straw at the market, though she had not seen her for a while. The miners used the straw on the floor of the mine tunnels where springs dripped from crevices along the lamplit walls and turned the soil to mud. As a group, farmers appreciated expensive jewelry. Prasia remembered how her mother raised the price of her necklaces when she recognized the bell-rattle sound of a farmer's cart coming around the corner from the ferry.

This woman's cart had but one string of bells, and she only wore two necklaces made of inexpensive river stones and commonly found seeds. Prasia thought the woman must not be very good at the art of the trade. Her knuckles were fat from working the straw and she had no donkey but pulled the cart herself with a handle at either side, worn smooth and dark with use. The woman tipped the cart down carefully and braced one wooden wheel with a rock. She nodded and talked to them in the guttural clicks of her dialect.

"She says her brother told her we'd be needing a home," Prasia translated as the woman extended her arms to her load of straw. Prasia felt proud to be of use, and she let that pride dry up any remaining tears.

Sika was already shaking her head. She knew what kind of house she and her sisters should have. The house she saw in her dreams was a house of stones, like the houses where her mother fed fires, swept floors, hauled water, lit oil lamps, and started a kettle of soup on the fire each night. She saw the kettle they should have, too. A kettle made of copper. Care for your home, her mother had said. Sika wanted to urge her sisters on.

"Ask how much?" Zvina fingered the coins in her pouch.

Prasia translated the woman's reply and Zvina smiled broadly, "Tell her we can pay in coin."

The woman didn't lose her smile, but she nodded her

head back and forth, pointing to Zvina's necklace. Zvina didn't need Prasia to translate what the woman said next.

"Tell her I won't trade the necklace," Zvina said. She tried to sound firm, ignoring the tingling in her spine and the uncomfortable twist in her stomach.

Prasia chose her words carefully, hoping to be clear. She didn't believe her sister would trade the gift from her mother. The old woman shook her head again, then smiled and replied.

"She says she can send someone to help with the building, included in the price." Prasia said, "With the necklace." Prasia looked at her sister who glared back as if Prasia were the one asking for the necklace.

"Never mind about the straw, then," Sika said. "Let's move on, save our coins for now." She believed this place was not the North her mother talked about. She saw no flowers on the low-growing vines that covered the ground. The air still carried a taint of something unpleasant, and Sika could hear neither bird nor insect.

"It's a good price," Zvina said. She adjusted her scarf and then retied the knot at the back as if this would make her decision clearer. She recounted the remaining coin in her head.

"Tell her," Sika said, "she can have the necklace, but we want three helpers." She felt the straw was a good price but knew she and her sisters lacked the knowledge to weave it. She was certain her mother had given her the necklace for just this purpose.

On a small piece of land at the edge of town, the three sisters, plus two plump young women and a sinewy boy, began to build their new home of straw. Zvina was the quickest at the weave, and sometimes grew impatient with her sisters. Sika found the work slow and tedious, but her fingers finally learned the twists and turns that the grass needed. Prasia thought the grass sharp and deft at cutting her fingers. She cried often, not from the cuts, but from the place in her heart where her mother had been.

Gradually, however, the sisters found happiness in their new home. Life was simple. Svina's skill with the straw gave her a place among the weavers, and Sika and Prasia carried water to the fields from the two remaining springs. It was not hard work. Zvina took up the fiddle. Prasia danced and smiled and no longer shed tears for her mother. Sika found solace in her dreams, which was the only place where she could find birdsong and flowers. Still, she remembered her mother's word. She remembered to dance. But all three sisters misunderstood their mother's message to care for their home.

Then, one morning, when her mind was still in her dreams, Sika smelled a musky spiciness in the air. Usually, when she first awakened from a dream, she could smell the fresh air of the North, feel it wrapping around her before her senses returned completely to her waking body, and her nose picked up the acidic smell to the air. But this smell was different. It took her a moment to recognize the ruffling of the flax curtains on the windows. She pulled back the curtains, dyed blue with the woad cabbage leaves that had once been a major source of trade for the village, and looked outside. A twirl of dust danced across an empty field between their house and that of their neighbor. There were more fields like this, gone fallow in hopes the field could be coaxed to support crops again. Sika breathed in. It was five years since the Vik swept through their village, but the clutch in Sika's stomach came right back, as if she were a young girl again seeing her father flying into the air and nearly taking her with him.

Sika woke Prasia and set her to filling their water skins.

"Our home is sturdy," Zvina said in a dreamy voice when Sika alerted her to the Vik's approach.

Sika remembered this, the way her father smiled with half-closed eyes and said they should let the Vik in.

"I'm not worried about a little wind." Zvina patted the woven straw walls and curled back into her bedding. "Let it in, let it in," she said as she closed her eyes.

Sika tried to lift her sister, but Zvina was heavy in her arms, pushing and shrugging her off and trying to get back into her bed box.

"We have to go," Sika said as she began to gather what food she could.

"But Zvina ..." Prasia cried. "We can't leave her."

"Can you smell the musky spiciness of the air?" Sika asked. "That means a great wind is coming. A wind stronger and angrier than you have ever known." She didn't tell Prasia it was this same wind that whisked away their father and left them homeless, until a kind woman with wrinkled cheeks and white curls took them in. Sika knew it was already too late for Zvina, as it had been for her father.

"Please Zvina, please." Prasia wrapped her arms around her sister, who was curled tightly in her bed with closed eyes and a gentle smile on her face. "Please wake up, wake up," she said.

"It's no use, we have to go." Sika pulled Prasia away from the bed. "I'll finish loading our bags. You go and alert the others." One last time, she attempted to lift Zvina, and as before, Zvina fought to remain in her bed.

"Let it in," she said dreamily.

Prasia ran from hut to hut telling the villagers to flee. Her eyes were clouded with tears and her voice ragged and halting as if she had lost her facility with words. Some of the villagers were already under the spell of the Vik. Others found little believable in the halting story the young girl told of a wind she had never seen.

"It's too late for them," Sika said, hurrying Prasia into the forest as puffs of wind picked up speed around them. The hills echoed the far-off thunder of the Vik's approach. The Vik huffed and puffed and cracked and howled. As they ran, the air spun around them and threatened to lift them off the ground. Prasia cried for Zvina, for the loss of another home, and then for her mother. She heard shrieks and screams carried on the spicy scent of Vik's warning, but she did not look back.

The sisters ran until they were over a hill and deep in a thick forest where they sheltered in the dark overhang of a rock outcropping. The air was still and cool and smelled of rat droppings. Sika tried to soothe Prasia's tears by telling her stories from her dreams. She promised they would get to the North as their mother intended, that they would work hard and dance and take care of their home. But Prasia cried and cried, and finally, when Sika had fallen into a troubled sleep, Prasia crept off into the moonlight, determined to return to find Zvina, who she was convinced would be able to escape the Vik. Sika found Prasia the next morning, not far from their overhang, having walked in circles through the night.

"It's okay. It will be okay. We'll be safe now," she said to Prasia as she took her into her arms. The smell of the Vik had passed, but Sika knew in her heart that if the Vik had found them once, it could find them again. She knew her mother was gone, and so was Zvina, eaten up by the Vik. There was no reason to think the Vik wouldn't be coming for them next. This was a truth Sika didn't feel needed to be shared with her sister. She clasped Prasia firmly by the hand and together they continued into the forest.

Prasia cried for her sister and her mother. She was moody and short tempered, but she walked. When Sika tried to distract her with a game of toss, Prasia threw the sticks and scrunched her face into a frown. She refused to eat the meager meals Sika cobbled together from their packs and grew weaker and more irritable by the day. The sisters were barely talking to each other when they emerged from the forest into a clearing. Here they found a small village of stick-built houses with smoke curling through an opening in their roofs.

Prasia refused to try and communicate with the round-faced villagers and kept her focus on the short brown grass that covered the gray soil. Sika searched for words to convey their situation and their need for food and shelter. She resorted to using a charade of hand gestures and facial expressions, which successfully resulted in a plate of stew and a straw mattress in the corner of one of the village's tightly built stick houses.

Sika was grateful for the villagers' hospitality, but she knew the North was farther on. There were few birds and flowers here, and the air had a peculiar smell. As soon as Prasia grew stronger from her days of refusing to eat, Sika told her it was time to move on.

"Let's use the last of our coins to buy supplies and continue," Sika said.

But Prasia stuck out her lower lip and began to cry, whining between sobs in a dialect that brought worried villagers to her side with suspicious glances at Sika. After this outburst, the villagers concerned themselves with assisting Prasia, and her perhaps abusive older sister, in building a home of their own. Within days a sturdy stick structure lined with soft beds and a round center hearth stood on a cleared piece of land next to a stand of feathery-leafed trees.

Prasia offered her necklace as part of the negotiation for the construction of their home and found her smile again. She was certain that her mother had given her the necklace for just this purpose. She danced in their new home with outstretched arms and, in a flurry of animated speech, made a promise that she and Sika would be most helpful working in the gardens where vegetables broke through the ground and welcomed the infrequent rain.

This time, Sika's discontent did not wane. She couldn't get the dream of the stone house out of her mind. She imagined how she would care for it as her mother intended. Sika noticed the scent of flowers growing weaker. She heard fewer birds and no insects at night. Still, she couldn't bring herself to leave her sister behind. So, she worked in the garden and struggled to carry the wooden buckets balanced across her shoulders on the long walk to and from the village's last spring. She tried to convince herself that she and her sister were safe. But, then, one morning when she rose early to begin her trek to the spring, she smelled a waft of musk.

"Prasia, the Vik," she said as panic clutched at her stomach.

But Prasia said she couldn't smell anything different. "It's only the smoke from our morning fire and a bit of roasted vegetables from last night's meal."

Sika couldn't lose the last member of her family. She threw young Prasia over her shoulder, intent on carrying her to safety. But the girl kicked and screamed and brought a crowd of villagers to their house. Sika tried to tell them of the danger of the Vik. Perhaps it was her difficulty with their language, the fantastical nature of her images, the protests of her sister, or the Vik's spell already affecting them, but the villagers were not swayed by this fairy tale. Two tall men with red beards and muscled arms wrested Prasia away from Sika as the wind curled fallen leaves around their feet.

"Let it in," Prasia said. "We are not worried about a little wind." She loved her home of sticks. She didn't care that there weren't birds or insects or air that smelled like rain. She thought Sika sullen and judgmental and jealous of the villagers' fondness and protectiveness. "You can go if you must," Prasia said, "but I'm staying here."

So, Sika ran, with a few vegetables from their bin and a small skin of water, which was all she had time to take. She let the force of the Vik's huffing and puffing help her forward, even though the twirling leaves and dirt made it hard for her to see her way out of the valley. She ran through the forest, slept, then ran again until she came to a land broken with sharp towers of golden rock slanting out of the ground and gray hills cut through with rivulets of green water.

The air was dry, and yet it smelled as if it had just rained. Every breath of this freshness lifted Sika's spirit. Around her, yellow and orange flowers burst from thin stalks. Sika smiled at the way the vibrant colors of the blossoms waved like precious jewels over the sandy hills. A flock of red-headed birds sang from the short trees. Even though her heart held sadness for all she had lost, the birds' joyful melody made Sika feel like dancing. Which is exactly what she did, twirling beneath the trees that branched out as if they couldn't make up their minds which way they wanted to grow. Sika was certain she had seen these trees in her dreams. Certain that this was the place she sought.

There was no sign of houses, though footsteps in the pale orange sand indicated a path to the east. Sika smelled the air again, took one last twirl under the trees, and turned to follow the footsteps.

Soon Sika came upon a village of houses made of stones the color of the sand. A man with light yellow hair and matching crooked yellow teeth stood in the path, shading his eyes from the sun. Behind him, a green cart was piled high with these same dirt-colored stones.

"Bricks," the man said to Sika's questioning eyes. "Made from mud. You don't know them?" He pointed behind him, where brown rectangular blocks were drying in the field. Sika realized the man had spoken to her in the South River dialect. She felt a warmth wash over her.

"You are South River? Right?" The man nodded as if answering his own question.

Sika thought it might be her square face, strong jaw, and freckles that betrayed her birthplace, but then the man gestured to her ribbon and stone necklace.

"I worked for the lords on the stone houses on the hill. That's how I learned your tongue." The man pointed at Sika with a crooked finger, the only finger he had left on that hand. He saw her reaction and smiled. "A stone," he said, "fell hard." He held up his hand as if he wanted her to admire it. "Bricks, they're easier to work with." He gestured again to the pattern of blocks behind him.

Sika realized the house in her dreams wasn't made of stones. It was made of bricks.

∼

Sika had no coin to buy the bricks or pay anyone to help her use the mix of mud, sand, and grass to bind the bricks together. To earn coin, she washed clothes in the river, plucked chickens for roasting, and shoveled manure from donkey pens. Progress on her house was slow. Work stopped completely some weeks, but Sika knew she was in the North where her mother wished her to be. The air smelled like rain, birds sang from trees, and insects buzzed under the stars.

Sika built one course of bricks and then another. One thickness of walls, and then two, and finally three, even though the villagers thought this unnecessary and told her so.

Sika worked long into the evenings. When the villagers invited her to eat with them, she refused, saying she was too busy. Her dreams stopped; her body was so overtaxed that it didn't have the energy for imagination. She forgot how to laugh. Sometimes she forgot to eat. She didn't remember to dance. When the walls were finally finished to her satisfaction, she accepted the help of the village to put on the wooden roof and secure the chimney.

"One more thing," she said. "I need a copper kettle."

The man with the yellow hair and crooked teeth said he had such a kettle, but the price he asked was more than Sika could spare.

"Your necklace, then," the man said. "I would take it in trade, to remind me of my time in South River."

Sika hesitated. She looked at the kettle which shone so brilliantly she could see her reflection. The thought came to her with certainty that her mother had given her the necklace for just this purpose.

Sika had worked hard, but she forgot to smell the air and listen to the early morning voices of birds and the evening serenade of insects. She forgot, as she and her sisters had forgotten before her, to care for her home. She didn't notice the decline of the voices, the new acidic smell to the air, the way the water retreated in the springs. If she had been paying attention, she wouldn't have been surprised the morning she smelled the scent of the Vik.

On this morning, she listened to the sound of the wind twirling around her chimney, not realizing at first the connection to the sound and the familiar musk of the air. When she did, she didn't run. She believed her house to be strong. She heard the thunder of the Vik and felt its breath searching for cracks in her walls, but her walls were tight.

"Let it try to get in," she said to the strong brick walls.

Sika smelled the scent of the Vik curling down her chimney where her new shiny kettle hung waiting for a fire. The kettle faced the Vik when it whirled into the chimney. The force of the wind hit the rounded bottom of the empty kettle and spun viciously, ringing the kettle as if it were a bell, shaking the walls of the house and finally toppling the chimney. The Vik exploded through the collapsed chimney and pulled the last Varkin sister up the chimney with it.

THE SUIT
ELEANOR SHELTON

IN HIS HOUSE on the edge of a ravine near the woods, Irv Goshen stood in front of the locked closet off the kitchen worrying about the suit. His worst fear was that he'd be the last of the Bellingham, Washington Goshens to wear it.

His problem wasn't that he'd have a chance to wear the suit, only that it wouldn't fit. Irv's great-great-grandfather Levi was the first Bellingham Goshen. Measuring seven foot, four inches, height, not his Jewish religion, was the reason he'd left the small town of Szeged in the eastern part of the Austro-Hungarian Empire in the mid-1800s. Irv's great-grandfather was six foot nine, his grandfather six foot, seven inches, and his father six foot, seven inches. Irv was now the tallest male in the family at six foot four, which wouldn't do. The family tradition would be broken.

The Bellingham Goshens had run the Goshen Family Plumbing and Feed Store for over seventy-five years and eked out a decent living, paying for daughters' weddings, sons' bar mitzvahs, and community college whenever asked. There were few Jews in Bellingham, most of whom weren't practicing. Churches were fairly empty too. Former days of worship were now reserved for football, sleeping in, or brunch. It was different in October though, when there was anticipation in the air and the talk in town turned to scopes, binoculars, and camera lenses. For some it was hunting, for others it was a chance to catch a glimpse of the elusive beast, a sure sign that all was well in the community, and a year's worth of bragging rights.

The Goshen family tradition allowed only two people to touch the suit: the eldest female, who would maintain the suit, patching where it was wearing, removing dirt, and brushing out tangles. And the tallest Goshen man, who would wear it. When Grandma Mike died, all suit duties would fall to Irv's older sister. If Irv and Lydia had a son, then the job would eventually be Lydia's.

Reasons behind that tradition had been lost in the generations, but the Bellingham Goshens observed it with the dedication of a dying wish. Grandma Mike, frail but determined, held her responsibility close, keeping the key to the locked closet on a silver chain around her neck.

This October would be Irv's first time wearing the suit. The complications of his height weighed heavy. His father had barely made it work with padding and some platform shoes. For Irv the solution needed to be more radical.

"How about stilts or some kind of brace?" Irv's wife Lydia came from the garden with telltale dirt on the knees of her high-waisted jeans and a yellow dandelion stuck to the heel of her red Crocs. "The suit could be altered. Grandma Mike could take some off the legs, tighten the shoulders. If you walk far enough away you'd be seen but no one would know the suit wasn't the same. We'll use perception," said Lydia.

Irv knew it was a reasonable suggestion. "How about

our son? He might be tall enough for the suit. Then what? Once it's altered, there's no going back."

Irv and Lydia stood in front of the closet. They stared at the locked door as if waiting for a monster to emerge. Lydia slid her fingers through her husband's. After four years of marriage the coveted baby remained elusive. The night before, Lydia placed a tentative hand on Irv's chest and broached the subject of fertility treatments. Irv spent a sleepless night weighing medical treatments against the tenets of their faith. At least Lydia stood five foot ten. Their son would have a fighting chance to bring some needed height back to their suit.

The Bellingham, Washington Goshens couldn't let down the Eureka, California Goshens, the Riverside, Illinois Goshens, or the Williston, Florida Goshens. The pact had been made well over a century ago. Irv's great-great-grandfather had been shunned, harassed, and ridiculed for his height in his native village of Szeged, motivating him to leave. The villagers forced the tall Goshen men to wear a scratchy camel hair shirt inside out to reinforce the fact that God found them perverse. Decades later, the Goshens found out that they carried the HMGA2 height gene. For the last two generations the Goshen men chose a wife who also had the HMGA2 marker. Height above all things must be maintained. And yet Irv, at six foot four, was tall for a normal man but short for a Goshen. And short a son to carry on the tradition. A tall son.

"Or a hoverboard? One of those motorized things?" Lydia reached out to turn the closet doorknob then remembered and let her hand drop.

"They have to see me and believe. That's the whole point. How will it work if I glide?" Irv shook his head. "Feet must be firmly planted. I must take strides. That's how it's always been done."

The two of them stood a few minutes longer looking at the closet door, hand in hand, heavy with the burdens of family traditions.

It was agreed. They would use construction stilts. The family—Irv's older sister, her husband and daughter, Grandma Mike, and Lydia—collected an extra three hundred dollars. They drew more customers by lowering the price of organic cat food and dog treats at the feed store and placing a coupon in the paper for environmentally friendly greywater installations. They purchased a Serv-A-Lot stilts model with a wide foot plate, adjustable heel bracket, and a leg brace with wraparound safety bands.

In less than eight weeks Irv needed to master his gait while balancing on a narrow strip of grippy rubber, while wearing the suit. At first, Irv tried them in the house, taking slow, purposeful steps from the kitchen to the dining room table. Lydia followed two steps behind, arms outstretched.

After a few days, and in between greywater installations for the Bellingham nouveau hippy crowd, Irv transitioned to striding from the kitchen all the way to the front door, past the living room, raising and lowering his arms in an exaggerated manner, as he'd seen his father and grandfather do. His father, now safely tucked away in a retirement community, had passed on the suit to Irv and moved as soon as his wife had died.

Irv fell seriously enough to cause injury once. He had been distracted and didn't notice the bunch in the carpet. He knocked over a bowl of Lydia's tomatoes as he toppled and the broken glass sliced into his back, the red of the tomatoes mingled with his blood. Usually, Lydia acted as his pilot, but she was at a doctor's appointment having her uterus and fallopian tubes examined. His sperm, already analyzed, appeared to be normal. He'd grown to love Lydia even though their meeting was predetermined at an HMGA2 gene gathering.

With Lydia it had been easy. She'd taken to running the feed store along with Irv's older sister. With her love of cultivation, she created a large vegetable garden at the back of their property, supplying the family with organic carrots, peas, bell peppers, cucumbers, and any number of herbs.

Over time Irv got used to his new height with the stilts. The way he saw the world altered with his new stature. Things that seemed unreachable were suddenly closer. Problems such as piles of magazines on the coffee table or dust collecting in a corner were now too far beneath him to address.

As he became more comfortable, he suggested to Lydia they take their practice outside. Branches that he once passed under now smacked his forehead. Picking a fallen apple was impossible. Tree roots were a danger and uneven ground became natural landmines. It was Lydia who suggested they practice on the path he would take the day he put the suit on.

With the stilts strapped snugly around his feet and legs, Irv, with Lydia's guidance, took his first few steps in the US Forestry Service lands a few miles away from their home. They had predetermined the route he should take the day he wore the suit. It was relatively flat, with few adjacent trees, and close enough to popular hiking and hunting sites, where he would be seen. That was the point. The suit had to be seen.

"There's a slight slope and a bend just ahead," Lydia said, her hands raised above her shoulders, poised to catch her husband if he faltered.

"I'm doing okay." Irv's stride was slow and purposeful with a hint of unnatural.

"We are, aren't we?" Lydia spoke as if tentatively asking for a second helping of pie. "We'll figure this out, right? I mean science can make anything happen these days; catch a killer, land on Mars, make a baby."

Irv grunted as he negotiated a patch of mud. "Sure, sure." Irv developed a headache from focusing on any imbalances that might drop him in an instant.

It was eventually an old gopher hole that nearly did it. The edge of his foot plate tilted into the soft earth and Irv felt his delicate balance slant. A last second grasp of a tree branch and Irv's grace at bracing his other stilt over the crunch of brittle leaves prevented his plummet.

Lydia gasped and briefly lowered her hands.

Irv took a steadying breath and recalibrated. In the suit he would need to walk at least thirty minutes straight, depending on his audience.

The night before Irv was to put on the suit and take his walk, the family gathered for a special prayer service. Grandma Mike lit three vanilla-scented candles and handed Irv the Siddur, removing a thin piece of paper deteriorating with age. Irv, the male head of the family, opened the Siddur and read,

Blessed are You Lord God, King of the Universe Who bestows good things upon the unworthy and has offered us the gift of Belief. I am your Loyal Servant to pass on the Binding that Faith

and Belief yield. Although your Children know You not. God takes on many Forms and through your Wisdom and Love, our Small Sacrifice Furnish our Brethren a means of Knowing You.

With that, the family sat at the table for a meal of organic kale, vinegar potatoes, venison, and bread. The bounty of the earth for all of God's creatures, even the ones that didn't exist.

It all began in 1858, when Levi Goshen arrived in the Pacific Northwest, all seven plus feet of him, along with the family camel hair shirt the Goshen men were forced to wear back in the old country. The scratchy camel hair shirt was meant to be worn underneath the cotton tunic as a way for the town to remind the overly tall Goshens that God was displeased with their abnormal height. Forced to marry only within their circle, their giant frame became embedded in their DNA.

Having grown tired of his outcast status, Levi Goshen and his new, tall wife (a Goshen second cousin) left Hungary in 1849 for better prospects in the United States. A gold rush in the California territories drew them to the west coast. With enough money, Levi headed north to buy a homestead and put down roots in the Pacific Northwest, far enough from the settlement to be away from pestering eyes and religious persecution. Out of habit, Levi brought his camel hair shirt, passed down from generations.

Back then, the small settlement, called Fairhaven, was a rough place with little law and a lot of crime. Bar fights, burglary, murder, all the evil trappings of a group of greedy men without the balance of women, families, and faith. Nothing to care for except acquiring wealth and felling trees. Levi and his wife stayed away from town as much as possible, not having a healthy view of folks there.

Then one warm fall day, when the sun was dimming and weak, Levi put on his camel hair shirt with the cool silk lining inside and the prickly camel hair out. He wore hide pants and a beaver hat to check his traps. His long stride and loping arms caught the notice of two drunk, near-sighted local elders.

They ran back to town to report on a large creature, ape-like with fur from head to toe, haunting the woods. The town elders consulted with local native peoples who decided it must be their creature, Sasq'ets, a godlike spirit who takes the shape of a large ape but can shapeshift into a wolf, a bear, or a mountain lion. A Sasq'ets, or "Sasquatch," sighting was said to be the harbinger of good news, that the gods were watching over the raucous community.

The Sasquatch spotting changed the town. Before, it had been every man for himself. Now, groups came together to discuss why the creature was there. What did it portend? Recently, a preacher had wandered to the area, drawn by the prospects of timber riches as much as the godlessness. Small miracles began to happen: a skull-shattering boulder fell where Benjamin Lynch had been standing moments ago, surely he would have died; a colicky baby slept through the night for the first time; a wild turkey just laid down and died practically at the feet of Zachariah Evans, who'd not had a meal in days. The list of wonders continued to grow.

Living out by a ravine and a distance from the settlement, Levi Goshen still heard talk of the miracle creature. It wasn't until he wore the camel hair shirt again and the sighting claims came anew, he understood the godlike creature was him. But by then the town had become a community, drawn together by the grace of God incarnate as Sasquatch. Harvests were bountiful, salmon jumped into fishing nets, wives and babies became more plentiful. No longer did a person fear walking down the main street, ever vigilant of thugs.

The town had found their savior and it was a tall hairy creature that loped through the woods in the fall.

Irv bent his head after reciting the annual prayer. He thanked God for the opportunity to serve his community.

He still dwelled on all that could go wrong. Mostly, that he'd fall, not be able to stay a safe distance away, or, worst of all, nobody would see him, and he'd have to put the suit on again. He must be seen!

The next morning Irv put the stilts on and walked around the house, the gardens, and the yard for some last-minute practice. Lydia was with the doctor to get the results of her fertility test. On any other day Irv would have gone too. He was sad not to be there, but on this holy day, the day of a Sasquatch sighting and of family obligations, he needed to stay.

All day Irv shunned food and drank little. His nerves destroyed his appetite and there was no option to crap in the woods. Not in the suit.

Irv didn't notice when Lydia came home and sneaked into their bedroom, too preoccupied with the imminent arrival of Grandma Mike and the suit. The afternoon brought a gathering of dark clouds. Time slowed for Irv. Nerves wrestled within him. His hands and arms trembled with the desire to see an end to his walk. Irv never remembered his father or grandfather exhibiting such fear.

At three in the afternoon Grandma Mike, with a hand-woven scarf over her head, took the jumble of keys out of her wooden knickknack box and opened the closet door to reveal the suit.

Remnants of the original camel hair shirt could only be seen close up, as Grandma Mike laid the suit out on the bed in the guest room. The old hook and eye closures faced up, some rusty with age and exposure. Next to the bed were the stilts and some extra wool padding to augment Irv's other bodily failings. The head and face were made from an old ski mask with wool hair glued onto a mesh backing and a cardboard cup insert to resemble a protruding nose and mouth. As Irv placed the hood over his head, the cutouts for the eyes were a good half an inch too high.

"We'll have to pin the head to the rest of the suit so you can see." Irv hadn't heard Lydia enter the room. Her eyes were swollen from crying as she bunched the hood fabric to attach it lower and pull the eye sockets down.

"Yeah, that works," said Irv, too enclosed in his duties to notice his wife's sadness.

Irv's trembling irritated him because Sasquatch was not a fearful being and it shamed him in front of his wife.

"Let's put your stilts on first, then attach the padding," Lydia said. "We may need to alter the feet."

Irv sat on the bed as Lydia kneeled on the floor, gently maneuvering the brown fur feet with the brown leather soles over the rubber foot plates of the stilts.

"Wow, these are big feet," Lydia said, running her hand over the leather of the soles.

Irv tried to smile at her joke but didn't have the energy for a light comeback. It was his first time transforming and Lydia's first time helping her husband become the creature.

As she jimmied the fabric over the foot and a half of

metal firmly Velcroed to Irv's shin, Lydia gently placed her hand on Irv's fur covered thigh, calming the involuntary muscle quiver.

Lydia's hand jerked away from the suit as if from a flame. Her eyes met Irv's. She stood, pressing her hands to her chest, and backed away. Now locked inside the heavy suit, Irv lowered his head onto his hands, elbows resting on his knees. Neither spoke.

"At least you're on the lowest setting of the stilts. Should make a difference," Lydia finally said. "I'll get Grandma Mike to help you with the rest."

Irv lifted his head. "Wait. What did the doctor say?" Lydia, whose long brown hair was collected into a thick ponytail, so her face was wide and open, stared up at him not hiding her tears.

"My fallopian tubes are crooked." Lydia turned her face to the floor and began to sob again in earnest. "Maybe you need to find another wife. I've botched so many things now."

Irv's heart constricted. He wanted to reach for Lydia, hold her in his arms, but not wearing the suit. Not again. No son. No one to carry on the tradition. "I'm not Henry VIII, looking for the next wife who can give me a son." Although the thought had crossed Irv's mind—only because he was transforming into the creature.

"There are medical options. They can create an embryo in a petri dish and then plant it in my womb. It works sometimes."

In his imagination, Irv saw Lydia dressed in a hospital gown laying in a sterile room with a bunch of face-masked doctors.

"No, we will have a child if it's God's will."

"But what about the suit?" Lydia asked. "The creature is

God's will too. If he deems the town ready to move on without Sasquatch, who are we to meddle?"

Irv tried to imagine the Goshens without the suit and Bellingham without their Sasquatch. Would his life still have purpose? Could he let go? Irv maneuvered himself off the bed but slumped back. He raised his hands to his wife. "We started this. Let's finish it. Help me get dressed."

Lydia collected herself and helped Irv to stand. With his extra height he towered over her. She climbed onto the bed to attach more padding to her husband's torso and arms before easing him into the top half of the suit. Along the back were tufts of lighter, coarser hair from the original camel shirt. Even after two centuries, a slight odor of that poor animal clung to the worn strands.

"We could create a Little Sasquatch GoFundMe page." Lydia smiled at her humor and turned to kiss Irv but instead met a ferocious creature who stared back at her with alarmed eyes through hair claimed from several auburn wigs.

Lydia pulled off the dirt road about two miles from their home, by the ravine. Irv sat in the front of the feed store's small van with the passenger seat adjusted as far back as it would go. Before walking out the door, Grandma Mike had placed a prayer shawl around Irv's shoulders and asked God to protect this creature who was about to do his work. As she did with Irv's father, she keened as he walked out the door, anticipating and channeling the suffering of the Jewish people throughout millennia.

Sasquatch didn't move at first, reluctant to heave his unruly and long body out of the safe space. Lydia came around and wrapped her hands around his wrists, braced herself, and became the creature's leverage.

"You just have to be seen for a few minutes. This is your first time. Don't try anything extravagant. I'll be at the end, waiting."

Sasquatch relaxed his grip on Lydia and slowly balanced himself on the stilts, taking two tentative steps. Like a child learning to control his body, the creature held his arms out for stability, then lifted one foot and placed it purposefully, and then the other foot. Stop. Breathe. Focus. And again. Step. Stop. Breathe. Focus. More quickly. Step. Stop. Breathe. Focus.

By now the creature was moving a little more quickly.

Sasquatch's path took him on a slightly downward trajectory, around a bend, along a tree-lined path, and then up a short climb that circled back to where Lydia would meet him with the van. The whole route was less than a mile, but with the stilts it would take Sasquatch an unlikely twenty to thirty minutes. If he wasn't seen, he'd have to make the trek a second time. The townspeople must be reminded that there was something out there besides themselves and their personal problems. There were miracle creatures that God made and who portended wonders big and small. After a Sasquatch sighting, the community came alive with news, gossip, communion, and hope.

The creature grew more confident in his purpose. He alone was the revelation, majestic in his beastly ugliness. This was his duty. A sacrificial lamb to the greater good of his people. A burden he could shoulder.

As Sasquatch walked in and around the dying leaves, pools of shadows camouflaged his path. Other junctions were open and obvious. This was a popular area for hunters, which was one reason why he chose it. Sasquatch had carefully completed the part of the trail that dipped and was now at the longest portion, the flat expanse with trees on one side and open field on the other. Sasquatch was careful not to move his head, wary of the tenuous placement of his eyeholes. This section was his best chance at exposure.

Sasquatch concentrated on his gait so that he loped, rather than trotted. At each step he gazed around him, taking in his surroundings, aware of the danger. Soft earth, tree roots, slippery worms. There was only one section left of this mostly open area. His peripheral vision was limited with the hairy hood, but he didn't see any movement, neon orange hat, or the raise of a flask.

No one had seen him. Silence where he strained for an exclamation, a shout of wonderment. He'd made this trek for nothing.

With less than a tenth of a mile left of his path, he reluctantly understood he'd have to make this trip again. But then a shout, and the crack of a shot. The creature twisted toward the sound of the discharge to see two men running in his direction from across the open field. He had a good three hundred yards on the hunters but with the stilts he couldn't maneuver, duck, or twist. Normally, Sasquatch could disappear as quickly as he materialized. But not this time.

In the Bellingham Goshen lore, Sasquatch had never been shot at before, never seriously pursued. The stories passed down, from one generation to the next, Sasquatch was beheld in wonderment and awe. Perhaps these were not Bellingham hunters.

"Hey! It's him!" one hunter shouted. Sasquatch saw the

flash of a silver beer can thrown to the side for something more exciting.

"No way!" the other called back laced with excitement. "No way! Sasquatch. SHIT!"

"I gotcha Bigfoot. I gotcha on camera."

The first hunter lunged across the field, the second, smaller one a couple of leaps behind. Neither one was running fast. It crossed Sasquatch's mind that neither was he in his stilts and weighted suit. Picking up his feet with his wearying legs, he increased his speed only slightly. He needed to get into the thick of the forest. He'd been seen. That was enough. There was a picture, evidence, which was good. But now he needed to disappear.

His breathing became ragged as he tried to run, burdened by the extra weight and clumsiness of the stilts. When the creature twisted his head to find his upward trajectory, his eye holes shifted, and he was blind. He turned up a leaf-strewn hill, waving his arms in front to feel for impediments, the hunters' voices muffled through the pounding in his head. Behind him, long grass buffeted as it was torn aside. The hunters were closing in. With a rush, the creature lifted his legs and placed the stilts, one at a time, on the ground to propel him up toward what he hoped was the protection of the thick trees. He hadn't practiced on upslopes. He couldn't see his path. His ears became attuned to the grunts of effort from the hunters. If he could make it up the hill, he would be close to Lydia and the waiting van. At the crack from the gun, his body was thrown to the ground. Not by the passing bullet, but by an animal trap holding tight to his right stilt that he didn't see. The sharp teeth ripped through the suit and bit into his right stilt less than an inch from his flesh and blood foot. The hunters were closing in, convinced they had shot the beast. But Sasquatch was camouflaged among the trees and brown fallen leaves, for now.

Sasquatch knew there was a spring mechanism that would release him, but without his eyes, he would be fumbling and wasting precious time. He could get lucky and find it quickly.

Another shout but this time coming from above. It was Lydia, he could picture her head and shoulders over the rim of the slope, her hands desperately reaching with more impulse than expectation.

"Just a few more steps and I can reach you!" Lydia's stricken voice filled his stifling suit.

The creature had no time to decide.

He leaned down and placed his finger in the nearest small gash in the suit made from the trap and yanked upwards. The rip was like an explosion to Irv's ears. A small puff of ancient dust and debris briefly lifted and fell to the loamy soil. With the rupture of the suit, Irv knew this would be the last Sasquatch sighting in Bellingham. He would be the final Sasquatch. The community would have to find their own inner belief. There would be no more Goshen sons to inherit this burden.

The hole was now large enough for Irv to disengage his foot from the captured stilt. With two hands, he tore the suit up to the shoulders and emerged, like an exhausted caterpillar shedding its skin, on his padded knees and arms. With the Sasquatch head still on, he skittered up the slope into the waiting arms of his wife, leaving the molted skin behind for the bewildered hunters.

RACING THE MARINERIS

JOHN M. CAMPBELL

BRANDON HENRY STOOD beside his sister Johanna as they watched the network reporter open the coverage for the viewers back on Earth.

"Welcome to our broadcast of the race for the Martian Cup," Steve Amos said, facing the camera. "We are gathered at the race's starting line on the rim of Oudemans Crater located at the western end of the Valles Marineris, the largest valley in the solar system. Outside our dome, it is still dark as we count down to the dawn start. This is a cross-country race with four legs. Each team must pass through waypoints at Arima Crater, Saravan Crater, and Hawking Crater before ending in Vinogradov Crater at the eastern end of the Marineris. It is a match race between two cars, with the winner taking home the Martian Cup and $200 million in prize money."

Brandon wished he could just skip this part and get going. Sweat was dripping down the side of his torso even though he had his helmet visor open to provide ventilation.

"Hold my helmet, Brandy."

He peered up at Johanna. "Why the hell would I do that?"

"This is the best I'm going to look for the next two days," she said. "I don't want to mess up my hair."

He scowled, but he took her helmet like she knew he would because she was the star.

"Thanks," she said with a smile.

He never thought of her as pretty, but she had a killer smile. And with her tall, athletic body zipped into a formfitting pressure suit, he recognized some might consider her ruggedly good-looking. Indeed, Tortuga Rum had paid a wad of cash to have their name splashed across her chest.

Steve continued, "Joining me remotely from the finish line is Nika Ross, who owns one of the competing cars." Ross appeared on a monitor next to the camera. "Is this your first trip to Mars?"

"No," Ross said. "Ross Interplanetary runs several round-trip cruises per year. I recommend them."

"*His* hair was probably done in the ship's spa," Brandon remarked to Johanna. She laughed.

Nika Ross was a billionaire with an ego to match his wallet. He wasn't in this race for the prize money. He wanted another bauble to demonstrate to the world what his money could buy. He tried to recruit Brandon to build his car, but Brandon refused to be bought. Ross hated to be told no. In pure spite, Ross tried to intimidate their suppliers into cutting them off. And he really didn't appreciate Johanna retaliating with the fundraising slogan "Be a Part of Beating Nika."

"Your car is the first in a Martian Cup race driven solely by artificial intelligence," Steve addressed Nika. "Why did you make that decision?"

"Because it's the future of racing. An AI fits in a shoebox, has quicker response times than a human, and doesn't require all the extra equipment needed to support a human in this environment. The less weight, the faster and farther you can go on a battery charge."

"The rules of the Martian Cup stipulate a human must be present in the car during the race. One would expect your passenger to be a mechanic, but you went in a different direction."

Ross showed off his perfect teeth. "For each leg of the race, I offered a seat to the highest bidder, which included a round-trip ticket to Mars on Ross Interplanetary. The proceeds after expenses go to the Ross Foundation to provide college scholarships."

"And you didn't have to pay a dime to ride with me, Brandy," remarked Johanna.

"You're not driving my car without my supervision," Brandon shot back. "Besides, you wouldn't get to the first waypoint without me."

"What happens if something breaks down?" Steve asked Ross.

"We constructed our car with redundant systems and control pathways that minimize the possibility a failure will ever bring us to a halt," said Ross. "Our self-healing technology detects a failure and brings the backup online automatically."

Steve thanked Ross and waved Johanna over. Brandon trailed behind.

"Now we are joined by the competing team led by that Steel-Drivin' Woman, Johanna Henry."

"Good to see you, Steve," said Johanna. "I grew up driving steel, but now it's all carbon-nanotube composite construction." She flashed her winning smile.

Steve loved it. "You're facing some stiff competition.

Nika Ross seems willing to spend any amount to win the Cup."

"We've got a million small contributors back on Earth," said Johanna. "We don't intend to disappoint them."

Steve nodded. "Can you give us an idea of your strategy for the race?"

"We've got a few tricks up our sleeves," said Johanna. "Plus, I've got the best mechanic and navigator on the planet."

"You're speaking of your brother, Brandon Henry, who designed your car." He turned to Brandon. "Can your car beat Ross?"

Another drop of sweat trickled down Brandon's side. "In a drag race, probably not."

Confusion crossed Steve's eyes.

Brandon continued, "Mr. Ross likes his cars fast. Fortunately, this race is thirty-three hundred kilometers long. A lot can happen over that expanse. Top speed is not as important as navigating through the obstacles the Martian landscape throws at you. I'd like to see how his passenger reacts when they're stranded hundreds of kilometers from a waypoint in the middle of the night—"

"Sorry, Steve," interjected Johanna, "but we need to get ready for the start."

Brandon gritted his teeth so he wouldn't say what he thought about her interrupting him.

"Of course, Johanna," Steve said. "Good luck to you."

Brandon handed Johanna her helmet as they strode to the airlock. She put it on and inflated the neck doughnut to seal it in place. They entered the airlock, and Brandon closed his visor.

They stepped out onto the dusty red surface of the Sinai Planum. Although it was summer here near the equator on

Mars, the nighttime temperature had dropped to minus sixty Celsius. Their pressure suits were well insulated, but the cold still seeped into Brandon's feet through the soles of his boots.

Floodlights lit up the two racing machines. The sleeker car was painted in Ross's trademarked corporate colors of forest green and gold. A long chassis housed its battery packs, with bulges at the front and rear to protect the massive motors that powered the wheels. Mounted at strategic points on the body were radar and video sensors that allowed the AI to monitor its environment. And, of course, the car's length provided enough real estate to emblazon the words "Ross Interplanetary" along each side. In between the front wheels, an attendant belted Ross's first victim into the car's cockpit.

The maroon-and-black paint job of the Henrys' car gleamed under the lights. Brandon prized stability over sleekness in the low gravity, so he chose a wider wheelbase. Their car sported large titanium wheels and a heavy-duty suspension for high ground clearance. The wide construction allowed the seats to be placed side by side in the passenger compartment. Behind the cab, solar cells covered the body in a convex arrangement of hexagonal brackets. The press dubbed it the "turtle shell." Of course, Ross's car also used solar cells, mounted on deployable panels that detractors had labeled "rabbit ears."

The press billed this race the "Tortoise versus the Hare." Running with the turtle theme, Johanna recruited Tortuga Rum as a corporate sponsor.

Johanna and Brandon climbed into their vehicle and pressurized the cabin. On the horizon, a narrow line of red signaled the coming sunrise. Brandon activated the hydraulics, and behind their heads the shell of solar cells tilted forward to catch the sun's rays. Beside him, Brandon saw Ross's solar cell "ears" rise from their stowed position along the rabbit's back to a vertical configuration facing the sun. It looked ridiculous.

The countdown clock outside read twenty seconds. Brandon scanned the instrument readings on the monitor in front of him. All systems reported green. Connections to the navigation satellites were strong. Another screen showed the broadcast from Race Central, which received feeds from their onboard cameras and telemetry that they shared with the audience, but he had turned off the sound.

"How's everything look?" asked Johanna.

"I'm 90 percent sure we're good," Brandon deadpanned.

In silence, they watched the clock.

Three. Two. One.

Brandon leaned back into the seat cushions.

Zero.

Johanna jammed down the accelerator. The force clamped him to his seat as the first brilliant rays of the sun leaped over the horizon directly ahead. Out of the corner of his eye, a cloud of dust scintillated in the sunlight. The dust emanated from the churning wheels of the Hare, which already held a slight lead.

The speed on Brandon's monitor climbed past a hundred kilometers per hour. Johanna kept accelerating. Past one-fifty. Past one-seventy.

Brandon peered over at the Hare. It was in front, but not far. He had built the Tortoise for the long haul, but that didn't mean his car was slow. The Hare edged in their direction.

"Watch it, Johanna."

"I see it," she said.

"What's it doing?" he asked.

"Trying to cut us off," she said.

Brandon peeked at their speed. She wasn't backing off.

The Hare veered into their path. Its dust cloud enveloped them, and Johanna juked right. Just as the dust cleared, they sped past a three-foot-high rock outcrop. It missed their front wheel by inches.

"That rat bastard!" Johanna yelled.

Brandon's heart pounded in his throat. "What the hell?" You never put a rival in danger intentionally.

Johanna cursed, banging the steering wheel with her fist. She maintained her distance to the side, but her speed crept higher. "He's not getting away with that crap." She slowly closed the gap.

Brandon could only imagine what she had in mind—and didn't like it. "Ross isn't in that car, Johanna. It's an innocent civilian."

She steered past a crater, keeping it between them and the Hare.

"So what?" she asked.

"The best way to pay that jackass back is to win the race."

Johanna didn't reply. Instead, she found every opportunity to accelerate. She steered to avoid the shadows as much as possible while keeping the sun centered on their dashboard. Only when the shadows prevailed did she back off. At 180 kmph, she didn't have much time to react to the unexpected.

The Hare raced a few hundred meters to their left. Every so often, its wheels left the ground as it crested a bump in the low gravity. Brandon hoped its passenger was prone to motion sickness.

He checked his navigation display. Based on their position, the computer displayed a heading for Johanna. So far, she was matching the route as planned.

But who knew what surprises Mars—or Ross—had in store for them?

Three hours later, they approached the south rim of the Marineris as it bulged out. The geologic activity that created this bulge also left parallel fissures that formed deep, curved arcs hundreds of kilometers long in the surrounding terrain.

"We're coming to our turn," said Brandon. "Then we've got another span of clear country before we start threading our way through craters and canyons to curve around the bulge."

"Okay," said Johanna. "How's the power holding up?"

"Fine," said Brandon. He swayed to the side as they avoided a small crater. "We're getting good supplemental charging from the sun."

Johanna executed a zigzag past a pile of rocks. "How long till we get past the craters and canyons?"

He consulted his map screen. "Maybe an hour and twenty minutes. Then it's clear again for another hour."

"Where's the Hare?"

He checked the screen. "It peeled off to the southeast a while ago. It's maybe seventy kilometers south of us."

Through her visor he saw her frown and purse her lips. "Why didn't *we* go that way?"

Brandon bristled. "They're heading into variable terrain. We're going farther east, so we can maintain our higher speed for longer."

"Okay." The doubt in her voice had disappeared. She tilted her shoulders to guide their car around a dip.

Two hefty craters had created a splash zone that stretched tens of kilometers away from their centers.

"There may be debris ahead," said Brandon, "so take it slower. Once we're through, we have almost two hundred klicks of clear sailing."

Johanna lifted off the throttle and eased into a left turn. After twenty minutes of picking her way through the debris field, she headed southeast and bumped her speed up to one-eighty again. The midday sun afforded perfect visibility—until a bump sent them airborne.

Brandon reached out to brace himself on the dashboard. He glanced at Johanna. Both hands were on the steering wheel as the car touched down. The wheels on the left landed before the right. But she aligned the front wheels with the direction of motion, so after a brief fishtail in the back end, she regained control. Not only had his driver done her job, but so had his heavy-duty shocks.

They swung south to avoid the worst of the fissures. Then they navigated west to east across a series of parallel canyons that flowed north toward the Marineris. If Mars still had water, they'd be seeking out the crossings shallow enough to ford the streams. Between canyons were stretches of twenty to forty kilometers where they hit top speed again. The final two hundred kilometers to Arima Crater offered no easy way through a terrain filled with craters and crisscrossing canyons.

"Where's the Hare?" asked Johanna.

The question startled Brandon. He'd been so immersed

in navigating them through the canyons he hadn't checked the Hare's position for hours. He zoomed out the map screen until the forest-green dot appeared. Could that be right? He traced the Hare's path backward before he convinced himself.

"It's now leaving the fissures," he said.

"You said that way was impassable."

"I guess it found a way through."

"So, where the hell is it?"

"Eighty kilometers north of us."

She turned her head to dart a fiery glare at him. "How close to the waypoint compared to us?"

He estimated the distances. "The Hare's two hundred klicks away, and we're around one-eighty. It has to go around the splash field of a crater before it can head for the waypoint."

"What's it facing after it rounds the crater?" she asked.

"Crisscrossing canyonland, same as us."

"So, the race boils down to who gets through the canyons fastest?"

"Right," Brandon answered.

"Okay." Johanna's voice was calm. "We've got a twenty-klick lead. Let's hold it."

As Johanna sped forward, Brandon zoomed to maximum magnification on his map to verify the best way through. During his prerace prep, he'd covered this ground countless times. His chosen route seemed the best they could do, but the map resolution was six meters per pixel, which was plenty wide enough to hide a dangerous feature. A lot still depended on what they actually confronted on the ground.

"Okay," said Brandon, "we're coming to a chasm. I can't

tell how fast it drops off, so slow down as we crest the ridge."

They paused at the top. To their left, the ground plunged into the chasm. To the right, an air gap separated them from the clear terrain beyond.

"Now what?" asked Johanna. "Should we go north?"

"This valley runs north for hundreds of kilometers and drains into the Marineris," Brandon said. "My terrain map seemed to show a way past around here."

"Use your eyes," Johanna said. "Do you see a way past?"

Brandon's stomach tensed, and his ears heated at her tone.

"What if we go farther south?" she asked.

"The canyon ends in a crater debris field," said Brandon. "It would be risky."

"How far?"

"Fifteen kilometers."

"Let's try it," she said. She accelerated to a brisk speed alongside the canyon. "Where's the Hare now?"

Brandon blinked at what he saw on the map screen. How did it get so far? "It's approaching the northern end of this same valley. It'll have an issue getting through."

Up ahead, low hills emerged that marked the edge of the debris field. A minute later, the ravine they were following disappeared into a pile of house-sized boulders.

Johanna slowed. "Does the map show any way through that?"

Brandon started to sweat. "I'm not seeing anything."

"Okay, we go to plan B," she said. She turned the car around.

"Plan B is a hundred kilometers north," he said.

"Plan C, then," Johanna said.

"Plan C?"

"It's a short way back," she said.

Two minutes later they parked on a rise overlooking the ravine.

"How far across do you think it is?" Johanna asked.

"It's got to be thirty meters," said Brandon. "Why?"

"See this dip? It forms a ramp as it hits the edge."

Brandon knew how her mind worked, but he couldn't believe she would go there.

"I can make it, Brandy."

"Johanna—"

"It's a piece of cake. Knievel made a jump of forty meters in Earth's gravity. Mars's gravity is 40 percent of Earth's."

"Yeah, you could do it if we prepared a proper ramp and calculated the speed you'd need—"

"What other choice do we have?" she demanded. "We'll lose hours if we go north, right?"

Brandon bowed his head.

"If we lose this leg by hours, we'll never catch up." Her voice caught, and her eyes shone. "Brandy, you know what this race means. We bet our company on it."

Even with all the fundraising, they had borrowed heavily to complete the car and transport it to Mars. "All right," he said. "Let me think." He considered the angle of the ramp and the expanse to cover. "What speed could you reach if we started from here?"

She eyed the distance. "A hundred-ten. Maybe more."

"If you backed up, could you make it one-forty?"

"Hell yes, I could," she exclaimed.

"Are you absolutely sure?" he asked. "I'd rather not die today."

"I'm absolutely 90 percent sure." She smiled.

She backed the car away from their position, keeping

the wheels aligned with the ramp. Their wheel impressions traced parallel lines up the rise.

Johanna stopped. "Ready?"

Brandon sighed and nodded.

"Here we go."

The car advanced as the speed climbed on his screen. They rolled over the rise and dipped into the downslope. She gunned the four-wheel drive. The car hit the bottom of the dip, and g-forces pressed them down. They shot off the ramp into the pink sky.

Johanna let off the power. She tapped the brakes to stop the wheels spinning. Brandon's breath caught as he stared into the crevasse. It was wider than he'd estimated. The other side was too far away.

Somehow, the car kept flying. Impossibly far. They passed beyond the distant edge, but on they flew. On the ground ahead, a boulder awaited. The car descended on an impact trajectory.

As he stared in horror, the whine of the engines barely registered. The nose of the car dove. The spinning front wheels plowed into the ground. Brandon's body slammed into the seat harness. The inflated doughnut around his neck kept his head from snapping forward into the monitor. The rear wheels smashed down. The suspension compressed and the car bounced—toward the boulder.

Johanna steered, keeping pressure on the accelerator. The car slid sideways but still hurtled at the boulder. The spinning wheels churned up dust, obscuring the view outside. Brandon braced for impact.

A crunch issued from the back fender and thrust them to the side. Johanna corrected, and they raced onward, leaving the rock behind.

Johanna screamed in triumph. Brandon's screams were

even louder. He blinked away the tears of relief forming in his eyes. He reached over and squeezed Johanna's arm.

She nodded. "How much farther?"

He took a deep breath and let it out to slow his heart. Then he checked the map. "A hundred and ten klicks."

"And the Hare?"

"I can't believe it."

"What?"

"It found a way through the valley already," sighed Brandon. "It's a hundred klicks away from Arima."

"Plot the most direct route you can," Johanna said.

"You got it." He plotted a straight line on the navigation map. "Keep on this heading, and we'll adjust as needed."

Johanna showed her racing chops as she kept her foot on the throttle in and out of shallow depressions and drifted through turns around craters.

Both dots on the map converged toward the waypoint at the southern edge of Arima Crater, the Hare on an east-southeast path and the Tortoise headed east-northeast.

Johanna rounded a hill on the final stretch. Outside her window, a dust plume appeared a couple of kilometers distant. At the horizon, the dome of the waypoint rose above the surface with the ridge of Arima behind it. They watched as the Hare halted at the waypoint. Its dust cloud settled quickly in the thin air. A minute later, they parked next to it. The Hare's rider was stumbling out of the cockpit assisted by a figure dressed in a Ross Interplanetary pressure suit. The next passenger stood aside waiting to take their turn. Another technician was replacing spent batteries with fresh ones.

Brandon closed his visor and pushed the depressurize button. "You take care of the air and water," he told Johanna. "I'll get the batteries."

"Just like we rehearsed, Brandy-boy," she said.

They threw off their harnesses and hopped out.

He visited the restroom, and on the way out he spotted Johanna. She had removed her helmet and wore a headset. She yelled at the screen in front of her, "What the hell were you doing out there? You could've killed someone—like one of your billionaire buddies riding in the front seat."

Brandon edged around to see the screen.

"As I understand the rules, the car in front has the right-of-way," Nika Ross said with a smirk. "An accident would have been your fault."

"Yeah, go ahead and argue that at the murder inquest," she said.

Outside the dome, the Hare took off, leaving a cloud of dust.

"I'm loading the batteries," Brandon told Johanna. "Don't let him get to you."

She raised her hand to acknowledge she heard him—or to wave him off.

As he wheeled the replacement batteries into the airlock, he heard her yell, "Your pretty race car could end up spread across Mars in pieces." The door closed before a response came.

Brandon installed the new batteries and climbed into the cab. The battery status showed all connected and fully charged. The car rocked as Johanna climbed in. Air and water supplies showed green. He hit the pressurize button.

As she snapped her seat harness, he asked Johanna, "Was it worth giving Ross a three-minute head start?"

"No sweat," she said. "Have you seen the piece of crap he's racing?" She punched the accelerator and sped off.

With only an hour and a half of daylight left, they would reach Saravan Crater in the dark. The terrain ahead exhibited the usual fissures running parallel to the Marineris. For the first half hour, they wove their way past eroded hillocks, the remnants of Arima's ancient splash zone. Every so often, they glimpsed the Hare's dust plume ahead catching the rays of the late-day sun. When they hit the rolling, unobstructed plain, Johanna increased the speed to one-eighty for the last hour of light.

With shadows appearing, Brandon switched on the headlights. The Hare was racing a parallel path somewhere nearby to the north, but they hadn't seen it for a while. Johanna was following the rim of a shallow ravine when suddenly their lights glinted off a huge titanium wheel rising out of the depression diagonally across their path.

Johanna swerved and braked. The Hare's wheel climbed up and over their front-left fender. The snaps and pops of breaking carbon-nanotube composite filled the cabin. The Tortoise's front wheel dug in and seized. The right wheel lifted off the ground, and their car rotated about the buried fulcrum. The right wheel crashed onto the ground, and the car skidded to a stop. The Hare kept going, leaving the Tortoise surrounded by a haze of dust.

Fuzzy cotton balls filled Brandon's head. He blinked and fought to focus his vision. A familiar voice reached his ears speaking ... something. Finally, the words clicked in.

"Brandon?" Johanna's voice. "Are you all right?"

He swallowed. "I'm ..." He licked his lips and tried again. "I'm ... okay ... I think."

"I'm okay, too," she said. "Thanks for asking."

"What happened?" he croaked.

"Ross ambushed us." The tightness in her voice conveyed barely controlled fury. "Can you get us going again?"

He peered at the brightly lit status monitor. "Batteries

look good. Life support's good. Something's wrong with the left-front wheel. I'll get out and check it."

He decompressed the cab and stepped out. Darkness had fallen, so he switched on his helmet lamp to inspect the front wheel. He found it mashed into the surface down to the axle. The fender was cracked but still serviceable. "Johanna, see if you can reverse the other wheels and pull this one out."

A few seconds later, she dragged the wheel out of its hole, leaving a trench behind. Brandon retrieved a jack from his tool compartment and raised the front end. "The axle is bent," he reported, "but I can salvage the wheel."

"Can you fix the axle?"

"I think so, with some cutting and welding."

"How long will it take?"

"Maybe half an hour."

"Good," she said. "It gives me time to file a protest."

He took out his cutting torch, separated the wheel from the axle, cut away the damaged parts, and welded on a new section from the spare parts they carried. Squeezing underneath, he welded the wheel onto the axle and completed the final connections.

He slid out from under. "Try it out," he told Johanna.

She drove the car forward and tried the steering. "It's a bit stiff turning left, but I can make it work."

"Glad to hear it," said Brandon.

Back inside the pressurized and warming cab, he checked their race status. They'd lost the better part of an hour. The Hare was eighty kilometers ahead.

Despite the creaky wheel and reduced visibility in the dark, Johanna averaged one-fifty for the next two hours, pulling into Saravan at nine o'clock. The Hare had left forty-five minutes earlier.

The deficit rose to fifty minutes before they departed the waypoint. They faced nine hours of rugged terrain in the dark. Shortly after leaving Saravan, Brandon took his planned sleep interval.

He woke four hours later to discover Johanna had navigated the toughest part of this leg on her own in the dark. Maybe he was superfluous after all. Then he observed her closely. She was hanging on by her fingernails. After driving for nineteen hours straight, she needed rest.

"Time for me to drive," said Brandon. "We need you at your best for the final leg in the morning."

"It won't matter if we can't cut into Ross's lead," she said.

"It *will* matter if he runs into trouble," argued Brandon. "He's been lucky so far. It can't last."

She slammed on the brakes and skidded to a halt. That sort of juvenile petulance was further evidence of her exhaustion. They exchanged places in silence. He accelerated to a speed he felt comfortable sustaining in the dark. He glanced at Johanna. She was leaning to the side in her harness with her helmet slumped forward, rocking with the motion of the vehicle.

Dawn was breaking five hours later when Johanna woke. The terrain Brandon traversed had been gently rolling. A greater concentration of craters characterized the route forward. He needed to navigate, and Johanna needed to drive. She sucked down a tube of breakfast laced with caffeine. Then he stopped the car, and they exchanged places.

An hour and a half later they arrived at the Hawking

Crater waypoint. Brandon's slower driving pace had cost them. The Hare had left two hours earlier. This time, Johanna didn't bother yelling at Ross, and in two minutes they were racing again.

Satisfied with the initial headings, Brandon zoomed out the map display to find the Hare.

What the hell?

"The Hare is a lot closer to us than it should be," he said.

"Did it run into trouble?"

He switched to the television feed. "They're showing pictures overlooking the Valles Marineris taken from Ross's car," he said. "The arrogant jackass sent the Hare on a sightseeing trip a hundred kilometers north of Hawking."

"That idiot thinks he's already won this thing," said Johanna.

"We've got ground to make up," said Brandon, "but he's given us a chance."

"Let's make him pay." Her eyes flashed.

"Hell yeah," Brandon replied.

Johanna pushed the pace. Brandon concentrated on guiding them through a tricky cluster of craters with as little deviation as possible from their most direct route to the finish. A commotion on the TV link caught his attention. He turned up the volume.

"It appears the Hare has a problem," the commentator was saying. "The race car has not moved for two minutes."

"Did you hear that, Johanna?"

"Yeah. Keep on top of it."

They'd heard Ross brag about the self-healing features of his car. This incident would test how good they really were.

"More chatter on the TV feed." Brandon listened intently. "I don't believe it." He laughed. "It's stuck in a sand-filled crater. Ross told his passenger to get out and push."

Here was their opportunity. Every minute they closed the gap by another three kilometers.

Brandon returned to his navigation duties. The nearer they got to the badlands, the more rugged the landscape became. They had just entered the badlands when the news came through.

"The Hare's on the move again," he told Johanna. "It's ten klicks north of us. Whoever gets through the badlands first is the winner."

He guided her into a debris-free valley that traversed a twenty-kilometer S curve as it ascended the slope of the Vinogradov Crater wall.

The map showed the Hare on an intersecting path— and it was close.

"Watch out," said Brandon. "The Hare's approaching fast from an opening on the left."

It barreled out from behind a hill a hundred meters ahead. They were both aiming for the same narrow pass.

"At the top of this slope the route squeezes between two craters," Brandon said. "I'm not sure the path is wide enough for two cars. And we may encounter splash rubble."

"Then we better get in front," said Johanna.

Ahead, the gap between the two craters emerged—and so did a stretch of rubble cast up by the impacts that formed the craters. A narrow channel appeared. The closer they got to the gap, the narrower it became. On both sides, the crater rims dropped off vertically for at least ten meters.

Johanna accelerated into a rock-free opening and drew level with the Hare. Her maneuver forced it either to brake or drive into the debris. The Hare didn't brake.

It plowed into the rocks at high speed, scattering some

to the side and bumping over others. Johanna fought to keep her line to the channel as the Hare bounced and lurched beside her. An instant later the Hare twisted right and clipped the Tortoise on the rear fender.

The force knocked their back end to the side. Johanna corrected, but too much. They headed for the crater on the right with no room to stop or turn in time.

Brandon's heart exploded in his chest. Johanna accelerated hard. Eyes open wide, he clutched his armrests. The front wheels dropped over the edge. The nose of the car dipped. They fell in slow motion toward the bottom of the crater.

Dust and debris formed a short, rocky ramp at the base of the wall. Johanna used reverse wheel spin to stop their nose dipping further, but the ground rose to meet them. The front wheels impacted near the bottom of the debris ramp, blasting rocks aside. The back wheels hit and bounced the car forward.

They roared through the crater bottom toward a level exit point. Brandon unclenched his fingers and sucked in a breath.

"That was exciting," he rasped.

Behind her visor, Johanna grinned.

For the next fifteen minutes, Brandon focused on finding a new path through the badlands. Finally, they mounted a ridge and headed down a chute that emptied out into the vast floor of the ancient Vinogradov Crater.

He had to get them around a double crater that formed a hole twenty-five kilometers across. Once they cleared the crater, they faced a straight sprint to the end.

He checked on the Hare. The green dot had disappeared. How was that possible? Its last position was a few klicks north of their location.

A popup message from the race stewards appeared on their video streaming link. "RACING ALERT: Potential Danger to Life."

He turned to Johanna. "The stewards have posted a PDL racing alert."

"What?" She glanced in his direction. "Why?"

"I don't know, but the Hare's beacon is off." He listened in on the TV broadcast. "And the commentators are saying they've lost the Hare's camera feed."

They drove in silence, considering the implications. In a normal race, a PDL meant nearby cars should provide aid.

"It's another of Ross's tricks," she said. "He could've just turned off the locator beacon."

"Yeah, maybe," Brandon said. "But if it's a crash severe enough to take out the beacon, his passenger could be hurt."

They sat in silence as their car devoured several more kilometers of Martian dirt.

"I'm contacting the stewards," Brandon said. They lacked voice capability, so he typed in a text message that would travel up the telemetry link: "Are we required to provide aid?"

Two minutes later came the reply.

"Those slimy asshats," he said. "They punted. 'Race rules do not address this issue.' They're thinking the same thing we are. Ross is capable of anything."

"But if it's not a trick ..." Johanna said.

"I know." It was an unwritten racer's code. They all put their lives at stake, even if the racer was just a passenger. Nika Ross was a slimeball for putting them in this position. "What if we drive to the finish line? If the Hare's not there, we can go find it."

"That could take over an hour," Johanna said. "Remember Libya."

Her comment smacked him in the face. Twelve years ago, in a race across Africa, a PDL went out, but Johanna and Brandon had kept racing. They learned later a driver they knew bled out before the medics arrived. A simple tourniquet would have saved his life.

"But it's the Martian Cup, Johanna ..."

"Doesn't matter, Brandy," she said gently. She lifted her foot off the accelerator. "Tell me where to go."

They crested a rise. A rock-strewn stretch of the plain lay before them.

"I see it." Brandon pointed. "Down to the right."

Sunlight glinted off the Hare's green-and-gold paint. From this distance, it seemed to be in one piece.

Johanna picked her way along, avoiding the larger stones. They stopped in front of the Hare, blocking its way forward in case this was a ruse. Inside the cockpit, the passenger waved frantically.

Brandon depressurized the cabin and stepped out, taking his tablet with him. He approached the cockpit. Brandon used a gloved finger to write the word "Air?" on the tablet. He showed it to the passenger and received a thumbs down. Brandon frowned. He erased the tablet and wrote "Heat?" The guy held out his hand and tilted it left and right.

"He's got no air or heat," he reported to Johanna. They didn't have room for another person in their cabin. As it was, the guy was living off the small amount of air the suit carried to support him walking to and from the waypoint airlocks. The ambient temperature was currently warm enough that heat wasn't a major issue, but if Brandon couldn't get the air flowing the guy was a goner. "I'm checking the car."

He walked around the Hare, searching for the cause of the problem. He kneeled to peer under the car. He flicked on his helmet light.

Several dents and deep scratches marred the undercarriage. He leaned his head in further. There it was: a ragged hole the size of his fist deep enough to penetrate the battery compartment. So much for the car having a fail-safe design —or a safe driver.

He stood. "It's real, Johanna," he said. "Looks like a rock punched through the floor and ruptured a battery." He circled around and located an access panel over the damaged battery. He opened it, and inside, the compartment was black with soot. He opened the adjacent compartments and found the batteries clean. Maybe there was hope.

He went back to the Tortoise and retrieved his torch and a coil of wire. Returning to the Hare, he welded the end of the wire to one of the good batteries and stretched it across to bypass the bad battery. When the wire touched the connector of the next good battery, he saw a spark, so he secured the wire.

He returned to the front to check on the passenger. The guy had his hand raised to shoulder level and shook his fist with his thumb pointing up. Through the guy's faceplate Brandon saw a big smile. Brandon signaled an OK.

"I got the power restored," he told Johanna as he replaced his tools. "I'm going to rig up a tow line."

He had her swing around and back the Tortoise's rear into position in front of the Hare's nose. Inside their winch compartment, he grabbed the hook and unreeled a few meters of cable. Ducking under the front end of the Hare, he began threading the cable through the suspension.

Suddenly, the Hare moved. The cable tightened and ripped the hook out of his hand.

The giant wheels on either side of him spun backward, kicking up dust.

"Hey!" Brandon yelled. He flattened himself on the ground. Beside his prostrate body the wire spooled out of the winch. In another second, it would reach the end, and when it did—

Brandon pushed up and rolled his body to the side as the Tortoise lurched backward over the spot where he lay a second earlier.

"Brandy!" shrieked Johanna.

"I'm okay," said Brandon. His knees wobbled as he stood.

The Hare stopped and surged forward, bumping over the rocks in its path as it swerved around the Tortoise. The cable slackened, and an instant later the hook shook free, left behind in the dust as the Hare sped off.

"Get in," Johanna barked.

He ran to the Tortoise and retracted the cable. When his butt hit the seat, Johanna hit the accelerator. Brandon fought the acceleration as he squirmed into his racing harness.

Ahead, the Hare hopped and reeled as it sped over the rocky terrain, seemingly oblivious to any further damage it risked sustaining. A puff of dust appeared where each wheel alighted, maintained only until the next rock or bump sent the wheel airborne again. The resulting dots and dashes of dust formed a Morse-coded message from Nika

Ross that Brandon read as a combination of abusive impudence and sadistic laughter.

"What the hell was I thinking?" Brandon erupted. He should've just duct-taped an air bottle to the hose of the guy's suit. Instead, he put the Hare back in the race—and probably cost them their company.

"Not now," said Johanna. She stole a glance at Brandon. "We've still got a race to win."

Johanna picked her way through the rocks to avoid damaging their car. They fell farther behind. Up where the Hare drove, the debris was thinning out. The Hare hit clear ground, and its hopping shifted into a sprint. By the time the Tortoise reached the unobstructed plain, the Hare had disappeared over the horizon. They now faced Brandon's worst nightmare: a drag race against the Hare for the Martian Cup.

Johanna pushed the Tortoise to its maximum speed. He checked the map display. They were a hundred and two kilometers from the finish. The Hare had ninety-one kilometers left.

The Tortoise's speed topped two hundred. At that velocity in the low Martian gravity, any bump they encountered propelled them airborne. Johanna drove the Tortoise like it was a racing boat skimming from wavetop to wavetop.

All Brandon could do was hold on—and monitor the systems. The batteries were draining quickly, but they had more than enough energy to reach the finish line. He checked the map.

Was he reading it correctly? With sixty-nine kilometers left, the Hare's lead was down to seven kilometers. How could that be?

Then he knew. "The Hare is running on five batteries

instead of six," he told Johanna. "We're catching up."

"Okay."

With thirty-three kilometers left, Brandon spotted the Hare's dust plume peeking above the horizon. The Hare was three and a half kilometers ahead.

Johanna continued to press.

"Twenty kilometers left," said Brandon. The Hare was two kilometers ahead.

A big bump thrust the right wheel up and rotated them left. The previously airborne left wheel hit harder than usual and dug in. The back end skidded to the side. Johanna steered to correct, but the suspension over-compressed and the car bounced. The Tortoise threatened to roll onto its shell.

Brandon braced for the crash—but Johanna combined steering, brake, and throttle to keep the shiny side up. She wrestled them back on track.

Each minute, they pulled ever closer to the Hare. With four minutes left, it was one kilometer ahead. With two minutes left, the gap was four hundred meters. With one minute remaining, the Vinogradov waypoint dome peeked over the horizon. And still the Tortoise gained. Until the Hare was close enough to reach out and touch.

Johanna edged to the side to pass. The Hare made one last, desperate move.

It swerved into their path. Johanna was ready for it. She lifted off the throttle. As they dropped back, she turned toward the Hare. Obscured by the Hare's dust plume, she tapped the Hare's back fender with the Tortoise's front fender and put the Hare into a spin.

She punched the accelerator and veered around the Hare. Emerging from the dust cloud, the Tortoise powered across the finish line.

Brandon's chest filled with all-consuming ecstasy. He joined Johanna in pounding the dashboard and yelling himself hoarse.

Johanna circled around back to the dome and braked to a stop. The camera crews and reporters gathered around. She opened her door, stepped out onto the shell behind the cab, and punched her fist at the sky. She hopped off and led the throng to the dome's airlock.

Brandon opened his door and stepped down. An attendant was helping the passenger out of the Hare's cockpit. Freed from his prison, he slung his arms around Brandon. Pressing his helmet to Brandon's, he shouted his thanks for saving his life. Then he added, "That was a sleazebag move Ross pulled out there." Brandon slapped him on the shoulder, and they turned to enter the dome.

Johanna was holding court in front of the cameras. She had removed her helmet. Her hair was a tangled, sweaty mess, but her smile was angelic. Ross stood watching from behind the cluster of reporters with his arms folded across his chest and a frown on his face.

Johanna finished a remark and glanced in Brandon's direction. She spotted him and waved him over. He deflated his neck seal and removed his helmet.

She stepped toward him and pulled him into an embrace. "We did it, Brandy," she murmured into his ear. He squeezed her tight. Before he released her, he reached up to wipe aside the hairs sweat-pasted onto her forehead.

"Now, to present the Martian Cup," said the network host, "here is the president of the Martian Society, Emil Cornwallis."

"What a wonderful display of racing skill and sportsmanship we have witnessed today," said Mr. Cornwallis to the cameras. "Johanna Henry has won many racing titles in her illustrious career. But I dare say, this one is surely the most magnificent." He faced Johanna. "You are the Conqueror Queen of Mars. I present to you the Martian Cup. Congratulations."

Johanna climbed onto the podium, accepted the sculpted platinum cup, and raised it before the flashing cameras. Hugging it to her chest, she stepped up to the microphones. "I'm thrilled and proud for myself and my brother, Brandon."

She called him up and handed him the Cup. He raised it for pictures.

"I'm also thrilled," Johanna continued, "for our supporters who helped us achieve this tremendous accomplishment. Thanks to you and our generous corporate sponsor, Tortuga Rum."

The network host stepped forward to interview the winner. "Congratulations, Johanna. How does this victory compare to the others in your career?"

"This was our ultimate challenge," she said, "but we never quit."

"On this last leg, we saw how you broke off racing to go to the aid of the Hare," said the host. "What transpired out there?"

"A fellow racer was in distress," she said. "We had an obligation to help him out. Brandon repaired their vehicle, and the race resumed."

"And the Tortoise beat the Hare, just like the fable." The host turned to Brandon. "Is there a new moral to the story?"

Brandon's grin spread across his face. "I don't know. How about this: A harebrained driver in a million-dollar car will come to an un-hoppy end."

Across the room, Nika Ross turned and walked away.

THE EMPEROR'S NEW SHOES

JENNIE MCDONALD

A YOUNG PIGEON pecking the ground near the feet of a small boy heard it first.

"But he has nothing on at all!" the boy exclaimed.

The pigeon looked up at the approaching procession, saw the emperor, and saw what the boy had said was true.

The boy was shushed and whisked away, scuffing his brass-buttoned shoes to delay leaving as long as possible.

The pigeon flew into the trees to tell her friends.

A passing dove could hardly believe her ears and mentioned it to a robin, who told a bluebird, who told a cardinal, who thought it a good joke and shared it out among the chickadees, finches, and swallows.

And then the tale was in the wind, spiraling down into villages and towns, rattling newspaper printing presses into action and brushing past the ears of people who lived too far away to attend the procession and hadn't been invited anyway.

Someone giggled, someone else joined in. A collective chuckle became a chortle, a guffaw that grew to a belly laugh in the far reaches of the empire.

Over the following days a chorus of laughter crept, then rolled, then surged across the land toward the palace.

In the broad avenue before the ancient gates, the laughter skirted carriages and coaches and caught at the brass button of a boot worn by a small boy, who shook it off and ran to catch up with his friends. The laughter curled up next to the curb where lords and ladies alighted from their conveyances. Eventually, someone would let it in.

The emperor couldn't remain holed up forever, could he?

A tradeswoman carrying a banner emblazoned with two shoes stepped over the laughter and presented her card at the gate.

"What kind of trade has she?" asked a young page, watching her pass into the foyer.

"Shoemaking, of course," replied the silver-polisher. "Shoemakers must have everything in pairs."

"My old dad has just one leg," said the page. "What would he do with a second shoe?"

"Give it to an old dad with one leg who wears his shoe on the other foot, of course." The silver-polisher had an answer for everything.

The shoemaker was shown to the emperor's dressing room, which had once been a ballroom. But as the emperor had so many clothes and the palace several ballrooms, he'd long ago ordered this one fitted up to serve his greatest pleasure: displaying his lovely wardrobe on an army of mannequins and sharing this breathtaking sight with specially invited guests.

In one niche slept a baby mannequin dressed in an exquisite lace gown and bonnet knitted by the emperor's grandmother. In another, a tiny boy mannequin wore velvet breeches and jacket for riding his mannequin pony. It was this charming suit and brocade cap festooned with one long peacock feather that had turned the young emperor's head to the delights of clothing.

The acquisition of every other article of apparel in this vast hall—every cloak, cape, coat, blouse, shirt, vest, tie, cravat, tunic, sash, belt, trousers, robe, turban, helmet, uniform, dressing gown, and pajamas—had each been part of his quest to discover once again the rapture of that very first ensemble and the intoxicating response to it that fed his pride.

As days passed after his public humiliation, the emperor could be found slumped in his gold-leafed chair at the center of the room, sighing one heavy sigh after another. Newspapers lay scattered about his feet, the staff having stripped them of front pages that continued to carry headlines like "Emperor's New(d) Clothes" and "Man Finally Cured of Hiccups Caused by Laughing That Day."

"Boy Speaks Up Where Adults Fear to Tread" featured an interview with said child, whose biggest regret was missing the sweets thrown by the emperor's retinue to distract the crowd. His mother's biggest regret was the child's tantrum thrown at her tea party the afternoon of that same day. "My carpet will never be the same!" she lamented. But the emperor just couldn't help pulling the front pages out of the recycling bins when no one was looking.

With such news and the fact that no one could take his calls without bursting into laughter, the emperor had fallen into a deep depression. The two swindlers who had taken advantage of his love for beautiful clothes had fled, but not even the thought of pursuing and apprehending them made him feel any better.

His wardrobe no longer pleased him. Since that day

he'd gone through the habit of dressing but without the pleasure that once attended this sartorial event. Within weeks he'd even stooped to throwing together his daily outfit without any assistance at all. No one said a word when he shrugged on an old cardigan over his fine silk waistcoat and buttoned on his sailor's trousers. Waving away a proffered breakfast tray (usually he tucked into the most important meal of the day with early-morning enthusiasm), he wondered if he should just go back to bed. But then he remembered commanding his counselors to find him a new source of amusement.

"Your shoes, sir, have never disappointed," his good old minister observed.

The emperor regarded his tall black shoes with silver buckles. "That's true. Even on the worst—that very worst—of days they bore me through to the end of the street. I shall have a new pair, the best in the land."

His good old minister had hastened to the Office of Imperial Decrees. A "Notice to All Shoemakers" was composed, printed, and dispatched throughout the land. Days passed. The staff grew anxious. The emperor could be found despondently feeding pigeons in the garden.

Only one shoemaker responded to the imperial decree. The rest were all still laughing and feared they couldn't keep their faces straight during an interview.

Now the shoemaker bowed before the emperor. "Your Imperial Majesty, I have brought you the finest shoes in all the land," she said. With a flourish, she lifted the lid from a simple wooden box.

The emperor leaned forward eagerly, but his face crinkled with disappointment. He sighed and fell back in his chair. "They are terribly plain. Can you not add a lace or bow at least?" he grumbled.

"I'm afraid such decoration would alter the shoes altogether, change the balance, the center of gravity, your very ability to walk in them," the shoemaker answered. "With your unquestioned sense of style, Your Imperial Majesty must see these shoes have no need of embellishment."

The longer the emperor looked at them, the more extraordinary the shoes appeared. Graceful but sturdy, the toes curling up ever so slightly. The thought of wearing them, walking in them, became irresistible.

"Oh, do put them on!" he exclaimed, extending his stockinged feet.

The shoemaker knelt. With no laces or bows the shoes simply slipped on. The emperor stood and wriggled his toes. There was plenty of room for toe wriggling. He liked that.

He took a step, then another, joy rising in his heart. He walked all around the room, jigged a little with a mannequin wearing a harlequin costume, and gazed at the shoes in the mirror for a long time. Then he rushed upon the shoemaker and shook her hand so roughly his good old minister feared it might come off.

"You have made me the happiest emperor in the world, my dear woman. I must have ten more pairs."

The shoemaker bowed and took up her banner once more. "You shan't require any more pairs. These shoes will last forever. You need only take one long walk in them to make them yours."

The emperor threw on his oldest overcoat and started for the door. "Whatever price you name, my good old minister will pay you," he said.

"Are you sure?" she asked. "I require but a trifle."

"Name it."

"The peacock feather from your childhood riding costume."

A gasp went up from the courtiers and staff.

The emperor froze, his gaze seeking the object in question. The eye of the feather seemed to wink at him, that old familiar wink reminding him of the glorious moment when he first heard someone say, "Oh, dear emperor, how handsome you look!" How his heart had warmed with pride. How he'd known then the course of his life—to acquire and treasure such beautiful clothes.

"Surely not," he whispered. "Name anything else."

"No. The peacock feather is the only payment I'll accept."

"Then I must decline." He reluctantly held out his feet so she could remove the shoes.

"As you wish."

The emperor jerked his feet back. They felt so warm and cozy in the wonderful shoes. He just couldn't give them up.

The shoemaker smiled a little smile. "I'll tell you what. You may pay me when you return—if you're content with the shoes."

The emperor, unused to bargaining, agreed. "And now," he said to his good old minister, "I'm going for a long walk."

The servants watched the emperor depart the palace without fanfare, without accompaniment, without even a picnic lunch for later. He'd dressed himself that morning, indecisively piling layer upon layer, until he was quite bundled up. This turned out just as well, as he emerged to find a chilly day awaiting him.

The laughter biding its time on the curb trailed after him but easily got distracted and drifted away.

He walked down the avenue where he'd been so publicly humiliated and felt not the sting of it. He passed through the business district, waving at bakers, bankers, and the candlestick maker. Burghers and their wives drew back to line the storefronts, but children ran into the street and followed the emperor until they got too tired and went home for tea.

In the evening he passed through the city gates into the countryside. No weariness claimed him, but he suddenly felt hungry. He knocked on the door of a small cottage where crickets sang in the thatching. The farmer's wife was taken aback, for she recognized him from his portrait on pennies earned by selling eggs.

Curtseying, she offered him some rough but fresh bread with warm cream and strawberries. Her several children watched him with moon-round eyes, except for one little girl who lay in a bed in the corner and coughed without ceasing.

"What ails her?" the emperor asked.

"Cold at night has got into her lungs," she said. "But we've no money for a good blanket or the doctor."

The emperor was baffled. He'd never heard of such a thing. He wanted to help, and that was a strange feeling. He found his toes were tingling with excitement.

"You shall have my overcoat!" he exclaimed. "And the gold coins you find in the pocket."

"Bless you!" gasped the farmer's wife. "Never did I hear you were a generous man—well-dressed, but not generous. But I see now that's not true."

This troubled him greatly as he partook of bread and strawberries and sipped the cream. In the wonderful shoes, his feet itched to be moving. He rose to depart.

"Where will you be going now, Your Imperial Majesty?" the farmer's wife asked.

"I am going," he paused, "to find out."

Another mile fell behind, and he came to a crossroads. There he met a pair of shivering movers struggling under the weight of a heavy dresser. The emperor gave them his old cardigan and quilted jacket, enabling them to pick up the dresser with renewed gusto. Like the farmer's wife, they too were astonished to find him so indifferently dressed and yet so kind.

To a trembling youth begging in the next town the emperor gave his silk waistcoat, flannel shirt, and watch, helping him to put them on. Speechless, the youth flung his arms around the emperor.

Even reduced to his cotton shirt and trousers, the shoes kept the emperor's feet moving and warm, and that warmed the rest of him.

He walked on through the evening until he found himself in a clearing at the center of a forest. He'd met no one else and felt strangely dissatisfied, despite the encouraging encounters of his day. He paced the forest floor, recalling those he'd met, the farmer's wife with her children, the movers with their heavy dresser, and the youth with his ready embrace.

The pole star directly overhead told him it was midnight, when the heart is cloven in two, for yesterday and for tomorrow.

He thought of his yesterdays, back to his first wearing of the riding habit with its winking peacock-eyed feather. How vain he'd become.

Yes, that was it. Vanity, not mere pride, had driven the acquisition of his fabulous wardrobe. Transfixed by each new ensemble, he'd lost sight of all else, of the empire and its people, the beauty of these lands, and the wonder of all they contained. Absorbed in these thoughts, he walked faster and faster through the forest.

The ground began to fall away below him. The shoes were carrying him along the curve of the atmosphere, exiting to a starry blackness stretched between the planets.

The shoes held him up, steady in a solar wind, and he saw the people of the world for what they were: microscopic filaments hurrying about a planet of ice and fire, buffeted by worries, greed, striving, and fear, yet bound together by warm hearths, by hands held out in friendship, by love.

A meteor blazed before him, dazzling his vision, its light scattering all around, accompanying him in a spiraling waltz back to earth.

The emperor could walk no more. Sinking down beside a horse trough, he fell asleep. When the sun rose hours later, a stable boy found him, his head upon a dandelion tussock and all the florets blown away by his snores.

The boy alerted the sheriff, but clad only in his cotton shirt and sailor's trousers, no one recognized the emperor until a telegraph operator wandered by with the news he was missing. "You will know him by his new shoes," went the description. "Perfect fit, very plain." The sheriff could scarcely believe her luck (usually bad) and sent word to the palace. The lottery ticket she bought that afternoon was a winner and paid for her new uniform.

A carriage soon arrived to take the emperor home.

"The shoemaker was right," he said, embracing his good old minister. "I've walked a long walk in the new shoes. I've met many people of the kingdom and given everything away, except for these shoes, which were the making and means of my journey. We've traveled to the sky, walked above the atmosphere, and waltzed in the light of a meteor, together. They are mine now. But I am also theirs." He watched a young pigeon flying about the palace garden.

In the shoes his feet itched to be moving. "Come, walk with me, my friend!"

In time, the rest of the emperor's beautiful clothes were sold for money that ensured no small children suffered from cold and no tramps and beggars from want. The dressing room was made over again into a ballroom. Everyone was invited to the palace to celebrate, and not just the lords and ladies. All came to dance with the emperor they had grown to love and respect.

At the end of the avenue the shoemaker watched the wave of laughter sit up eagerly on the curb. The palace gates stood open, but it waited. A hand beckoned it to come in. The laughter rushed forward, straining the palace walls, spilling from the windows, the chimneys, and the crevices where swallows came and went. Up in the belfry, bats caught rides on tendrils of giggles, spinning out into the night.

With a smile, the shoemaker returned the emperor's feather to the peacock at her side. She pulled up her hood. The two stepped into the shadows and went upon their way.

THE DIAGNOSTIC DEMON ON SKILLMAN AVENUE

MEL LAKE

I PERCHED on the cleanest-looking chair in the waiting room, curving my spine even though I knew better, staring at the fish tank across the room. Whirling schools of neon tetra and an ancient receptionist ignored me, though every now and then the clouds of tiny fish paused long enough to point their perpetually open eyes my way. This place smelled like feet and cleaning solution. It was a "Save As" version of every other waiting room I'd been to in the borough. But once you were ushered through the door of this one, you'd be possessed by a demon for a sliding scale fee.

I wrote my story on the medical history forms, skipping the pain scale because it's bullshit. One of them had a diagram of a human body that you marked up like a reverse voodoo doll to indicate where you wanted the pain to go away. He looked too much like the guy from the Operation board game for me to take seriously. Skip. I scanned the HIPAA forms, tapping my foot on the floor to distract me from the electric ripples going from the base of my spine down to my right pinky toe.

There was an extra form at the back, printed in dark red ink on bright red paper. I moved it to the front of the stack and squinted but couldn't actually make out the words. I signed the bottom of the red form anyway, then handed the clipboard back. The front desk lady's lipstick wedged into the wrinkles around her lips as she gave me a perfunctory smile. With only the two of us and the fish in the room, silence hung heavy in the air, even though it was two in the afternoon and we were right off Skillman Avenue.

Ten minutes later, Dr. Jones came and beckoned for me to follow him back to an exam room. I'd expected an assistant to do this part but there didn't seem to be anyone else in the office but me, the receptionist, and Dr. Jones. He was a small man. If someone was going to play him in a movie, it'd be that squinty guy from *The Princess Bride*. Inconceivable! That guy. He wore little glasses on a chain around his neck and his arms were so fuzzy they looked like they belonged on a Muppet. I tried not to stare at his hands as he moved me this way and that. His fingers were dark and fat and gentle.

He put his glasses on the very tip of his nose and peered at me, head tilted back so far I could see up his nose.

"You have been told about the procedure, then, yes?" It didn't really sound like a question.

"Umm..."

"It's very simple for the patient and usually quite pain-less. I can show you a pamphlet?"

He patted his pockets, then swiveled around on a squeaky stool. He riffled through drawers that were filled with things that looked like they belonged in a pawn shop, not a doctor's office. I scanned the OSHA reminder on handwashing taped to the wall while he muttered to himself. Next to it was a poster with anatomical drawings labeled in a language I couldn't read. It could've been Latin. On it, a man and a woman stood with only half their skin on, staring at each other like they were about to star in a very awkward porno. Above the door to the exam room, a single horseshoe had been nailed to the wall.

"Here we are," he said, handing me a pamphlet that had been laminated far too late to preserve it.

The bullet points read like every other presurgical pamphlet I'd ever been handed, except for the title, which read, "Demonological Diagnostic Services: What to Expect When You Are Possessed." No food twelve hours prior, only clear liquids. Dizziness is to be expected, but if severe, call the office. Tingling and numbness at the injection site, perhaps minor swelling. Call 911 if you experience any of the following. Nothing seemed out of the ordinary on the list except speaking in tongues.

"Yes, thank you," I said. My body didn't seem to register that it should be nervous.

"Very good. We'll schedule you for your initial appointment Thursday, come back Friday for exorcism. Then consultation in two weeks."

"Two weeks?" This was costing me a thousand bucks, so I'd hoped it would be quicker than going back to the specialist recommended by my insurance.

Dr. Jones looked apologetic.

"The diagnostician must recover. This is not as easy a procedure for the entity as it is for you."

I nodded, feeling childish.

He ushered me out of the exam room and the front desk lady ran my debit card through her machine. She handed it back pinched between two enormously long acrylic nails. I smiled thinly at her, then shrugged on my purse and

walked back out to the streets of Sunnyside with something
churning in my gut I couldn't name.

On Thursday, the front desk lady ushered me into the office
instead of Dr. Jones. I'd been offered general anesthesia or a
local and a Xanax. I took the Xanax that morning as
instructed. I wore my "outpatient procedure" underwear. It
suggested, "this is normal and I'm cute, not just your
average chronic pain patient," while not being too flashy or
suggestive. At least that's what I was trying to project.
Statement underwear wasn't an exact science. The exam
room was colder than it had been before.

When he entered the room, Dr. Jones looked the same,
but something about him felt heavier. More serious. I swallowed an icebreaker comment.

"I will need to dim the lights, Miss Porter," Dr. Jones
said, adjusting his glasses. The front desk lady stayed in the
room this time. She lit six candles and placed them around
the room in locations that seemed random. I glanced down,
expecting to see a pentagram in blood with the exam chair
in the middle of it. All I saw were a few dust bunnies
loitering on scratched linoleum.

Dr. Jones touched my arm gently, then began saying
things in a language I didn't understand. It wasn't scary.
His voice washed over me like a gentle wave of fatherly
concern. I breathed in his cologne, which mostly hid the
antiseptic smell of the office. I thought about my dad,
always wearing Hawaiian shirts and those cargo shorts
they seemed to make specifically for dads. He always
squinted when I talked about my body in any way, and
although he cared about me, I don't think he'd summon a

demon to find out what was wrong. Dr. Jones swayed a little and the glasses slipped down his shiny nose. Tears welled in my eyes before I could stop them.

After a ceremony consisting of chants, handling of symbolic items, and a rush of cold wind, Dr. Jones sat down heavily in the unoccupied chair. I didn't feel anything.

"Is that it?" I asked, and immediately felt bad for phrasing it like that. "I mean, sorry, can I move now?"

"Yes," he said, still looking a little dazed. The front desk lady blew out the candles and collected the items Dr. Jones had brought out for the ritual.

I stared at the horseshoe on the wall above the door, trying to figure out if I had just been scammed for a thousand bucks. If I wasn't actually possessed by a demon who would provide Dr. Jones with valuable insight into the severity of my ailments, I would have a funny story to tell at parties. I could tell it at happy hour while standing at a high table instead of perching on one of those stools you can't sit on without flashing everyone and making your ass go numb. I'd laugh telling the story, not explaining that when you live with constant pain, you forget what it's like *not* to feel it and then you forget to feel the good things because all you're focused on is getting through the bad. Then when doctors shrug at you or ask if it's just your period, they act like *you're* the crazy one for screaming. Everyone would laugh.

"Why does he do this? The, you know, demon."

Dr. Jones stood. His face was getting its color back. He took my hand and felt my pulse, then prodded me in several places, muttering.

"We have an arrangement."

"An arrangement?"

"Yes." He adjusted his glasses and, for the first time

during my appointment, seemed impatient. "You needn't concern yourself with the details."

"But you made a deal with the devil, though? Sorry, it's just hard not to be curious." I felt myself spiraling. I was giddy, sitting on an exam table, supposedly possessed by a demon. The dull pain in my hips and legs hadn't changed in any way. "He does this because you made a deal?"

"*He* is a rather limiting term to describe an entity such as this being," Dr. Jones said.

"Oh, yeah, right, of course," I stammered, feeling foolish for having misgendered the literal devil. After fifteen minutes of watchful waiting to make sure I didn't pass out, they let me go.

I left the office with a reminder card in my hand for my return appointment. I felt both strange and not.

I didn't go right home. It seemed like a waste of a PTO day to get possessed and then come straight home. I hadn't brought gym clothes and still had a bit of Xanax in me, so a swim was out. The rest of Queens didn't give a shit about my demon or the chronic pain that led me to him (it?), so I wandered, feeling the energy of a crisp Thursday morning and trying not to freak out.

Three blocks from Dr. Jones's office, I almost died.

A cab careened around the corner, tires squealing— they *actually* squealed, apparently that's not just something they put in the movies for dramatic effect—and I was right in its path. Until I wasn't. My body jerked back onto the sidewalk, and I fell on my ass, hard. The painful impact and the adrenaline rush that followed made me feel like I could rip the cab in two and eat it.

"What the fuck?!" I said to no one.

"Bloody hell, this person is my host for five seconds and almost gets us killed."

"Hey!" I yelled, frantically turning in a circle to find out who I was yelling at. A group of kids clearly skipping school passed me, along with a pair of tourists, some locals, the guy who owned the Korean restaurant a few blocks over, and an Orthodox man in a hurry. No one paid me any mind.

"Just go home. I've got twenty-four hours with you, don't make me save us again."

I didn't move.

"Holy fuck," I said. "It's you."

Silence. Or, rather, no more voices in my head. All I heard was the ambient noise of the city.

"Hey! I'm talking to you."

"You're attracting attention, just move along," the voice in my head said in a distinctly annoyed tone.

I moved along. To Starbucks. Wasn't Starbucks where everyone went when they had no idea what the hell was going on?

While in line I practiced talking to my demon without actually saying the words out loud. "What am I supposed to call you? Demon? Do you have a name? Is it, like, cursed so that humans can't pronounce it?"

Nothing.

I ordered a triple-shot latte and watched all the screenplays being written with the free Wi-Fi.

"Oh come on, it can't be *that* embarrassing. I mean, my name is Rachel. I guess you know that. Do you have access to all my memories? I didn't really think about that part of the deal. Don't look at prom, 1999."

From my head, a pointed silence.

My feet ached. My hips ached. I wanted my latte. A

group of moms sat gossiping in the corner while glancing every now and then at their strollers, presumably filled with future screen-raised babies. A shot of lightning went down my leg and I hated everything.

"I'm going to call you Todd."

"You're not supposed to call me anything. I'm not supposed to talk to you," he said. Or rather, thought. The demon in my head sounded annoyed, even though *I* was the one experiencing a botched possession. "Just forget I'm here."

"Okay, but like, no," I said. Or rather, thought. I was getting better at thinking in his direction instead of talking out loud. "I can't just forget that there's a demon in my head. I have a million questions and I hurt, and this latte is taking for-fucking-ever."

"I will not answer your questions. You must forget that I'm here, Miss Porter, so that we can get this done."

"How can I forget there's a demon in my head? There's no way you could forget something like that."

"You'd be surprised."

He sounded amused. I felt a little ripple of it, tickling the back of my brain. Inside me, he'd chuckled and because it hadn't come out of my mouth, it felt like an aborted burp.

"Fine. But if I need you again, I'm calling you Todd."

"You can't need me. That's not part of the deal."

I felt frustrated, but it wasn't just my feelings anymore. His frustration layered on top of mine, bleeding through my emotional state like a watercolor in the rain. I could feel through him (it?) that this wasn't right, he wasn't supposed to bleed into me like this. The mental traffic was only supposed to flow one way.

"Okay, I won't need you. But I'm calling you Todd all the same."

The demon was silent for a moment. I could tell he was thinking because it felt like my brain was struggling to keep up and the cursor in my head was blinking slower than it should've been if it were just me in there. The barista chose that moment to call my name. I reached for my drink with all the speed of a sloth.

A few sips into my latte and several zaps of electricity down my leg later, he said, "Todd is fine."

He was quiet the rest of the walk home.

I logged in and checked emails from home even though I said I wouldn't. I made tea. I sat in my comfy reading chair and fidgeted, trying to arrange myself and my laptop in a compromise position that didn't exacerbate my mild carpal tunnel syndrome, didn't send any more zings down my legs than usual, and allowed me to actually see the screen. After about fifteen minutes the toes on my right side were asleep anyway. Another ten and the ball of my right foot was out. After my feet went numb, little zaps of electricity started pinging through my body like a manic pinball determined to win a prize. I kept my out-of-office message on, but people messaged me anyway.

Todd was quiet. He was right, earlier. If he hadn't pulled me out of the way of a speeding cab and saved my life, I'd have had no clue he was there. In between emails, I burned with curiosity. What had he witnessed while possessing people? How old was he? Had he been inside kings and queens? Presidents? Cowboys? Literally *anyone* more interesting than a thirty-two-year-old data processor from Sunnyside with chronic pain no one had much interest in resolving?

"Todd, who is the most interesting person you've possessed?" I asked.

A tiny ripple in the very back of my consciousness was all the response I got. He heard me, though.

The afternoon passed as all afternoons do. My hips got stiff from sitting, then ached from standing, then ached in a different way when I put my laptop on my belly and collapsed on the floor. I asked Todd who his favorite Beatle was, whether he'd possessed any astronauts, and if vampires were real. No response. I asked him if he'd been cast out from heaven and if hell was anything like Dante described and if so, was endless wind really the worst thing in the world if it meant you got laid while you were alive? No response. I microwaved dinner and sat at my kitchen table scrolling through Twitter for as long as my lower body could handle. Finally, Todd and I watched Netflix for an hour while little zings went from my hip through my upper thigh, gathering together under my kneecap until it felt like there were bees buzzing about just under the bone.

Todd was silent as I brushed my teeth. He remained hidden, wherever he was, while I set my phone on its charger and didn't say any prayers before pulling back the covers.

The night started fine, then got not-fine real fast.

Pain in the night is the same as it is in daylight. But without the rest of the world to interact with, the only thing helping you through it is your own mind. My mind turned on me a long time ago.

"Todd," I said, out loud. My head was too full to not say something with my mouth. If I didn't call him out I would have to scream. "Do you feel this? It's fucking—it's —Todd?"

He didn't answer.

"Fine. I'm not supposed to talk to you, but I have to talk or I'm going to go insane," I said. "It's not always like this. I can handle it until it gets like this and then I don't even want to—"

I felt him squirm. Inside my head, he shifted, and I realized he *did* feel it. All the electric shocks going down from the base of my spine, pinging off my kneecap and lighting up the nerves in my feet—he felt them too.

The sheets drifting over my body felt like knives, so I threw them off. I started shivering immediately and slipped them back on. My hip and knee joints felt like magnets, pulling me down to some invisible node on the mattress under me, painfully dragging the rest of me with them. I felt the concave curve of my kneecaps, and it was like they vibrated in a frequency that was at odds with the rest of my bones. At night I felt *everything*, every random piece of flesh no one ever thinks about until it's on fire—and he felt them too.

"Look, I can't quote Goethe right now, but I fucking *get it*, man. Deal with the devil, sign me up. I just ... can you end this?"

Todd sighed. My ribcage didn't move or expand at all but in my mind I felt a weary sigh.

"That's not why I'm here," he said at last, speaking inside my brain. The words echoed around in my skull a little, like he was having trouble containing them.

"I know, I know," I said. My fist was clenched again, and I made myself release it. The pain in my limbs and joints didn't subside. But having someone to talk to other than the aloe plant dying a slow death on my windowsill helped.

"I just ... nights, man. I can deal in the day, you know? But nights it's like, all I am is pain. I can't remember a night that wasn't like this."

"Don't." His voice was firm, but it sounded like it was coming from behind clenched teeth.

"Don't what?"

"Speaking of pain is not the same as experiencing pain, which is not at all a true reflection of pain itself."

"What the fuck does that mean?"

He was silent for a long time. I felt him, crouching in the back of my consciousness. Todd the demon was a little wisp of a feeling, cornered in the back of my hypothalamus, suffering a pain I was used to, but he wasn't. For the first time since Dr. Jones had done his song-and-dance routine, I realized maybe I should feel sorry for the devil who'd made an arrangement with a sketchy doctor with an office in Queens.

"When you speak of your pain, you put it through a lens. It is the lens of your life, but it is not the lens of mine. Do you see?"

"No."

Then, for a fraction of a second, I saw lives. I felt the shadow of endless cycles of this, as experienced through borrowed brains. Screams in the dark. Fists bitten into until the skin broke. So many humans crying in so many bathtubs while the shower ran to drown out the sound. And always, the wisp of Todd crouching in the back of their brains, feeling it all.

"You adjust," Todd said. "Humans. You adapt. It's your gift and your curse. What you experience as pain is a complex reaction of your body to stimuli. Sometimes the stimuli are imaginary, but your body doesn't care. You have no scale that can measure pain because you are both the scale and the thing being measured."

I thought for a moment. That stupid Pink Floyd cover with the prism flashed before my eyes and I tried to ignore it but once it was there I couldn't stop thinking about my ex-boyfriend, who had a fabric tapestry of it pinned across his wall like he was proclaiming loyalty to the douchebag navy.

"So? Then what the fuck is the point? What is the point of this if you can't tell me how bad it is? How bad it *really* is?"

He smiled inside my head, though my lips didn't move.

"*You* were the one who invited me in, Miss Porter."

I swallowed, tasting my own sour breath and the remnants of wine my toothpaste hadn't washed away.

"Goodnight, Todd."

"Sleep well, Miss Porter."

"This is for you," Dr. Jones said, handing me a thick folder. "It is two versions of your medical history, summarized. For you is the, ah, layman version. And for the doctors you see, the ones you go to in the future, there is a physician version. They may not accept it without tests, but they will trust this more than they trust your words. It has letterhead, you see."

"Oh," I said, not really sure what else to say.

"And this is the supplemental report." He handed me an envelope. It wasn't sealed, and it contained about five folded pages inside. "This is what you miss."

"Huh?"

"While you have pain, you miss things," Dr. Jones said.

"This is what you miss because you are busy dealing with your pain. I have not read it. The diagnostician provides this for every patient as a service to you for allowing entry into your world." Dr. Jones smiled and it was so genuine that for a second I wondered if he was about to try and sell me a nutritional supplement.

He stood up and I followed him out of the exam room, past the neon tetra swirling in the waiting room.

The little envelope from Todd sat on my kitchen table for three days.

It took half a bottle of wine before I had the courage to open it, knees folded under me on the thin cushion of my orange IKEA couch. I knew better than to fold my knees under me, but I did it anyway.

Halfway down the page, the tears started.

"You smile with half of your face when you're being self-effacing, and you don't realize how much more of your face lights up when you're not. Your feet are very large. This isn't an insult, Miss Porter, though I know you'll take it that way. You are not a graceful person, and you know this. It's because you're in pain, Rachel. Grace is of no concern.

"Buy new furniture. You can afford it.

"Your apartment is well decorated, furniture notwithstanding. You're self-conscious about it because you live in New York and humans here have convinced themselves that this tiny stupid place is the most important strip of land on the planet, but you need to get over yourself and realize that you like the color orange and you've filled your living space with a color that pleases you. Embrace it.

"Out of the humans I've inhabited, you have an average sense of smell and excellent hearing. At night, you can hear the wind whispering through the trees that line your block, especially the one that occasionally taps on your window like a friendly neighbor. Listen to it.

"You like the way it feels when you crack your knuckles because it's a thing your body does that doesn't hurt in any way. It's a neutral activity your body does and no, it won't lead to bone disease, and you can do it as often as you like.

"Your shower wash smells nice.

"You asked if I could end your pain. I could have. It would have ended everything else too.

"The barista at the Starbucks you frequent would be open to a sexual encounter with you, should you so choose to initiate one.

"The yogurt in your icebox is very expired.

"You are both the scale and the thing being measured, which means you can never know how your suffering compares to others. But nor can you truly know your own strength. I do.

"Live well, Miss Porter, and look more carefully before you cross the street. —Todd."

SOMETHING IN THE AIR

RICK DUFFY

A GRAY-HAIRED MAN in stocking feet unwound a red woolen scarf from his neck. Worn leather gloves, caked with snow, lay on the hearth. Tiny runnels melted near the fingers.

"Wood's high and dry," he said, his face winter-ruddy in the firelight. "What you got going, Anna?"

Anna sat hunched in a stalled rocker, her skin like museum parchment in the window's frosted glow. Knitting needles lay across her lap. She held up a red scarf. "See if it fits, Joe."

Joe came near and stretched it out. "Perfect," he said, though he had three others now, just the same. Two hidden in drawers.

Anna gazed across the room. Or into space, or another world. "I forget—did I put up the peaches?"

Joe hesitated. "Cellar's crammed. Not much now except wait out the winter." He planted a kiss on the galaxy of age spots dotting his wife's temple. "And think up new ways to warm our old bones."

Anna's focus resurfaced like a diver from the deep. "You cad," she said with feigned shock.

"Don't tell your parents." He poured himself a coffee from the pot on the hearth.

Fat white snowflakes drifted outside the window, like pale algae in a colorless sea. The pines beyond the fences blurred into a dim black wave, frozen in time.

Joe warmed his hands on the cup and licked his chapped lips. "I still need to get the shutters up."

Anna sighed. "With spring so near?"

A chill ran down Joe's neck, though not from a draft. He'd noticed that Anna's absences, her slips of memory, had gotten worse. Yesterday he'd found her sitting with the window wide open, a light shroud of snow covering her thinning hair. Each year he'd hung the shutters to protect the cabin from the winter winds. This year, that wouldn't be the sole reason.

Joe eased into his chair. "Winter's just beginning, dear." He lay a gnarled hand on hers and squeezed. "But spring's always in the air with you. Remember when we met?"

Anna squeezed her husband's hand back. She knew her mind was going. Sometimes, as she sank into that cloudy, frustrating dream, she wondered if living was still worth the effort. Then Joe would reach into the murky shadows and lift her again into the sunshine. The smile in his eyes brought back all her colors.

"At the fairgrounds," she said. Anna could see it as if it were yesterday—the best parts of her life remained intact.

He nodded. "It was raining. You were dancing."

"Spring." She smiled. "I remember."

A log cracked and spit up a cloud of sparks, the souls of yesteryear's snowflakes released from their wooden tomb. Wisps of steam rose from the wet gloves. Silence settled over the room.

A delicate tension disturbed it.

Anna sensed it first. She slipped her hand from Joe's and returned to her knitting. "You're worried about something."

"Well," Joe said, "wondering."

"Oh?"

Joe's thoughts had strayed like the sparks from the fire. "When I was outside, I heard a bird."

"A bird?" Anna fiddled with a ball of yarn. "We do live in the mountains, dear."

"Yes, well." He sipped his coffee. "I heard a warble out past the fences. The birds still around tuck in for winter, at least the worst of it. They don't sing during a snowstorm."

Anna paused her work. Crimson light from the fire flashed along her needles. An unsettled silence returned before she looked up and said, "My mother once told me there are three reasons a bird sings in a storm."

Joe leaned forward, eager to encourage any exercise of his wife's failing memory. "Tell me."

"First," she said, "it may sing in distress. Hungry, or hurt, or for another."

He shook his head. "It's fussed too steady for too long."

"Like your wife," she grinned, "when her sciatica kicks."

Joe grinned back. "Like your husband when he stubs a toe."

Anna chuckled. "Second, it sings because it's old and confused, gone addle-brained. Don't try to compete with me *there*."

Joe pushed down a brief swell of sorrow at Anna's little joke. "And the third?"

Her eyes seemed unusually bright. "The creature has discovered a great truth, an awful secret. The bird is beyond madness. Its soul burns and it must tell."

The man crinkled his brow at another uncomfortable stirring in his chest. Joe respected the forest, the mountains, especially in winter. He accepted these places held secrets, like any neighbor. Yet there was something else, quiet and intangible, that one sensed outside the safe harbors of cities and towns. He couldn't quite put it into words. As if, among the creeks and pines, the green hills and river willows, something watched—and judged.

Anna continued, "My mother said that when winter comes, the animals don't take to their holes to sleep. They go there to hide."

"Hide?" Joe asked. His wife's eyes held him. "From what?"

Her face became at once unreadable, and more present than Joe had seen in years. "From the thing that brings life. And takes life. And turns the great wheel of the seasons."

Anna's hand relaxed in his. Her eyes shifted out of focus as she let herself drift. Joe was here, so even in the fog, she knew she'd be safe.

Joe sat a moment longer, wondering at the strange tale. Then he smirked, happy to have seen Anna so attentive— while it lasted.

He stood. "I'll start supper. Then we'll snug into our own cozy burrow."

The next day arrived with new winter bluster. Anna dozed in the rocker. The cheerful cackles from the fireplace and the guffaws of the storm became happy crowd noises, taking her back to parties of long ago. She hoped someone would ask her to dance.

When Joe felt she was settled and safe, he wrapped himself from head to heel and trudged through the piling drifts to their shed. Regardless of his layers, the frigid winds clawed through his coat and scarf, picking at his skin with icy fingers.

He found the shutters where he'd left them, beneath a canvas dusty with the seasons. As he hauled one out the door, a gust nearly knocked him off his feet.

"Shit," he hissed and retreated into the shed.

He waited for the wind to die. There was nothing in here to keep his thoughts upbeat, and soon his darker ones crept out—the things he didn't dwell on when Anna was close.

The time was fast approaching when he could no longer care for her alone. They'd have to give up their mountain home and move closer to town. They both loved it here, but Anna saw the mountains in a way Joe couldn't. When he gazed upon their blue and white summits, he felt, deep inside, their grand independence, their eternal majesty. But she saw a wild beauty, forever changing. Unstable, in Joe's opinion—like his wife.

Still, his fear of losing Anna softened at the image of her passing, peaceful and happy, surrounded by the hills and forests she adored. If possible, he'd stay with his wife right here, until their lives came to their natural ends.

Another howl of wind blew his thoughts to the memory of his wife resting before an opened window, exposed to the killing breath of winter. For the next few months, he'd stay close to the cabin, keep her in sight.

But he was no spring chicken either. What if he died first?

The stubborn winds refused to calm. He abandoned the shutters and pushed out into the cruel white gusts.

Halfway to the cabin, again he heard the bird.

It warbled through the tempest, sometimes clear and

constant, sometimes bizarre, indefinable. It came from no direction, every direction, urged on by the feral winds.

"What do you want?" Joe shouted to the storm, surprising himself at the venom in his tone.

The birdsong paused, then continued as indifferently as ever.

"Get off my property!" he yelled.

The strange cries went on and on.

He clenched his gloved hands. "Fine. Freeze, for what I care."

Joe slogged to the cabin. Anna stood by her rocker, one hand on the window latch.

"Wind's too high," he said, and kicked off his boots. "I'll try the shutters tomorrow."

She didn't turn around. "Can you smell the cherry blossoms, Joe? Let's air the place out."

He reached her before she'd undone the latch, helped her into her chair. She seemed content in whatever world she now wandered. He wouldn't pull her out. Yet he couldn't share her bliss.

And still the bird sang, the wind carrying the song even into the cabin.

Or, he now wondered, was it the bird that carried the wind?

In the morning, Joe rose tired and early to hang the shutters.

Anna still didn't understand the need, but let her husband have his way. She knew there was no point arguing when he was in a grump.

But Joe was in more than a grump. He'd slept little. The

wind's incessant whistling reminded him always of the bird.

The gusting snow again frustrated his efforts. He covered half a window—the one nearest Anna's rocker—before a sudden blast pushed him off the stepladder. He banged his head on the window box and had to come inside.

Anna treated the bump and scrape. Then she began a new green scarf, because she couldn't find the red yarn and didn't want to ask Joe. She was well aware of his worries about her memory.

Joe had hidden that ball as a gentle way to stop her from making another red scarf. He sat at the corner of the hearth, snacking on sunflower seeds, spitting the shells into the fire. Outside, snow rushed against the cabin in angry waves, a frothy sea against his bulwark.

As Joe listened to its bluster, he found that, if he held very still, he could just make out the bird.

"Maybe a hawk," he said.

"What?" asked Anna.

He looked up, not realizing he'd spoken. "I saw a hawk, couple days back. But—no. This thing's got less shriek. I think."

"Like a mourning dove?" she asked, loving all the birds in their little world.

"Can't be. The hawk would've eaten it by now."

"An owl, then? A woodpecker or a crow?"

Joe closed his eyes, listened, and shook his head. "Sometimes there's a melody—sort of."

"A tree swallow?"

He considered. "Well, it *is* a little crazy like that."

"The finches are my favorite," Anna said. "They'll be back now, with the spring."

Joe grimaced as her delusion again invaded their cabin. Crowded it. How, he wondered, could he stand being trapped with it, as bad as it'd become, the entire winter?

The noise of the bird pricked his ears. His eyes snapped wide. "A bat. A rabid one. Some kind of squealing, ugly—"

"You said it had a melody."

"No." He huffed and stood up, swung an arm toward the door. "It's got a grate, like a bad hinge."

"Joe—"

He turned, eyes wild, and laughed. "Or a chicken with a wrung neck."

"Joseph, please."

Joe was at the window. He startled at his own agitation and took a breath. "This was a mistake."

"What's that, Joe?"

Trying to ride out another winter together, is what he was thinking.

"The shutters," he said. "Should've put them up earlier."

She sighed and repeated, "With spring so near?"

He clenched his jaw, his eyes searching the writhing veils of snow, searching for that bird.

That goddamned bird.

Wind roared through the eaves. Anna slept peacefully, but not Joe. In the heights of the storm, rode again the bird. Its sharp, crazy notes pecked into his ears. Ate at his brain.

He scowled and got out of bed. Snow rushed sideways past the windows. Nights such as these, in the lightless mountains, made it appear the cabin had been dropped into an abyss. His wife's curious fable returned, about a frightful thing in the wilds that moved the seasons, or whatever.

He forced a smile. And drove birds mad?

As a rule, Joe took reality head-on. He scoffed at baseless fears and the imagined monsters under the bed. Yet, this bird's incessant screech—not only in midday, but now in the darkest night—stirred in his heart an inexplicable despair. A prick of an unfamiliar nerve. He tried to shake it off. He didn't abide the unexplained, the unknown, around his property.

With little chance of seeing anything outside, he returned to bed. But the mind-grating warble continued. It dove and swooped over the roof and around the eaves.

Again he rose, his frustration mounting. To a window. To another. To the door for a blustery peek. Still, he couldn't locate the source. When he returned to the bedroom, Anna was awake.

"Damn bird," he growled.

Anna perked an ear, and for a moment, heard a strange lilt and cadence beyond the wind. But she felt as if she were eavesdropping on a private conversation. Out of an instinct of decency, she shut it out. "Come back to bed, Joe."

They tucked themselves under the covers. But the bird's song had set a hook in the man's brain. It pulled and yanked. He became convinced the creature was taunting him, or asking him an unanswerable question, or…

He was at the door, wrapping himself in his coat. "Fucking bird, Anna. Damn fucking bird."

"Joe," she said, "it's none of our business. Let it be."

His laugh was almost a shriek. This was *his* home, *his* property. Nothing had a right to invade it. Certainly not some abomination in the belly of night. Of course it was his business. He'd *make* it his business.

Joe jammed his stocking feet into his boots, pulled on a woolen cap, grabbed a flashlight, and burst out the door.

Anna slid from the bed, wrapped herself in a robe, and hurried barefoot to the window. The wind howled through the black, dimensionless void. Her husband's light shrank to a dot, then to nothing.

She gripped her robe tight at the neck. She'd never seen Joe like this and didn't know what to do. Her mind began to drift with the snow, darken with the night.

The flashlight's returning orb, like a weak sun in a low black sky, brought her back from the edges of a dream.

Joe rushed to the cabin and banged through the door. "Impossible," he stammered, his eyes wild and white. "I can't—it can't..."

Anna opened her mouth to speak, but Joe's eyes froze her words in her throat.

He hurried across the room. "Where's the shotgun?" He found it, shoved in the shells.

"Joe, please—" Anna reached out a begging hand.

He stepped toward the door, but stopped before her, fingering the gun. His eyes softened. He came closer, leaned in, pressed his stiff lips to her mouth. Then his face twisted again. He turned, rushed out the door, slammed it shut.

She stood trembling before the window, terrified to look, terrified to look away. The flashlight grew smaller, smaller, until the very maw of night swallowed it down.

Then, Anna heard it again, that odd something she'd shut out. It wasn't at all ugly, as Joe had said. Yes, it was wild, evasive, always moving. But there was also a loveliness, a whisper of magic and divinity, that tamed the mysterious strains. The music swelled and filled the world. She staggered before its majestic beauty.

It was shattered by a sharp ringing *bang!*

"Joe!" Anna screamed.

She lunged toward the door, cracked it open. But the roaring wind pushed her back. The ever-lurking fog in her brain rose up, that haze waiting to take her away from life. From Joe.

"No." The words came slurred. "Not now. I've got to... to..."

She leaned against the wall and closed her eyes, reeling before mounting waves of despair. An ocean of sadness washed over her, coaxed her away. She had no strength to fight. Joe was her anchor. Without him, she must drift. She must sink.

But as Anna felt she must surrender to the call of that bottomless gulf, a final distant chord, like the pure, dying echoes in a cathedral, touched her ears, and her mind. Her darkness drew back, thinned, dissolved into fleeing shadows. A dream she'd had.

Anna opened her eyes. The cabin stood silent, the ashen fireplace, cold. Her cloudy breaths came slow and stuttered. She went to the window, grasping at the dream. But it had gone.

At last she shook her head, took a deep inhale. "It's so stuffy in here." She unlatched the window, opening it wide. An icy blast tossed her hair.

Anna staggered back. "Oh! Such an impish spring."

She sat in her chair, closed her eyes once more, weary from—something. From everything. Now she would rest.

The storm gusted. Snow swirled into the room. Anna pulled a quilt close. Soon, the cold and wind seemed far away. Flakes of white collected on her shoulders, in her hair, in the little valleys between her pale knuckles. The night passed. The cabin grew gray and lifeless.

Another winter day arrived. The sun sped above the clouds in its celestial pursuits.

The night came.

And the day.

And the next.

The wheel of the seasons ground forward. Snow melted, fell anew, melted again. Clouds were born over one horizon and died beyond another. Bright green shoots sprouted from the damp, musky earth. Animals awoke and sniffed the air. The sun and stars shifted to higher grooves.

One warm morning, a small white bird fluttered onto the window sill. As the bird sang its fresh and soaring notes, the woman's gray, stiff skin loosened. Sunlight fell on her tangled white hair, filling it with gold until it shone lustrous. The spots on her forehead evaporated as had the snow, and her wrinkles smoothed like a glassy lake on a calm day. Color returned to her body, and to her mind.

A young woman drew in a sharp breath and opened her eyes. She sighed at the fresh, fulsome scent of evergreens. She noticed the bird. "Why, hello. Is it afternoon already?"

The bird twittered.

Anna tossed aside her quilt and rose from the chair. "I've napped too long."

A memory lingered out of reach, something she'd planned to do. She stretched, her mind clear now from her rest.

Then, she remembered. "The fair! And the dance. I hope I haven't missed it."

The bird warbled and flew off.

Anna smiled and brushed the wrinkles from her dress. "Maybe I'll meet a nice fellow. It feels like something's in the air."

THE AUTHORS OF THE BIZARRE BAZAAR

Francelia Belton's love of short stories came from watching old Twilight Zone and Alfred Hitchcock Presents television shows in her youth. In 2021 she published a collection titled, Crime & Passion: Three Short Stories, and her fiction has appeared in various publications, including "Dreaming of Ella" in the Denver Noir anthology by Akashic Books. Her short story, "Knife Girl," was a finalist in the 2020-2021 ScreenCraft Cinematic Short Story Competition and a semi-finalist in the 2021 Outstanding Screenplays Shorts Competition. Her short story, "The Brotherhood of Tricks and Tricks" was a quarterfinalist in the 2022 Screen-Craft Cinematic Short Story Competition. She is an active member of Sisters in Crime and has served as Vice President (2015-2018) and President (2019-2021) for the Colorado chapter. She is also an active member of Mystery Writers of America and Crime Writers of Color.

John M. Campbell is a winner of the Writers of the Future contest that recognizes science fiction and fantasy short stories. John grew up reading science fiction and loved imagining a future extrapolated from what is currently known. After building a career in the aerospace industry, he now speculates on the worlds unknown to us that science and engineering may unlock. He hopes his stories will motivate young readers to pursue careers in science and engineering as the authors he read inspired his career. He lives with his wife in Denver, Colorado. For more of his stories visit www.JohnMCampbell.com.

Doug Christi began writing, part-time, as a photo journalist. He has completed two novels and is currently trying to find representation. Doug is married to his best friend and has a son and two grandsons. He is retired from the Postal Service after 40 years as a Letter Carrier and Union Steward.

Rachel Delaney Craft is an engineer by day and speculative fiction writer by night. Her short stories have appeared in publications such as Cricket, Spider, Cast of Wonders, Metamorphosis, and Luna Station Quarterly, and her novels have won the Colorado Gold and Zebulon contests. She also edited the 2020 RMFW anthology, WILD, a finalist for the Colorado Book Award. When not writing, she enjoys hiking with her dogs, baking vegan goodies, and trying to keep her garden alive. "We are Celia" was inspired by her ever-growing succulent collection. You can connect with Rachel on Twitter @RDCwrites or at racheldelaney-craft.com.

L.V. Ditchkus is the author of the Sci-fi award-winning Sasquatch Series: Book I - Crimes of the Sasquatch, Book II - Mission of the Sasquatch, and Book III - Legacy of the Sasquatch, and Book IV - Passage of the Sasquatch. These stories will make you question who sits on the top of the evolutionary ladder. The first book in her new series "Chrom Y Returns" is about time traveling women from 200 years in the future who are trying to save humanity despite a virulent man-killing virus, activists trying to stop them from re-introducing men, and questionable actions from their powerful employer. While writing these series, she's led adventure travel trips, hiked and snowshoed hundreds of miles, and volunteered for wilderness advocacy and writing organizations. Besides being an active member of RMFW and their Spec Fiction Critique Group, L.V. is a Board Member of the CC Writers Exchange, and a member of the Colorado Authors League. She and her husband live in a rural mountain community in central Colorado, where she gains inspiration from the five 14,000+ foot tall peaks viewable from her window.

Rick Duffy is retired and writes from his home in a peaceful Denver suburb opposite the magnificent Rocky Mountains. His stories have appeared in Tales From the Old Black Ambulance, Adventures in Zookeeping, the Zoetic Press Literary Journal, the Providence Journal, the Pike's Peak Dream anthology, and the RMFW anthology, Wild. His coming-of-age novel The Sigil Masters won a FireBird award, a Wishing Shelf Award, and an IndieBrag. Connect with Rick at rickduffy.com.

Prior to becoming an elementary school teacher, **B.J. Eardley** was a counselor, an organic farmer, a bookkeeper, a travel agent, a tour guide, and an executive director of tourism. A long-time resident of southeastern Utah, she has also published articles focused on the cultural and natural history of the area. She enjoys hiking, camping, birding, and appeasing the voices in her head by writing fiction.

Jill English Johnston pours her heart and soul into writing both fiction and non-fiction. Ever since childhood, she's appreciated the power of story and the delight of putting pen to paper, fingers to keyboard, wings to words. Seeking to fulfill her life-long dream, Jill diligently works on her light sci-fi/fantasy series and composes numerous short stories, including a collection dearly titled the Peddler Series. The Peddler and the Goatherdess is Jill's first foray into traditional publication. With opportunities abounding, Jill combined her passion for writing with her husband's love for photography and they independently published a photo devotional series. Their sixth book in the Be Still series is planned to release on Amazon in November 2022. Jill currently live in New Braunfels, Texas and spends her time writing, watching sunsets, kayaking, hiking, cycling and traveling to visit grandchildren, children, family and friends around the country. Connect with Jill at tablet-sofhumanhearts.com

Mel Lake is a copyeditor who lives in Denver with her partner and a very good dog. Her short fiction has been published in Twin Pies, Stratum Press, and Land Beyond the World. Her CNF essays have been published in The Mark, Capsule Stories, and The Human Touch. Mel is a contributing writer to MultiversityComics.com and a reader for Capsule Stories. She's querying a vampire detective novel and always forgets to tweet @melofsometrades.

Kelley J. P. Lindberg writes award-winning YA and adult fiction, and sometimes admits to having penned several best-selling how-to books in her early career. When she isn't writing or reading, she's traveling as far and as often as she can. Kelley has spoken at numerous writing conferences and workshops. Her fiction and essays have appeared in The Baltimore Review, The Citron Review, 99 Pine Street, Chicken Soup for the Wine Lover's Soul, and others, and in the Tellables app for the Amazon Alexa platform. Visit Kelley's website and blog at www.KelleyLindberg.com.

Award-winning author and playwright **Jennie MacDonald's** publications include an edited collection, plays, poetry, short stories, fine art photos, and articles concerning 18th and 19th century Gothic literature, theatre, children's culture, and visual and material culture.

Vista McDowall is a fantasy fiend who enjoys anything to do with magic, fairy tales, or period-accurate fashion. She lives in a mountain town in rural Colorado where the people are often stranger than fiction. Most days she can be found trying to write while covered in cats. During her spare time, she sews clothing and costumes, plays video games involving moral dilemmas, or enjoys tabletop role-playing games with similarly nerdy friends. She has published an epic fantasy trilogy, The Lantern-Lit City, The Fading Glow, and The Enduring Flame, as well as a myriad of short stories. Though still a new author, she's already developing her next set of books and stories involving diverse characters and places, philosophical quandaries, and retellings of classic literature.

KL Mendt recently sold her Colorado home and put her belongings in storage, allowing her to travel around North America and immerse herself in locations pertinent to her current project—a historical novel set mainly in Manitoba, Canada. During breaks from working on the novel, she challenges herself with short stories and flash fiction, where she experiments with fantasy and explores social issues.

Way back when shoulder-pads were in style, **Susan Schooleman (Cepa Onion)** wrote for Roseanne Barr, was a member of the Denver Center Theatre's Playwrights Group, was published by Self magazine, and Samuel French. She then chucked it all for adventures in parenthood. Three grown kids and a retired math teacher husband later, she has begun inching her way back into the business. Her short stories have been included in two Rocky Mountain Fiction Writers (RMFW) anthologies. She was also a winner in the 2019 RMFW Gold Contest.

Eleanor Shelton lives in Northern Colorado and works as a writer for the USDA as well as owning a freelance writing business. She is active with the Northern Colorado Writers as well as the Aspen Writers Network. She received her M.A. in English and writes fiction as often as time permits. Eleanor has had her fiction published in The Huron River Review, Current Magazine, and Offbeat Literary Journal and non-fiction published in the Ann Arbor News, The Aspen Magazine, The Aspen Sojourner, Edible Aspen, Career Focus magazine, The Welding Journal, Cornucopia Magazine (Turkey) and several others. In 2019, Eleanor's novel Bangkok Butterflies won first place in the Colorado Gold Fiction Competition for the mystery/suspense category, and it was a Finalist for the 2020 Write Start Competition.

Alison Thayer lives with her family in the foothills of Colorado, where she enjoys reading and writing stories that are magical, mysterious, and spooky. She is an active member of the Society of Children's Book Writers and Illustrators and Rocky Mountain Fiction Writers.

Natasha Watts, a.k.a. Tasha Christensen, is a writer and audio producer living in the foothills of the Rocky Mountains. She is co-editor of the short story anthology, WILD, and has work featured in Leading Edge Magazine and Found. Her debut novel, AS YOU WERE, is a YA romantic comedy.